the
Devil's
Hearth

ALSO BY PHILLIP DEPOY

THE FLAP TUCKER SERIES

Easy
Too Easy
Easy as One-Two-Three
Dancing Made Easy
Dead Easy

the
Devil's
Hearth

PHILLIP DEPOY

ST. MARTIN'S MINOTAUR ✄ NEW YORK

www.minotaurbooks.com

Book design by Jonathan Bennett

Library of Congress Cataloging-in-Publication Data

DePoy, Phillip.
    The devil's hearth: A Fever Devilin mystery / by Phillip DePoy. — 1st ed.
        p.   cm.
    ISBN 0-312-28485-3
        1. Appalachian Region, Southern—Fiction.   2. Mountain life—Fiction.
3. Folklorists—Fiction.   4. Georgia—Fiction.   I. Title.

PS3554.E624 D48 2002
813'.6—dc21

                                                                2002069836

First Edition: January 2003

10   9   8   7   6   5   4   3   2   1

This book is dedicated to Lee Nelson Nowell, a girl named for a Confederate General, a Navy Admiral, and French Christmas, after which a name like Fever Devlin doesn't seem too far-fetched. (Thanks for keeping me from dedicating the book to Weezie Nodblocker, a person I don't know but whose name makes me laugh.)

Acknowledgments

Acknowledgment is made to Dr. John Burrison, from whom I took folklore courses and whose assignments introduced me to the people who became characters in this book. To Joseph Campbell, who visited Atlanta in 1979 and encouraged a similar project. And to T.D., whose work on the original manuscript made it better.

the
Devil's
Hearth

One

I was home, and the mouth of the corpse was open wide.

Like singing, I thought. *What would he have been singing when he died?*

His head was near the door and his legs were splayed in a sickening upside-down Y. He lay on his side, eyes wide as his mouth, and he was dressed in a dirty tan raincoat.

The small porch seemed otherwise normal. The old railing was only slightly in need of repair; the rocking chairs were protected from the elements by the small tin roof overhead.

"All right, then," the deputy told me slowly, his breath trailing upward like a ghost in the chilly autumn air, "welcome home, Dr. Devilin."

I looked out across the yard in the moonlight. A cold blue mist had drizzled over everything. The lawn that had once seemed so huge—enough room for playing baseball games, running endless races, and finding a kingdom of infinite hiding places—was in reality a mat barely large enough for ten blades of grass and a row of pansies. The house perched on the side of Blue Mountain—in my mind's eye a golden mansion of cathedral rooms and honeyed floors—was that night tilted, water-damaged, tiny, and gray.

Only the chestnut tree at the side of the dirt road, glazing the air, even at midnight, with auburn leaves, was undiminished—despite years of ruined expectations and failed promise that had surrounded it.

The sky above us staggered under the weight of stars. The night air, trembling with light rain, seemed uncertain that it would or even could support the weight of all that light. The little cabin, sad as it was, tried its best to lean into the moon's ladled silver—a heart-breaking attempt to present itself somehow better than it was.

All I could do was stare down at the corpse on the front porch. No amount of moonshine, liquid or light, could wash those steps clean of that stain.

Deputy Needle stared too. "I've never seen a dead body before. Seen lots of people shot up—but they were all still alive." He spent a moment thinking. "Seen lots of dead game, of course . . ."

". . . of course . . ."

". . . but this is my first real live person."

"Real live dead person." I felt compelled to clarify.

"Right." He nodded, still staring. "Any idea who he was?"

"No."

Skidmore Needle and I had grown up together in the hills, and even though we were the same age, it struck me, standing there in the cold rain, that I looked much older. His hair was still jet black, mine was white as cloud—colorless hair at thirty-one. His face was smooth, and careless with baby fat. Mine seemed a road map of the world I had traveled. I thought, for some reason, about an old joke: "What do you call a beautiful mountain dove that lives in the city?" The answer is: "A pigeon." That's what happens to anything that lives in the city—the angel wings turn gray, the clear eyes run sullied, and the body learns to live on refuse.

"Isn't it odd," I said to him out loud, "what your mind comes up with when you don't know what to make of a dead body." I looked away. "I'm just glad that you're the one who keeps the key to this place. What if I'd already had it—what if you hadn't met me here; I'd have come up alone and found this?"

And thank God, I thought, *that he got here before I did and saw the body first.*

He stepped off my porch and into the yard. His black rain slicker made him almost invisible in the shadow of the house. "Well, I believe whoever did this—they thought it was you."

"What?" The rain seemed ice, and stuck my face and hands with a hundred silver pins. My own gray wool overshirt was soaked, a wet rag clinging to my shoulders. My mind's eye looked through a catalog of a dozen questions, but none seemed adequate—though the worst of them must have played across my face.

"Well," he began, looking out across the night air, "nobody's lived in this cabin for years—you haven't even visited in over three yourself. Then, all of a sudden you come home, and we all know you're coming back, it's common knowledge. Everybody in town knows. So what's the next thing that happens? We got us a stiff here on your front porch that is exactly your same body type and general looks."

My eyes traveled downward. It was a little hard to tell in the dim light, but on closer inspection—closer than I wanted it to be—he did seem to be about my size. There was a slight facial resemblance, though he was at least ten years older than I. And his hair was albino white, paler than my own. "When did you get to be such a . . . perceptive person, Skid?" My voice was as calm as the grave. "You didn't used to be this smart, did you?"

"I know I got no college degree," he answered, raising up a mighty army of irony against my years at the university, "but I've done this job for a good while now, and by and by you get to be good at anything you do over and over again. Like playing a fiddle."

"Which you don't do that well either." I shook my head. "You're making too big a leap in your thinking here. You're wrong about this. He doesn't look *that* much like me." But the sound of my voice betrayed a clear lack of conviction.

"Shoot, Dev. You got to think a little bit more about it like *we* do up here in the mountains." He offered me the Devil's own smile. "For example, do you know this guy?"

"I said I didn't."

"Well, that's my point. Me neither. Which makes him a stranger." His smile grew. "And you're aware that we don't like to shoot at a person up here unless we *know* them real good." He even offered up a short, macabre laugh.

"Yes, well—very amusing. Very . . . what? . . . *gallows-humor* . . ."

But the rest of my objection to his was cut short by an explosive rifle shot from the nearby patch of trees, and the almost simultaneous breaking of a window on my front porch.

For a moment, neither of us moved.

"Dev?" He looked off into the woods. "I believe somebody's shooting at us with some kind of a rifle."

"You might be right, Skid." I looked at the window. "Whom, do you suppose, would care to do that?"

"Could be the Deveroe boys," he said calmly. "I believe I saw them out hunting earlier this evening."

"We don't look that much like wild pigs."

The Deveroe boys—three crazed, raven-haired orphan brothers—were famous for shooting feral swine. They were also often mistaken for same.

"What should we do?" I asked Skidmore.

"Well," he answered with a little jut of his chin, "I believe I'll get out of the way. They might be trying to shoot at something behind us, and I don't want to confuse them."

"You're probably right," I agreed. "Mind if I join you?"

We walked to his patrol car, it was closer than my old Ford truck. We sat down behind it.

Several other shots were fired.

Anyone less familiar with my world might have found our behavior strange, but Skid and I knew quite well that if anyone in that particular part of the mountains had actually wanted to kill us, we'd have been dead with the first shot. Hunting was a serious matter in Greenwood County, Georgia—and fine marksmanship a necessity. It never occurred to either of us that the person shooting might have been from somewhere else. The obvious sound of a hunting rifle—so familiar to us since childhood—just seemed like a local weapon. And one has an intuition about such things.

As we sat there in the darkness, I was attacked, as so often happened to me, by a razor-toothed moment of reflection—always a dangerous moment for me. Close proximity to my childhood home seemed to force my mind's eye to watch strange images of my past. I saw, as I had in so many nightmares, my parents' *Show*. It was a sad parade of dream-ghosts that were always there, ready to dance, at any moment the mind idled. This had been my malady since childhood: an inability to calm my mind. Because of the attendant worry and fretting, my mother, God rest her soul, had dubbed me *Fever*. It was a nickname that had withstood the test of time despite my best efforts to the contrary.

There they were—in my mind's eye, Horatio—like ether-visions: the flatbed truck with the painted carnival sign TEN SHOWS IN ONE; the five-piece string band playing "Devil's Dream" over and over again; the sad and beautiful magic act that my father had concocted out of a dangerous knowledge of chemistry and the human propensity for foolishness. And in the center ring I saw my mother moving in her bizarre, hilarious *Dance of Eve*—at once sensuous and laughable, lewd and righteous. This was the way they had always made their living: a traveling show, part magician's illusions, part tent revival—all surreal vaudeville.

With images of that sort pouring like a cavorting in the mind, a few stray rifle bullets seemed almost a welcome distraction.

Skidmore, squatting down behind his car, pulled a cigarette out of his shirt pocket. "So, it's nice to have you back, Dev. How was the drive?"

"Seemed to take forever." I sat cross-legged on the drenched ground. I was already so wet, what did it matter? And I was happy that his question had invaded my *danse macabre*. "What time is it, do you suppose?"

"It's almost midnight now."

"I didn't leave Atlanta until early evening. Took my time up through Dalonega and Clayton."

"It's a pretty drive." He pulled on his cigarette, the orange tip glowed like a tiny jack-o'-lantern in the dark.

"Can be. Seems more . . . filled out since I was up here last—more building going on."

"Oh, it's grown." He let go another ghost of smoke. It hung in the air between us, interested in the conversation—or afraid to leave the company of men. "It's not at all like when you was a boy up here." He grinned. "We got us a strip mall in town."

"Ah. Good. A strip mall—the absolute worst Western civilization has to offer."

"Oh, I don't know." He blew silver. "They got a K-mart."

"I see."

"Listen." He inclined his head. "I believe the shooting might have stopped."

Silence.

"Yes." I nodded. "What now?"

He held up his index finger and then yelled out across the night. "Are you all done with your shooting?"

No answer.

He flicked his smoke into the air and started to stand. "Well, I'm getting up and going on in the house now."

He stood.

Still nothing.

He looked down at me. "Want to go inside with me?" He offered his hand.

"I suppose."

He helped me to my feet and we headed for the front door.

No more bullets.

His eyes were, as they say, glued to the corpse—although I don't know why they would say a thing like that, given the grizzly image it created.

"Well, your timing was good in one respect," Skidmore said, stepping a foot onto the steps and leaning forward, his eyes still on the corpse. "I just got back in town, myself—just tonight. If you'd come up last night? You would have been standing here with Sheriff Maddox instead of me."

"Oh." I was suddenly very happy to be standing over a dead body with an old friend. I looked up at the front door, avoiding the body, finally aware of just how wet and cold and tired I was. "Can we go inside now?"

"Yup." He went first.

I stepped over the corpse and made it up the stairs in three steps. My key clicked clean the lock—like a dry bone snapping. I froze.

"Skid?"

"Uh huh?"

"I think someone's been using my cabin."

The covered porch was drier, and there were spiderwebs everywhere. In the corner by the door a hornet's nest decorated the beams overhead. But the key had gone too readily into the tumbler, and turned without a catch.

"What makes you say that?" His voice was only a little hoarse.

"The lock just turned very easily. I think it's been oiled. And there's no dust on the handle—no cobwebs directly in front of the door." I moved the door a little. It was silent. "And listen." I pushed the door open. It swung wide easily—and made no sound.

He watched and listened. Then: "I see what you mean." He tried to peer past me into the house. "How's she look inside?"

"Why don't you go on in and see?" I stood my ground.

"I'd like to, Dev," he said, hesitating, "but this is your house. It would be unmannerly of me to barge in."

"It's all right." I stepped aside. "I always bow to the power of the badge."

"You do?" He looked me up and down. "Since when?"

"Since there was a dead body on my porch?" I twitched my head sideways, encouraging him to precede me.

"Okay," he said, gazing into the darkened room, "but you come on right behind me, and light some of them lamps."

"Don't you have one of those police flashlights?"

"It run down," he said firmly, giving the only indication he ever had of being angry. "My boys went night-fishing while I was gone these past few days and they kept it on half the night cleaning fish." He rubbed his right eye. "They got a mess of bream."

"Could we go in now?" I insisted.

He paused, as if I had been rude interrupting a story about his sons catching fish, then sighed and stepped into the darkness.

I moved immediately behind him, then to the mantel, found matches and a glass lamp. I struck the box, lit the wick, and a kind of honey poured out all around me—but it only confirmed my suspicions. Newspapers, clothing, plates—all in disarray—cluttered my ordinarily spotless refuge. Someone had been in the house.

Still, it was home—the place to which I would always return in my dreams, the eternal return. Whenever the word *home* occurred to me, I saw that cabin. High roof beams sheltered one large room downstairs—the kitchen area was to our right. A cast-iron stove, black as a raven's eye, was settled into the stone hearth to our left by a window that looked out over the gorge. The furniture was ancient and mostly made by friends or relatives—ladder-back chairs, a solid oak dining table, two ornately carved rockers, a pie safe, a long bookshelf, a sofa shoved to one side, as if a dance were about to be held. A "rug from Persia" that my father had taken as payment for

7

one of his shows covered half the floor. The quilts on the wall, bright as stained-glass windows, were a hopeless attempt to keep out the chill and damp. The staircase at the other end of the room led up to the bedrooms, but the big room downstairs was flooded with more light than I would have expected from one oil lamp. It revealed the shambles.

"See?" I turned to Skidmore, only two steps away. "See this mess?"

"Okay, I got a new idea." He stepped carefully over a pile of papers. "Here's what I think now. That dead body there—I mean the one on your front porch . . ."

". . . I know which dead body you mean, Skid . . ."

". . . he had taken this place over as his own. Your place. He's been living here."

"Living here?" I took in a larger portion of the air in the cabin. "Couldn't he just have been a burglar, throwing everything around looking for . . . loot?"

"Loot. Maybe." He nodded. "Or maybe you're not the smart boy you think you are. You figured out something was wrong just by looking at the door frame. I'll give you that. But you missed a key clue."

Despite our years of friendship—or even because of them—our competition had never abated. He was always ready to beat me in baseball, catch more fish, or, later, to prove that his "natural instincts and mountain ways"—whatever *those* might have been—were ultimately better attributes than my intellect and education.

"And what might that be?"

"Exactly what I said." He motioned for me to come with him once again to the door frame.

I set the matches down on the mantel and moved toward him with the lamp in my hand. I followed his gaze, stared down at the corpse.

"Key," he said. "Like I told you."

It took me a moment, but I finally saw it: a door key in the man's right hand, clutched in the tight, cold fingers.

Two

"You know," I said slowly, staring down at my door key in the hand of the corpse, "you and I—together—might make one fair detective."

"Right," he agreed. "If it don't rain."

The wind picked up, and blew the raindrops across the dead man's hand. I couldn't look at it. I looked out, instead, across the rising pines and up the mountainside.

"Aren't you going to do anything," I asked calmly, "about the people that were shooting at us?"

"What you want me to do?" he answered. "They've quit shooting, they're most likely gone, and I think I need to stay with this body."

Skidmore and I had torn through the woods and mountains around my family's cabin for most of our childhood years. My family had traveled around a lot, but whenever our show rested, the cabin was home. Even at that, my parents were nearly always gone somewhere or other. I was often left blissfully on my own.

Skid and I had solved many a mystery of life when were were eleven—just by discussing it over two fishing poles. We wore sunlight for clothing and ate from the apple trees on the bank. And had it not been for the water moccasins, my worst terror, the lake where we fished would have been Heaven—instead of merely Eden.

The day I was turned out of our garden, and left town for college—it had been a matter of a few weeks since my father had died—I was only sixteen. Skidmore cried like a child at my leaving. I didn't. I had already learned that attachments to people only caused problems—pointless problems. Parting from someone you cared about was a painful moment, but there was no use wrenching and tearing. The laws of our physical universe will never be forsworn: Distance engenders separation. It's not possible to be with someone if they're a thousand miles away—in space, in time, or even in attitude. Better to eschew attachments in general. The physical universe would be a happier place.

"Dev." His voice broke in upon my reflection. "Has it really been three years since you was up here last?"

"Three years, yes—I think." I turned to look about the place again. "What a wreck."

"This?" He looked over the same area. "Hell. My kids can make a better mess than this in five minutes. This is just what comes from living in a place."

"So you actually think someone has been living here?" I tried to think what to clean first.

"I do," he answered. "And then somebody else shot him."

"The same person who was just shooting at us?"

"Not likely." He shook his head. "That body out there appears to me to have been shot with a pistol—it's a smaller hole in him than a bigger gun would make. And the one that shot at us sounded like a deer rifle, didn't it?"

"It did."

"Well, then."

"He couldn't be carrying two guns?" I watched him grind his jaw. "The person out there shooting?"

"Why," he began, "do you want to contradict every one of my guesses?"

"Because," I shot back, "that's just what they are: *guesses*. You have sloppy thinking. Good observational skills, but sloppy thinking."

He folded his arms. "Then I guess you'll just have to give me a hand figuring out all this trouble."

We stood in the room, two actors on a stage of recollection. His challenge, like a thousand others from our childhood, had been played out by other good friends in other places all over the world since the beginning of human civilization: *I can't do it alone. I need your help.* Just what neighbors always said in times of need. Just what Cain said to Abel about the farming business.

"No, I won't." I shook my head. "I'm up here to research, to write. I don't want to be stirred up. I've had enough of that."

"You've had enough of what?" He smiled strangely.

"Enough . . ." But what was it, exactly, of which I had had enough?

He leaned back. "All right, I'll tell *you* what you've had enough of, then. You've had enough of Burrison University, enough of the city—but mostly you've had enough of running away . . ." he looked around the cabin, ". . . from this here."

I stared at him. "Running away from what?"

"Home." He was staring back at me. He took a deep breath. "Past. Family." He let out the rest of his breath. "I know how you are, Dev. I've known you for a long time. You, my friend, are afraid that you might get snakebit by your own life. That's what you're running away from. That's why you're here now."

I leveled what was intended as a withering look at my so-called friend—a look that had reduced many a graduate student to tears. "I am not afraid of snakes, nor of Freud—only of well-meaning friends."

"Okay." He had finished his amateur sermon. "Want me to give you a hand cleaning up in here?"

"All right, then." I looked around the room once more, heartsick. "Yes, I would like a hand cleaning up." I avoided looking at him, and tried for nonchalance. "By the way, I'm not quite settled in my mind about staying the night here. I don't really care for sleeping anyplace that combines a dead body with live ammunition."

"I understand." He started gathering up newspapers. "You know I called everybody already—the boys over at the funeral parlor, and some lab help from my office. They're on their way. That body'll be gone in an hour. If you like, I can leave the state vehicle parked outside and take your truck home with me, kind of scare away the pikers."

"I was thinking," I tried, "that I might come over to your place tonight instead—actually."

"Naw." He made a face. "You don't want to do that. The middle boy's had the flu the past few days and Girlinda don't like nobody in the house when it's such a mess."

"I see," I said, gathering up dirty plates. "How is your wife?"

"Best there is." He moved across the room.

Girlinda Needle was, in fact, as fine a person as had ever been allowed on the planet. She was fierce in her love of her family, quick in her mundane county job, hilarious after five-thirty post meridian, and as pretty as a picture, if that picture had been painted by Reubens.

"Please tell her I said hello."

"Sure thing," he answered absently.

Suddenly he stopped cleaning and stood stark still. "Hold it, Dev. Hold it. Don't clean up this mess no more."

"What?" I held the plates steady.

"I think," he said as he put the papers back down very precisely on the table, "I'd like to have a look around before we do anything else."

"What are you talking about?"

"Put those plates back near as you can to where you got them from, would you? Damn."

"Fine." I did.

He rubbed both his eyes hard. "I don't know what I was thinking. This here is a part of the crime scene too."

"Oh." I stood back from the dining table. "I guess you're right. What made you think of that?"

He motioned to me. "Come over here."

I came to his side.

He pointed. "Look."

There was a newspaper article on the table. It was not casually turned to, but deliberately folded open and creased hard. It was a short article in the *Atlanta Journal and Constitution*. It had a little picture of my face and the title was "University Professor Seeks Roots." Beside it was an ashtray filled with Camel butts and burnt kitchen matches.

Skid looked up. "I told you that everybody knew you were coming home."

"It would appear."

"How about," he said as he blew out a breath, "if I stay here with you tonight?"

I looked over to him. "Well—thanks. That would be great."

"Let me call Linda."

"I haven't had the phone turned on yet," I told him, looking around the room to see if I could even find the thing. "Can you use your police radio somehow?"

Before he could say anything, or move at all, the phone rang. It so startled us both that we froze for a moment.

"That's somebody calling the dead man," I whispered.

"The dead man," he agreed, "who's been running up your phone bill, apparently."

It rang again.

He stared at the phone. "Well, get it."

"You get it." I was still whispering, as if the person calling could somehow hear me if I talked too loudly.

"It's not my house. Just pick it up and say 'hello' and wait to see what they say."

The phone rang a third time, demanding to be answered.

I hesitated, then picked up the receiver. "Hello?"

"Dev?" The voice was light.

"Andrews?"

"So," he barreled on, "you made it in one piece. Sorry to call so late, but I can't find the damned directions you left me and I wanted to leave first thing in the morning. I didn't wake you?"

Skid moved closer to the phone. "Andrews?" he whispered.

I nodded, covering the phone for some reason. "My colleague, Dr. Andrews, from . . ."

". . . the Shakespeare guy? The guy you always talk about? That's who you're talking to?"

"Our campus Shakespeare scholar, yes," I told Skidmore, "from Manchester—if that's not too much an oxymoron."

"Why is he calling at this hour?" Skid was whispering too.

I held up one finger and spoke to Andrews again. "From where you are, take 75 north to 575—it's not as scenic as the way I came today, but it's faster, and I know how you feel about *speed*."

I looked at Skidmore on the last word, and did my best to communicate the state of Andrews's late-night frame of mind.

Skid only blinked.

"So I've made it clear," the voice on the other end of the phone intoned, "how I feel about your so-called *vistas* in the north Georgia hills. What is it you see in them, again?"

"I've told you," I sighed, repeating the answer for the tenth time. "It's in the old shape note song: 'In these hills, the sky goes on forever, and I can own eternity,' remember?"

"I see. You want to be the king of infinite space, then."

"Oh." I grinned. "That's me in a nutshell."

This was the game he often coerced me into playing: worming Shakespeare quotations into daily conversations—this particular reference from Hamlet: *I could be bounded in a nutshell and count myself a king of infinite space.*

"That's good," he said. "Nice work, ' . . . me in a nutshell.' "

"I'm glad you're amused." I nodded. "I was hoping to be content here." I stared out the window.

"It's home," he said, as if it were obvious that contentment and the old home place were one and the same.

"I envy your childhood," I told him, tight-lipped.

"Well, you'll be bored in a month and come limping back down here." He sighed. "But in the meantime, I'm coming up tomorrow to see what all the fuss is about. It is my opinion that you're looking down the barrel of years and years of boredom."

"Being bored generates creativity." I believed that.

"In aberrant types such as yourself, I suppose it might. Look, is someone there with you? You keep covering the phone."

"A friend of mine," I answered, "an old friend, visiting me at the cabin. You remember my talking about Skidmore Needle. I've mentioned him."

"You have." He paused. "But what's the deputy of police doing in your little blue heaven at this hour? And your voice sounds . . . odd."

"It does?" I looked out toward the front porch. "Well, Skidmore keeps the keys to my cabin, and he came here with me because we're boyhood chums, but, look—something's happened. You may find it difficult to believe." I took a deep breath. "When Skidmore got here, he found, on the front porch of my cabin . . ."

The deputy lurched, nearly grabbing the phone away from me. "Don't tell him about that!"

I moved away from Skidmore, turning my back. "There's a dead body on my front porch."

"What?" I could barely hear Andrews.

Skidmore's shoulders sank noticeably.

"That's right." I nodded.

Skid's face was hard.

"Well." Andrews gathered his thoughts. I knew he was pulling on his left earlobe, an absent gesture he always made when he was thinking. "Are you all right? Who is it—the dead body? Who killed it? Man or woman?" He paused to breathe. "Dev? Are you there?"

I took a moment. I held out the phone.

He shook his head.

I put the phone back to my head and spoke into it again. "Why don't you just talk to Deputy Needle. He's the curious sort too—and a policeman."

"Right!" Andrews barked. "Give him to me."

I offered the phone to Skidmore again. He still wouldn't take it.

"You two talk," I begged him. "I can't answer his questions right now. I can't think. I'm starting a fire. I have a chill, suddenly."

Skidmore stared at me, sighed like a dying man, then took the phone.

I went to the cast-iron stove in the hearth. The fireplace had been made to burn wood, but in the forties, after the war, the house had been modernized: running water, electricity, and the best stove heater money could buy.

I wasn't sure why I'd just handed the phone to Skidmore. It was a collision of worlds: my best friend from childhood and my best friend at Burrison University. But the shock of seeing a dead man was wearing off, or getting worse—hard to tell which. The effect was that I was shivering, overly hot, confused, and bone-tired. I simply didn't feel I could talk any more.

The fire was roaring ten minutes later, and I left the door of the stove open. The blaze was really larger than needed to warm the room, but the psychological effect was quite bolstering. I was out of my wet overshirt and slumping in one of the rocking chairs, feet up on a small wooden ottoman, before the telephone conversation was over.

Skid finally stopped talking and placed the receiver in its cradle. He blew out another long breath, puffing his cheeks, looked around the room as if he were deciding what to do next, then took off his coat and laid it over the back of a dining chair.

"Well, that does it, Bud. Dr. Andrews agrees with me. Somebody just might want you to get dead. That boy surely can talk, can't he?"

"Wild speculation from *both* of you." But I wasn't as convinced as I had been. "Only a few moments ago you thought the Deveroe boys were shooting at us. And they certainly don't want me dead."

"Well, on second thought," he said, moving toward the other rocking chair, "those boys are loud when they shoot off their guns. We'd have heard them whooping and yelling. The point is that it's just possible somebody thought the boy on your porch was you."

"I'm less skeptical about that supposition than I might have been a half an hour ago."

"Good. I need you to be alert to every possibility. Andrews agrees with me that you got trouble your way. He's madder'n hell about it."

"He's angry?"

Skid allowed himself a look of superiority. "He thinks it's somebody from the university."

I didn't mean to smile, I just couldn't help myself.

"You don't see it that way?" he asked.

"I'll tell you what I see. I see that the Court of the Borgias was probably a more comfortable place than Burrison University sometimes was—but I find it hard to believe that someone in the academic environment would have the gumption to try to shoot me, let alone any reason to do it."

He nodded, and his face relaxed. "I expect." He stared into the fire. "The Borgias. That's the Italian family that killed everybody—poisoned each other."

"And they say public education isn't worth a dime."

"Well, Dev, you know I like to read a lot on my own." He sat down in the rocker and closed his eyes. I could tell he was tired.

We listened to the fire's white pop and sizzle for a moment. We knew what we were doing: trying to pretend it was an evening like so many gone by, when we'd sit in front of the fire, stare at the flames, and talk endlessly about everything important—fishing, great books, Mozart, the importance of the mandolin, Lucinda.

But that night we were trying to avoid talking about the most important issue: the body not thirty feet from where we were sitting. We were whistling in the wind, trying to convince each other that we were safe and warm.

"Skid?" I had to break the illusion.

"Uh huh?"

"Who *is* that man out on the front porch?"

"Yeah." He closed his eyes. "We do need to find that out right quick."

"You didn't check his wallet or anything? Before I got here?"

"Naw. I'm just the lowly deputy." He sniffed. "I'm supposed to let the county coroner have a minute, then I'll start really looking around—some of the others are bringing the lab tests that we've got over at the office. I'll try not to let them mess up your place any more than they have to. You go on to bed if you want."

"No."

He opened his eyes. "There's nothing you can do now. And you need to get right in your head about some of this. Sleep's what you need."

"And you don't?"

He smiled. "I slept last week."

We heard cars pulling up outside and saw the headlights. I got up and moved to one of the front windows; he was right behind me. We both peered out carefully. There were two dark sedans and an ambulance beside my truck.

"That's them—laboratory people, and all." He put his hand on the doorknob. "You care to watch all this? It's kind of interesting."

I only had to picture someone rolling the dead body over on its back to reconsider my stubbornness.

"Now that you mention it," I said, rubbing the back of my neck, "no. But I might try your other suggestion."

"Sleep?"

"Sleep," I agreed, " *'that sometimes shuts up sorrow's eye.'* "

"Sounds like more of that Shakespeare to me."

"You do read a lot, don't you?"

He opened the door and started out. Then he stopped, looked at me as if we were both idiots, and tried the light switch. The porch light blinded us both.

Skid squinted my way. "If he had the phone turned on and he was living here, I guess he might have had the electricity on too."

"Glad you thought of it," I told him ruefully.

He stepped out onto the porch.

"Don't forget to call your wife," I reminded him. "If you're still staying here tonight."

"Yup." He headed out the door.

I could hear him greet the coroner and the other men the way he might if he'd happened on them at church. I stood for a moment, listening, but when the talk turned from casual conversation to the thing at my door, I moved away, toward the staircase.

As I walked the few steps to the other side of the room, I also waded through a thousand memories—as well as the clutter left in my home by a stranger, clutter I did not want to see. I thought of the countless nights I had headed up those same stairs to my room, alone in the cabin, wondering where my parents were, what they were doing. I never failed to dream about them: every night a terrible vision, waking alone, hot even on the coldest night, afraid even to cry out.

As I began my journey upward, I felt the weight of all those other nights, those boyhood fears, making each step heavy. Every move was not so much a step up the staircase as it was an expedition backward in time, a year, or ten, with every stair.

When I reached the top, I was a boy of nine, eyes burning, facing the black cave of my room, where a cauldron of visions cooked and steamed.

I made it to the door, fumbled for the light switch—glad the electricity was on.

The room was not, in fact, a chamber of horrors. It was comprised of a sweet bed, a dozen quilts, pictures of great men—my heroes—a mandolin case in the corner, and a round rug on the floor that my mother had made herself.

How could nightmares live in such a world? I thought.

I took three steps, collapsed into that bed, rolled onto my side, and plunged deep into the ocean of night.

Three

A snake wound its slow way around my mother's throat. Her porcelain face grew paler and paler until it was the face of the dead body on the front porch of the cabin. That face was singing an old shape note song, but I could not quite make out the tune. All around in the woods there were wild swine, and the lake where I'd gone fishing, on endless summer days, ran red with blood.

"Are you dreaming? Or is all that twitching insomnia?"

I sat bolt up in bed at the sound of a real voice in my room.

Wrenched from a black vision of singing dead bodies and churning blood, I had a disconcerting second's thought that the voice might be my father's—despite the fact that he'd been dead for nearly fifteen years.

So my response was the soul of wit: "Who is it?"

"Sorry," Andrews laughed. "Didn't mean to startle you. I guess you were sleeping." He moved to the window and pulled back the curtains.

"Andrews?" My eyes were adjusting. I began to see his face. "What are you doing here?" A foolish question, but all I could think of.

"Don't you remember? Last night on the phone?"

Dr. Winton Andrews, son of a theatrical producer in Manchester, as proud of his rugby skills as he was of his education, stood nearly six full feet above me. His Hawaiian shirt and khaki pants, the unkempt blond frizz that covered his head, made him seem more a wayward surfer lost in the hills than a man who knew more about Shakespeare than anyone else in the state.

"I know," I managed, "but after what I told you . . . the body on the porch especially . . . I thought you might reconsider."

"Are you kidding?" He tugged at his earlobe. "That's my primary motivation for visiting."

"What?" I thought I hadn't heard him correctly—sleep clouded my ears.

"Let's wait until you're awake," he concluded, looking around the room. "I've never seen your little log cabin home in the sky. I'll want to take a look around when you're ready. Is that a mandolin?"

"Wait." I held up my hand. "You're right. Let me get out of bed, get some espresso, take a few deep breaths, and let's try this over again—in a few minutes."

He nodded. "Good. I'll be downstairs. Although where you're going to find espresso up this way I have no idea."

I shooed him away. "I'll be right down."

Five minutes later I had thrown on a black sweatshirt and some dark green corduroys, slipped into my walking boots, and found my way down the stairs.

Skid and Andrews were at the table, sipping coffee.

"So you did stay," I said to Skid.

"I said I would." He winced. "That damned sofa's too soft." He wasn't awake yet either.

I went to my smaller suitcase, which, it would seem, Skidmore had been kind enough to bring inside for me. I only spent a moment rummaging before I found my prize.

"Ah." I withdrew a small espresso machine, a coffee grinder, and an airtight container of whole beans. I headed for the kitchen area.

The whole place seemed better by day. The certain knowledge that there was no body on my porch—though I could not bring myself to look—did a great deal to brighten things up, I thought. And somehow everything seemed more tidy.

I stopped what I was doing.

"You cleaned," I said to Skidmore.

"Not really," he answered. On closer inspection, the dark circles under his eyes had deepened—his imitation of a raccoon. "I dusted for prints, bagged a few dozen items for the lab, that sort of thing." He looked at Andrews. "I don't do windows."

"But *he* does espresso?" Andrews could barely contain himself.

He glared at me and asked, incredulously, "You carry around your own espresso maker? We already made coffee."

"That's not coffee," I sniffed, staring down my nose at his cup.

"Don't speak to him until he's finished making that stuff." Skid set down his own coffee cup. "He can't drink our coffee like a normal person, and you don't really want him talking until he's had him a little sip of his own."

"Yes." Andrews seemed—what would be the word?—annoyed. "I know that."

I didn't even look back at them. I had business with a grinder. "Perhaps both of you wouldn't mind taking a flying leap—off this very mountain, in fact."

I spent a good five minutes in the process of making my morning refreshment. I could hear the two of them chatting, but I couldn't really make out what was being said over my deliberate racket—nor did I care.

The matter came to rest when I sat down with them at last, demitasse in hand, and I was vaguely coherent. I took a seat that I judged to be equidistant between them both, though I was not entirely conscious of doing so.

"Now. Andrews." I clasped my hands. "When did you get here?"

"An hour ago?" he asked Skidmore.

"I believe it was just about the time I had just fallen asleep," he answered.

"What time is it now?" I wanted to know.

Andrews checked his watch. "Just past eight-thirty."

"Christ," I exploded. "What time did you leave Atlanta?"

"Mmm," he told me, thinking, "about five."

Golden mallets pounded the floor soundlessly, and the silent sun made the wood glow bright. The air outside the windows seemed magnified and polished, clear and cracking in the morning's eagerness for light.

"All right, so you woke Skidmore up—you've met then," I said finally.

They looked at each other, sharing a secret smile.

"And so what is it that the two of you have been talking about that merits such a look?" I wanted to know.

"You." Skid finished his American coffee.

"I should have seen through all this mess at the university," Andrews said to me as if it followed directly from the word that Skidmore had just uttered. "The English Department's closing down its folklore section was just an attempt to try and squeeze you out—into a very early retirement—you thought. But you could have stayed on."

"Teaching *Beowulf* to freshmen and playing Folkways records in some introduction class? Not likely. The folklore section was doomed after Dr. Bishop retired . . ."

"Shut up, I'm not talking about that. I'm saying that I've changed my tune on that whole business. Someone has quite another agenda, I now believe. They don't want you to be retired at all. They want you to be dead."

I stared. I hardly knew what to say. "What an astonishing . . . why on earth would anyone want something like that?"

Skidmore sipped his coffee. "That's what we have to find out." But I could tell from the tone of his voice that he had something else on his mind too.

"Andrews," I looked at the both of them, "you've only been here an hour and you've already been infected with the local brand of faulty thinking."

"Faulty thinking?" Andrews was slouched comfortably, his legs stretched long under the table, his face perfectly content.

"You've both jumped to so many conclusions I hardly know where to begin. And maybe it's the odd circumstance in which you find yourself, but a phrase the likes of 'they want you to be dead' belongs on a television show—not in a real conversation."

Andrews turned to Skidmore. "He doesn't like me as much as he used to."

"Not true." Skid shook his head. He was leaning over his coffee cup, one hand on top of it, one hand on the handle, staring unfocused at the tabletop. "You just have to understand what makes him tick. What makes him such a good folklore guy, for example, is exactly this resistance to the kind of thinking that you and I apparently share."

"I know how he works." Once again, for some reason, Andrews seemed irritated and he shifted in his seat uncomfortably. "I've seen him in action. There's a kind of weirdly calm precision that he likes to employ in his work. When he's collecting a story, for example, it's so important to him to transcribe, exactly, each pause and 'um' and extraneous word or noise. It takes a great deal of time."

"Hurrying makes things messy," I replied breezily, sipping my espresso. "Otherwise one's apt to leave something out, forget something, overlook something. Slow and steady wins the race." I took another sip to punctuate the sentence.

"Original phrase," Andrews shook his head, "and I'd agree with it, except for the other phrase 'the quick and the dead,' wherein *slow*, you see, equals *dead*."

"Yes," I told him. "Well, my phrase comes from a story that exists in folk wisdom, and yours comes from the Judeo-Christian Bible. Is it obvious to you which is more important to me?"

He looked at Skid. "He's not a religious man."

"With his upbringing?" Skidmore shook his head, then gave a teasing glance my way. "I'd say not."

"Could we just examine," I began, ignoring their air of derision, "your wild speculations? In the first place, the plural pronoun 'they,' which you employed with such reckless abandon a moment ago, does not actually tell us anything. Your pronouncement that the anonymous 'they' from the university want me dead, is, in a word, ludicrous."

"You have to admit, Dev," Skidmore began softly, "that you don't get shot at that often."

"Yes," I answered him, "but the actual facts are these: Someone fired at a stranger coming into my house—and killed him—and then someone fired at me when I was with you, a policeman who must have dozens of opportunities for being shot in a given week. There's nothing to be inferred from those facts at the moment—they simply are what they are and nothing more."

"But it's obvious." Andrews was growing angry.

"Nothing is obvious." My voice was rising as well. "That's the point. We start from the unknown and *proceed* to the obvious. You have no grasp of fieldwork techniques whatsoever."

"Don't see the need of being riled, Dev," Skid said softly once again. "He did come up here to help us."

"Help?" I looked at him quickly. "Us?"

"Oh." His face relaxed into its natural grin. "Did I forget to mention? While you was asleep I talked to Dr. Andrews and he's going to stay on for a while and work with us."

I leaned forward as suddenly as my muscles would permit. "What are you talking about?"

"During our phone conversation last night," Andrews answered, "Deputy Needle and I discussed the situation here and I told him I wanted to help."

"This is something," I insisted, "for the police."

"Shoot, Dev." Skidmore coughed a scratchy laugh. "I *am* the police. And I say . . ."

". . . Skidmore . . ."

"Look," he interrupted, "you said yourself that you and me together make one fair detective. If you add Andrews to the list, hell—we got us a fair chance of actually doing something in the way of solving this mess. And if we don't—who will? Maddox?"

I stared at both of them. They stared back.

"Sheriff Maddox," Skid went on, looking at Andrews, "is one sorry pain in the butt—and he's got a kind of grudge against Dr. Devilin, here. I can't do this business all by myself—I ain't never had to solve a crime worse than goat-stealing or vandalism."

"From what I already know about the doctor's work," Andrews agreed in the same tone as Skidmore's, one that gave the impression that I was not in the room, "it's not much different from yours anyway."

"Really?" Skid turned his way. "Why do you say that?"

"Well, these so-called folk informants? He tells me they're harder to find nowadays than a witness to a street crime. And then once they're found? You've got to do all sorts of tricks to get them to talk, to make them tell you their stories. Finding the *genuine* folk today? It's as hard as finding answers in a homicide investigation." He turned my way. "You've been a detective all your life, Dr. Devilin—you just haven't known it."

"See what he means, Dev?" Skid looked at me very oddly then. "And I agree—except I think you've known it all along. You just don't admit how much of a detective you really are, or want to be—especially in your personal life."

It seemed a very pointed, odd expression he was wearing, and I had no idea what he meant by it.

"I agree," I considered, "that Sheriff Maddox is not the man for the job."

"That's right," Andrews announced, glowing. "This is a job for the Three Stooges."

"Why can't we be the Three Musketeers?" Skidmore wanted to know.

"Have you ever seen him walk?" Andrews answered, giving me a sidelong glance.

"Oh." Skid nodded. "Okay. I get to be Moe."

"Stop." I stood. "More espresso."

I moved to the kitchen, aching from hard, dead sleep. But the sun poured through the kitchen window, the wild ageratum leaned purple and feathered in the autumn breeze, and the slope of the road went to blue obscurity down the mountain. These images were so real and healing that they massaged my muscles, repaired my anxieties. And another shot of espresso, black as night, sharp as steel, turned me around in the kitchen.

"Andrews?" I announced. "Would you care to take a look around my mountain?"

"God." He stood up immediately.

"Detective Needle," I said, "if that is your name, get home to your lovely wife, apologize for me—for my keeping you here last night—and do whatever it is you do for the rest of the day, then meet back here tonight for our first planning session. What do you say to that?"

"That's it," Skid said, finishing his coffee in one gulp and standing slowly. "We're on. I do have a report or two to write, and Maddox won't be easy to get around, but I think we got us a shot at figuring this thing out."

"Which will be remembered at election time," I told him, teasing, "as the most sensational crime-solving epic of the decade, and you, my fine friend, will be the new sheriff."

"Maybe we ought to see if we're any good at this thing," he said dryly, moving around the table, "before I start my campaign." He glanced behind him. "Dr. Andrews."

"Deputy Needle." Andrews saluted ridiculously.

Skid moved toward the door, retrieved his rain slicker from a hook by the frame, and stopped halfway out.

"You know, Dev," he said without looking back at me, "this ain't really like your folklore research. If it's what we think it is, you got to be real careful."

"I understand," I said reassuringly.

He hesitated another minute, then left. The screen slapped closed, his boots thumped the porch—a second later the squad car rattled and started, and mud scratched up. Andrews and I stood silent until the sound of the car had completely disappeared.

"Well," said Andrews at last. "I thought he'd *never* leave."

"Hike?" was my answer.

"Lead the way."

The September day was crackling with perfect autumnal air, cold enough to relieve the relentless sun, clear enough so that every breath was like a sip of cold spring water.

The house tilted, and the wood had long since gone to gray, but dressed in sunlight and framed by purple at the base and blue at the roof, it seemed more a romantic explanation of the word *home* than an actual house. Heat from the still-warm stove in the fireplace inside made white steam rise from the chimney like smoke, but that steam rose upward and mixed with the clouds to give the illusion that the house itself had created the entire sky.

The mountain sloped radically downward only twenty feet from the left side of the house. Behind it a stand of pines rose dramatically enough to indicate the sheer upward slope of the hill that way. Only the roadway in front of the house seemed traversable. It was muddy, well-worn, and strewn with rocks and branches, but it was obviously the safest, easiest way to get anywhere. It ran downward toward town, and upward to the top of the mountain.

Andrews and I took the downward road a while until we came to a clearing in the trees and a stark drop-off to the left of the road. It opened on a view of seven mountains, and a valley wild with mirror lakes.

"Mother of Mary," Andrews said softly, gazing out over the view.

"This is my home," I answered. "All of this. And there's more to it for me than what you see. For me this road is the first road I drove a car on; that lake, the largest one down there, is where I caught my first fish, with my father, when I was seven. Just barely around the next bend in this road, very near to where we are standing now, is

27

the church where I first heard sacred harp music, shape note singing—"

"You've mentioned that often enough," Andrews interrupted vaguely, "but I never quite got the definition . . ."

"It was a way of teaching people to read music," I supplied, "in the nineteenth century in these mountains. Singing schools taught that a square was an A and a triangle was a D and so forth—Alan Lomax researched it heavily, made recordings—"

"No," he interrupted again, "I mean what does it sound like?"

"Oh." I groped to explain. "Well, my mother once told me it was called 'Sacred Harp' because every human vocal chord was a string in the harp of God."

"And you first heard it in this church we're close to." He returned his gaze to the astonishing vista.

"The same church," I went on, "where I first kissed a girl—felt the thrill of accomplishing something forbidden: kissing in the shadow of the Lord. Look all around. There's barely a stone or a clump of grass that hasn't endured my inspection. There's not a riddle here I can't unwind."

A breeze picked up, and the smell of pine straw in golden light washed over us.

"Except last night." Andrews folded his arms, suddenly understanding the true meaning of our walk.

"Except last night," I affirmed. "So I have to do this."

"Because if you figure this out," he said, still unable to tear his eyes away from the valley below us, "then you'll really, finally be home."

"Christ!" At the sound of my voice, a crow shot upward, like an exclamation point, from the nearest pine bough. "Why does everyone always play amateur psychologist with me? I only meant I had to do it to feel safe in my house again. Knowledge is security."

"Um," Andrews said, turning to face me at last, "isn't that what I just said?"

Four

That night the air remained clear. The stars so stabbed the sky that they threatened to break the black glass of night and let in the light-of-angels that lay behind it. Still, the human beings on the front porch of my house felt it necessary to have the porch light on and to bring two oil lamps outside as well.

I was in a ladder-back chair, Skidmore was in a rocker, and Andrews sat precariously on the railing.

"Repression," I intoned between sips of a certain glorious alcoholic drink, "is the mind's simple way of coping with impossible phenomena. Nothing unhealthy about it at all."

We'd spent all evening talking, arguing, eating, laughing, telling stories—as if we were old friends on vacation. It was what we all needed, in order to deal with the situation at hand—and to prepare for the situation to come. By the later part of the evening, we were all—what would be the proper phrase?—a little in our cups.

"Crap." Andrews responded to my psychological pronouncement with his louder voice. "Paging Dr. Freud. Please report to the front porch, Dr. Freud." His shirt was in anarchic disarray, twisted to one side. His pants had been stained with the contents of his glass by dozens of careless hand gestures. His face was red as a raspberry, and his eyes were made of glass.

"You'd think I wouldn't go in much for the Freudian side of things." I leaned forward in the chair, and all four legs came to rest on the porch floor. "But as a matter of fact, Freud is at the foundation of all my work—*along* with Jung, and Joseph Campbell, of course . . ."

"Could we stick," Andrews jumped in, "to one famous dead man at a time?"

"Very well," I said to him. "Freud is fundamental to the modern study of folklore. There. That's all I have to say on the subject."

"How?" He shook his head. "How is Freud? That doesn't seem right."

"Oh, it's right." I leaned back again, and sipped from my glass. "There was, for example, a movement in modern material folk culture research to categorize everything in the genre as either a womb form or a phallic form. Everything."

"I hate that." He tried to focus his eyes. "Give me an example."

"Well," I looked away, out across the sky, "let's say . . . corn husking or butter churning, those would seem self-evident images of phallic manipulation."

"That's disgusting," Andrews pronounced unequivocally.

"Nothing disgusting about it," I told him as I rolled my head. "And the guitar, there's an obvious female form."

"Uh huh," he nodded, "I can see that, but—"

"This categorization helped us to understand why certain tasks were thought to be masculine tasks and others thought to be feminine. For example, in a husking bee—"

"Stop!" He nearly spilled his drink. "A *what?*"

"Corn shucking," Skid explained. He was still in his uniform from a day at work, and as I looked at him then I could not remember a time in recent years that I had seen him in any other clothes. "Everybody'd come over to one or another one's house. All the took-in corn would be setting in the middle of the room, and everyone would get to shucking it. A way of making a party out of the work. You'd get all your corn cleaned in one night at a community get-together. I still remember them from when I was a little kid." He sipped. "It was fun."

"All right." Andrews looked back at me. "So as you were saying . . ."

". . . at a husking bee," I resumed.

"But why a *bee?*"

"If," I sighed, "you keep interrupting . . ."

". . . but I just want to know . . ."

". . . a husking bee," I raised my voice ever so slightly, "a quilting bee—even a spelling bee—these were ways of accomplishing work or learning communally—like busy little bees?"

"Oh. Like *bees*." Andrews took another sip of his drink, apparently satisfied with my explanation.

"At a husking bee, then," I told him, closing my eyes, "as I was saying, men were allowed to remove the husks from the corn, but only the women were allowed to clean the ears of silk, because of the manner of gesture used. You see, a man was allowed to take his ear out of his husk, but he wasn't allowed to rub it up and down because—"

"Yes, I get it." Andrews slung his glass, spilling a little. "Enough." He looked at Skidmore. "What the hell is this I'm drinking?"

"Yeah, it's good." Skid grinned his trademark expression. "It's Dev's own brew."

"I mean, what exactly," he said looking down into his glass, "is it?"

"Homemade apple brandy."

"Got a kick." Andrews had leaned far back on the rail, trying to concentrate. "Is it like moonshine? Is this what they call moonshine?"

"Andrews," I said, carefully pronouncing each syllable, "your position is dangerously precarious."

He looked around, obviously unaware of the incline of his angle on the rail.

"Moonshine," Skidmore explained, "is illegally distilled corn mash. Apple brandy is a legal household concoction from a secret family recipe. And if you think this has a kick, moonshine might could kill you."

"Well," Andrews pronounced, "this drinks quite well." He polished off his third large glass and swiveled his head wildly, taking in the panorama of the world around him.

The evening was cool. The crickets and tree frogs were loud, and the moon was low on the horizon.

"Jesus." Andrews suddenly brought down his legs and shot forward, standing and staring out into the night, and up the mountainside. "What the hell is that?"

I didn't even bother to follow his eyes. I knew what he was looking at. Skidmore knew as well.

Still, I humored him. "What do you see?"

"That . . . glow . . . up at the top of the mountain. That eerie light up there. Looks like fire—or a UFO. Look!" He pointed.

"That," I began, suitably hushed, "is Wicked John's Folly—on top of Blue Mountain."

"What's he saying?" Andrews asked Skidmore.

"It's nothing." Skidmore looked at him. "It's just a rock outcropping."

"Some of it is petrified wood," I added. "It's fairly large—and all covered over with phosphorescent lichens. That's what you see glowing, the lichens. Impressive, isn't it? Doesn't happen every night."

"Sometimes," Skid agreed, "if the moon's too bright, you can't see it at all."

"Would you like to hear the story?" I asked him.

"Story?" Andrews's eyes were still on the bizarre glow.

"That's right." I settled my own chair. "Many folk stories are etiological in nature. This particular one tells how that place got its name."

"Yes, all right." He settled a little more comfortably, back on the rail, leaning on the support post. "I suppose I could hear that. If someone will get me another glass of this apple juice."

Skidmore leaned forward silently and found, just out of the light of the lamps, the fifth mason jar that we had opened that evening. The brandy had been sitting in a dark place in my cabin for years, and Skid knew better than to frighten it with light.

He poured for us all, set the empty jar down, and slumped back down in his chair.

I stared up at the strange light on the top of Blue Mountain. All the night seemed suddenly to prepare, to set a stage for the play in our minds, the unfolding of a story that had been told on a thousand and one nights—and for a thousand and one years. Though I would not tell Andrews, or even Skidmore, I had collected variations of the story I was about to tell in Ireland and Scotland that were well over five hundred years old, about other mountains in other countries.

The crickets stopped for a moment, a black cloud dragged itself across the face of the moon, darkening the woods all around us, and even our breathing stilled. The cloud lifted, the curtain rose, and the dialogue began.

"There was a man in our little town," I said softly, "a very long time ago, known to all as Wicked John. He was the meanest man in the county. A blacksmith by trade, he loved to play cruel practical jokes. One day, as the sparks flew all about his face, an old ragged man came to the door of his smithy.

" 'Sir,' he said, 'can you help an old beggar?'

"Wicked John first thought to chase the old man from his door with a hot poker, but then he settled on something he felt was worse.

" 'Sit you down, old man,' he cackled, 'and I'll fetch you some vittles.'

"So saying, John ran to the house and found the rotting leftovers of his wife's last meal.

"*My wife is the worst cook in this nation*, he thought to himself. *That old man will surely choke on this food—which will teach him to come begging at my door.*

"He took the moldy food back to the forge, and offered it to the man. But no sooner had he done so, than the old man's guise fell away, and who should be standing there but St. Peter himself—who had not even looked at the food.

" 'I go about this earth from time to time,' St. Peter told Wicked John, 'searching for good men, and your kindness to a poor stranger has touched me. I will grant you one wish in this life.'

"Well, John didn't mention the nature of his wife's cooking then, nor the true intention of his bringing the food to the old beggar. He just set about to thinking what his wish might be. Finally, he came upon the perfect solution.

" 'I wish,' he told St. Peter, 'to make anyone who sits in my rocker chair to get stuck there in it—and they can't get up until I say so.'

"St. Peter thought this a strange request, but granted it nonetheless, and vanished.

"For years afterward, Wicked John made all manner of devilment out of his wish. Fine folk would sit in the chair for a rest, and John would refuse to let them out until they had given him money or favors. As he grew old, he was quite well-to-do.

"Alas, he also attracted the attention of another Wicked John, none other than the Devil himself. So when the Devil saw it was nearly John's time to die, the Devil set out to fetch the old man.

"The Devil came to the door of the smithy.

" 'John,' he announced regally, 'you must come with me. Your time has come.'

"John saw that he was in trouble, he recognized the Devil—he had seen the face often enough in his dreams.

" 'Well,' he answered, pounding on his anvil, 'I understand, and I shall be along directly. Let my just finish this one, last horseshoe.' He paused in his labor, a smirk on his face just out of the Devil's vision, and then continued. 'Have yourself a sit-down in my rocker chair . . . if you like.'

"The Devil looked around, saw the rocker, and sat. At once the Devil realized he'd been tricked.

" 'I can't get up!' he shrieked.

"John jumped around the chair.

" 'That's right!' he hollered. 'That's right! You can't get up until I say. And I'll *never* let you up!'

" 'But I'll freeze to death up here,' the Devil moaned. 'You've got to let me go.'

" 'I will,' answered John, 'on one condition.'

" 'What is it?' the Devil growled.

" 'You don't *never* come to get me no more!' John said plainly.

" 'Agreed.' The Devil spit to seal the deal. 'Let me go!'

"So John let the Prince of Evil up from the chair, and the Devil vanished. John lived on.

"But all men must die. And when it was finally John's time, Death itself would not be outdone. John was forced to leave his body behind, and his wandering spirit walked up to the heavenly gates. And who should be standing there but the very Saint Peter whom John had tricked so long ago.

" 'Who is it?' said St. Peter. 'You look familiar.'

" 'Well, I'm no one much, St. Peter,' said Wicked John, hoping to fool the gatekeeper. 'You likely don't even recollect me at all.'

"St. Peter looked in his golden book, searched every page, and found the name at last.

" 'You're Wicked John. I do remember. You're the worst mistake I ever made. One so-called good deed in your entire life, and a wicked existence ever after.' St. Peter shut the book. 'Well, you can't come in here.'

" 'But,' stammered John, afraid for the first time, 'where'll I go?'

" 'The Devil will take you!' St. Peter pronounced, and with a wave of his saintly hand John tumbled down to the Devil's lair.

"But the Devil saw John coming.

" 'Shut up the gates, quick!' the Devil yelled. 'It's Wicked John. We don't want him down here! He's worse than all of us put together.'

"So when John came knocking at the gates of Hell, the Devil inched his way toward him gingerly. Through the iron bars he handed John a pair of tongs with a red-hot coal in them.

" 'Here,' he told the wandering spirit. 'It's a coal from my very own hearth. You go on now, and start your own hell somewhere else. You can do it. We want none of you here in Hell.'

"So John was forced to wander this earth, alone and lonely, until he found his way back home, to this very town, the place of his birth. Here he searched high and low, and finally found a place to rest: on top of old Blue Mountain. There he laid the Devil's coal, and tried to start a hell of his own—but it was no use. That place you see up there, on that lonesome mountaintop? It's too cold and desolate even for the lost souls of this earth. So John's spirit lingers on, a lost creature, no home in Heaven, or in Hades. He learned, too late, that one Hell is enough for any world, and since the Devil already has his kingdom, best not to make another one of your own here on earth."

I leaned forward; my voice barely audible.

"Now—on a night like this—you can look high up on Blue Mountain—and if the moon's not too full, and the leaves aren't too thick—you can still see a faint and eerie glow: all that's left of old John's folly. We call it the Devil's Hearth."

The wind sighed, a crow, way off down the valley, called out— but nothing answered it.

The three of us sat stock still—in a trance, a reverie of odd respect for the ache of lost souls.

From inside, the telephone rang—a distant spirit calling us back from the doorway to the other world.

It did little to alter the ghostly mood on the porch. We all sat, staring up at the odd luminescence on the mountain until the phone had called three more times.

"That's most likely for me," Skidmore finally said, standing slowly. "I'm expecting a call." He vanished into the house.

The moon seemed to lay a silver spiderweb over everything on earth, and the crickets, as if realizing the story had been told, started up again louder than ever. Above our heads, all around, pine trees whispered the sound of winding sheets wrapped around a dozen dead bodies, and the wind seemed colder than it had been all night.

Andrews shifted on the railing, his eyes still fixed on the Hearth.

It was easy to see, I was thinking, how the folktales and fairy stories that I knew from childhood had lived for a thousand years, had been able to survive brutal Irish famines, Scottish clan wars, months of bitter ocean voyage to a new world, and deadly treks into unmapped mountain wilderness, all the way to Georgia, to my little house in the woods. They'd survived because the daring night was still haunted with every spirit that had ever bowed an unholy fiddle, told a tall tale, or sworn undying love for someone seen only once for an instant at a county fair.

I could see them, the spirits, flying all around my porch, calling out their light to me.

Other people—scholars from other disciplines—might have mistaken them for fireflies. But from my porch, I could see the obvious souls flash and move in the black tension of the night air.

The porch door swung open, and even the scrape of the wood was alive, a voice, a haunting.

"Coroner," Skidmore announced as the door closed behind him.

"Excellent," I said. "What did he say?"

"He said that the boy we found on this porch last night," Skid told us slowly, taking his seat again, "had done been shot dead."

"What a moron," Andrews answered accusingly, rolling his eyes. He stood and stretched his legs. "He didn't have anything else to offer—except for the obvious? We don't know anything from that."

"How many times do I have to tell you: Start from the unknown," I insisted, "and *proceed* to the obvious. That way you know where you're going and you know when you get there."

"Sounds very nice," Andrews took a single staggering step my way, "but how, exactly, do you intend to *do* it?"

"Ariadne's thread." I smiled.

"Say again?" Skidmore was still clearly considering some other information that the coroner had given him over the phone—I could tell from the furrow above his eyebrows—but he leaned forward in his seat. "That's one I don't know. *Whose* thread?"

"Ariadne was the half sister of the Minotaur," Andrews explained, with a little scowl my way. "She was in love with Theseus, the hero who was to slay the monster. It was easy enough to find your way into the labyrinth. You just followed the sounds of the beast. The getting back out was the trick. No one had ever done it. But Ariadne came up with the clever idea of holding one edge of a thread at the entrance to the cave, and Theseus took the other end with him."

"That's right." I was still staring out into the woods. "When the hero killed the beast in the dark labyrinth, he was able to follow that thread—the thread of love—from the lost, unknown center of chaos, back out into the bright daylight, the obvious place. The thread was his lifeline, and the woman who loved him was at the other end."

"I see." Skid leaned back. "That's nice."

"Except for Ariadne's reward." Andrews shook his head. "Theseus dumped her on the first island they came to, and she was abandoned to the elements. He sailed away."

"That's not Ariadne's reward," I protested. "She was found on the island by Bacchus, the god of wine, and he fell in love with her. She lived, as it is so often said, happily ever after."

"What?" Andrews winked at Skidmore. "Live with a drunken old man? Call that 'happily ever after'?"

"We all define *happiness* according to our own—" I began.

"So how do you have Ariadne's thread?" Andrews wanted to know, too drunk to wait for me to finish my sentence.

"Oh," I answered him, "I just meant that . . . I suppose I mean that I love my work. I love not knowing, being in the dark at the center of the labyrinth. I love following the thread to its logical, obvious conclusion."

That seemed to satisfy Andrews at that moment. He might have sensed that my answer was not entirely forthcoming had he not consumed such a great deal of foreign liquor. He just lumbered around on the porch trying to stretch his legs and walk off some of the effects of the brandy.

I watched the side of Skidmore's face. He was absently clicking his fingernails together, almost to match the crickets, *his* habit when he had something on his mind.

"Of course, you haven't told us all the information the coroner gave you," I said.

"Nope." He didn't look at me. "I have not."

"Wait." Andrews caught on. "What else was there?"

"I'm just trying to think how to say it." Skid's face was pinched. His hands moved quickly, clicking his nails even more. He clenched his teeth and sighed, heavily, and looked my way. "How do I tell you a thing like this?"

"Tell me what?" I steadied my feet on the floor of the porch. I'd never seen him so reticent to talk to me—we told each other everything.

"Um," he began, "you know how your mother was."

"God." I had only to close my eyes a moment, and that innocent phrase set off another parade of images in my mind: I could see my mother in her *Dance of Eve*, half-naked, gyrating, a live snake crawling all over her, pulling at the edges of her harem pants and nearly striking off the flimsy beaded top she wore in the show.

As a small boy, I had been frightened by that dance. By the time I'd grown to adolescence and seen the effect that her performance had on the audience—men in the audience—I'd been repelled; sickened.

Still, I'd watched nearly every performance until the day I left home for college.

I'd heard stories time and again of my mother's wild nature, her infidelities, her strange passions. I had only confronted my father with these rumors once.

"Your mother does what she likes," had been his only answer.

"So do I." He'd slapped my shoulder. "So can you, as a matter of fact. That's a secret of this life: You can do just about anything you want to."

Then I'd helped him load his table, the magic-show table for his act. It was always filled with coils and hidden chambers—like the Minotaur's labyrinth—like the folds and creases, I'd always thought as a boy, in the human brain.

That thought came to me because I was so fascinated with the human brain exhibited in our sideshow. It had been pickled in a large jar. Swimming in viscous fluid, it had been advertised as the brain of a monster, a man named Ed Gein, who had robbed graves, butchered women, and performed unspeakable acts in a land far away called Wisconsin. This man had been twisted into the horror that he was by his strange mother. He was, I learned years later, the real-life model for the character in the movie *Psycho*.

Of course, as was the case with nearly everything else in our sideshow, the brain was a fraud. It was actually the only remains of one of our roustabouts. He'd left his brain, in his will, to the show— in order that he might always travel with us.

Still, the image of the brain was linked in my mind to the grue-some stories that the sideshow barker had told about the true-life deviant Ed Gein—a man who had found a way of dealing with the difficulties he had concerning his own mother. He had tortured, murdered, and eaten many victims, and then said that it relieved his troubles to do so—for a while.

I deliberately willed my mind to stop the flood of images, and fin-ished the last of my brandy in a long, slow swallow.

"Yes," I finally answered Skidmore, "I know how my mother was. Why do you bring it up?"

"Well, don't get upset about this just now," Skid told me softly, "because we don't really know whether it's the truth or not." Short breath. "No other way to say it but just blurt it out. It appears that old boy we found here last night might have been somehow related to you. Might have been, I'm saying, your older brother."

Andrews jaw fell. "What?"

"It's nothing." I turned a fairly cold eye his way. "I've always heard rumors that my mother had several children other than myself—

older children—although I am the only child of my father. I always put that talk right out of my mind."

"So you're not shocked by this news," Andrews asked me.

" 'Shocked' is, I think, not the correct word." I pulled in as much air as I could fit into my lungs, then let it go. "Perhaps a phrase like 'reassuringly disgusted' would do."

"Wait." Andrews turned to Skidmore. "How could the coroner know that at this point? He surely hasn't had time for the proper tests."

"That's right." Skid would look neither of us in the eye. "He wants to do all the DNA tests, of course, but right now the evidence he does have is fairly convincing."

"Evidence?" Andrews pressed, finally standing still.

"Well," Skidmore shifted uncomfortably in his seat, "I guess we could start with the fact that they found a birth certificate on the body—and Dolores Devilin was listed as the mother." He exhibited only the slightest of pauses. "Father unknown."

"Birth certificate?" I could barely get it out.

"It appears to us, me and Montrose the coroner, at the moment," Skidmore rambled as he stared out into the black woods, "that it was deliberately placed on the body. Somebody wanted you to know who that old boy was."

"You mean," Andrews was still piecing it together, trying to clear his head from the brandy, staring at Skidmore, "that you think someone may have killed this man and stuffed him with his own birth certificate just to leave a calling card? On this porch? I don't believe that."

"I'm not saying I believe it either, entirely," Skidmore answered, rolling his head to ease the muscles in his neck. "But you've got to admit that it is a theory."

"What do you think, Dev?" Andrews shot a look my way. "What's going on here?"

"I don't know," I answered steadily. "I believe I've just been saying that I *like* not knowing. A question, as they say, is the beginning of a quest."

"Well, you're certainly calm about it," Andrews said. "And you've absolutely got enough questions to go around."

He looked up at the eerie glow at the top of the Blue Mountain.

A shroud of silence threatened to keep us still for the rest of the night, but Andrews was still too drunk to keep silent for long. "It's stranger than hell, that's what I think."

"Welcome," I told him, watching the fireflies blink on and off all around the porch, even managing a kind of smile, "to my world."

Five

The next morning I was up before anyone else in the cabin. Andrews had taken my father's room and Skidmore, after a lengthy phone conversation with Girlinda about *just* how much alcohol he'd drunk on my porch, had spent another night on the uncomfortable sofa downstairs. We'd stayed up until two, but I'd set my alarm for six. I needed to be out alone that morning.

The air was still quite chilly, and a low fog clung—a gray desperation—to the valleys and hollows, afraid to relinquish its hold on the body of the earth; also afraid to reveal what it might have hidden there.

I stood on the porch, zipped my black cloth jacket, and sipped the last bit of my espresso. Making it without waking the others had been a minor challenge, but an extension cord to the porch had done the trick. The whoosh of the machine fit nicely with the wind in the trees and the calling of ten thousand birds.

I always forgot how many birds there were around my cabin until I visited again and heard them singing. As a boy, alone in the place for days at a time, I'd often spent the long afternoons drawing the birds I could see, imagining what it might be like to have wings on my back.

I unplugged the espresso maker, moved the cord aside so that no one would trip over it, and stepped off the porch toward my truck.

Originally made in 1947, rebuilt by a student of mine in 1997— for a surprisingly small amount of money—the old green truck had been my father's. Aside from a few antique ties and a strange sense of what was acceptable in life, the Ford was all I had to remember him by.

I had parked it just exactly as I needed it, with the front headed ever-so-slightly down the slope. All I needed to do was release the emergency brake, and I could coast silently halfway down the mountain before I had to crank the engine. I wouldn't wake anyone in the cabin.

I opened the driver's-side door as quietly as I could. I only looked back once, taking a moment to wonder how Andrews and Skidmore would get along without my intervention. Then I slipped in, pulling the door behind me, put the key in the ignition, and released the hand break.

Rolling down the mountain road, then gathering speed and flying, was always a giddy ride—seeing how long I could manage without tapping the brakes. It was a bracing thrill of danger, playing "Runaway Car" as my father had called it.

Or was that the concept I wanted, given Deputy Needle's insistence that I was always running away from something?

Still, falling forward with such abandon, like an avalanche down the road, was a sensation I could not resist, and so I ignored the brake pedal, even as the truck gathered breakneck speed and the turns grew nearly impossible to negotiate.

I was close to the bottom of the mountain, barely shy of the main road, when I finally tapped the brake, set the key, and popped the clutch, bumping off the car without actually turning the starter. It was just as I had always done as a teenager, escaping the house when the parents had returned. It was the closest experience to flying I would ever know—without the actual wings.

The main road wound like a river, black and empty, over the rises and turns of the lower land. I was filled with a kind of rapture I had known far too infrequently in the city or at the university: absolute freedom, bursting into the unknown morning with no expectation of what might happen for the rest of the day.

Although I did, in fact, know where I was going at that moment. I was headed to the county's primeval gathering place: Gil's Filling Station.

Most folk communities had such gathering spots: barbershops, gas stations, feed stores. Gil's was an old-style affair. The centerpiece was comprised of two ancient pumps that looked like museum pieces but actually dispensed petroleum products. Behind them was a small wooden building that had once been painted blue and white, but as most of the paint was chipped and gone, the building looked more like a ruined barn. To the side of it there was a double-wide garage door where all manner of internal combustion engines had been taken apart, examined, and made better by Gil's slow, sure hand. Inside there might be a rack of magazines, if Gil had thought to order any, and two shelf rows of automobile items: oil, transmission fluid, wiper blades. On the counter: a huge jar of pickled eggs and a rack of candy bars. To one side of the counter there was a Coca-Cola machine so old that it would only accept a nickel and a penny as payment for the small glass bottles inside. The floor was dusty, and smeared with grease, and the whole place was colored by the perfume from the pumps.

Women were always welcome, and treated with an astonishing degree of deference and respect—but women seldom came into the place, and they were almost always strangers from out of town. It seemed a place for men not because women weren't invited but because women had better sense than to spend time in a place as dirty and smelly as Gil's. I knew that even at six-thirty on a weekday morning, the men would be gathered there, as they always had been in my childhood, before their work began: Shoo Walters, Carson Howe, and Hezekiah Cotage. Among these three men, and their wives, all the secrets in the world were revealed.

Shoo Walters was the ladder-back chair maker whose work I wanted to study more, the subject of the first book I would write. He was round, bald, quiet—always dressed the same: clean white shirt, bib overalls, a brown felt fedora, a clean shave, and a secret smile. As far as I could determine, he was the only one of his kind left in Appalachia. He gathered the wood for his chairs from the trees surrounding his house, not a Home Depot. Then he cut the wood, bent it, and shaved it with implements exactly like those that had been invented in the Middle Ages—tools that had remained unchanged in design or usage since the twelfth century.

He was a great artist, if something of a simpleton. He claimed to believe that his uncle, who had taught him the craft, had invented the implements. When I had shown him, once many years before, a woodcut from the eleven hundreds that depicted the same chair-making scheme, he'd only smiled and told me, "I had no idea my uncle was that old." His nickname was acquired from that same uncle, who was always trying, unsuccessfully, to rid himself of the boy.

Carson Howe was a different story. I'd grown up around him, and he'd helped raise me. He was a tree of a man, silver beard to the middle of his chest, skin like a tanned hide, hands that looked too big and too rough to play the violin the way he did. Blind since an accident in the coal mines of Kentucky long before he'd come to Georgia, he'd survived quite well as the fiddler in our traveling show.

The third of our gas station trinity, Hezekiah Cotage, made his living predominantly as a charismatic preacher. He was short, nervous, always rocking, always dressed in a black suit, a thin tie, a wrinkled dress shirt—his hair in random disarray. His was the church made famous in academic folk circles by my mentor, Dr. Bishop.

I had heard of Dr. Bishop as a boy—he was a familiar figure in the community for years, collecting stories and songs, discovering folk artists. By the time I had decided to leave home for the university, I hadn't even considered any course of study other than his program at Burrison. Bishop's foundational research concerning snake handling, and most especially a certain remarkable item of material folk culture housed in that very church, had made his name recognizable to any true folk scholar in the world.

Hezekiah also worked a small farm, but that did little save distract him—and provide his wife with fresh vegetables for dinner. I had always been, in fact, closer to his wife, June. She played the plucked psaltry and sang in a soprano so clear and angelic that it defied description. Her curly brown hair and soft green eyes always reminded me more of the schoolgirl she had been than the woman in her fifties that she had become. I had long wanted to record her singing.

The psaltry was an instrument much like the hammered dulcimer—fundamentally a harp built into a box, the obvious precursor of early keyboard instruments. When it was called a dulcimer, it was played with small hammers, one in each hand of the performer. When it was called a psaltry, it was generally set on a table, or laid atop a specially built stand, and plucked with the fingers, as was June's talent.

Her husband, and other men from the community, gathered at Gil's nearly every morning before setting off on the day's tasks—long before Gil was there. And they often found their way back to the garage after hours to play music, share stories, and drink illegal beverages—long after Gil had gone home.

Carson had first introduced me to that, his "social club," on my tenth birthday: sitting me down amongst the throng and thrusting a musical instrument into my hands.

"Here's you a mandolin," he'd told me. "Put your fingers here to make a G chord, here's a C, and that . . . no, like that—that's a D. All you need to know right now. Just watch us and follow. You'll get it." He'd patted my shoulder. "Oh yeah, and here's you a drink of corn whiskey."

The other men had laughed when I'd taken my first sip from that mason jar. I thought my lips had been burned off. I thought they had tricked me into drinking gasoline. But I'd laughed right along with those men when they'd howled at my expression. I knew they loved me. I knew this was an oft-repeated ceremony, one that meant they were taking me in as one of their number. I knew that my drink was, in fact, a sort of Eucharist—and that day was my confirmation, my first as a man.

Without another word, they began playing "Cotton-Eyed Joe."

Cotton-eyed Joe, Cotton-eyed Joe,
Where did you come from, where did you go
Where did you come from, Cotton-eyed Joe?

They must have gone through twenty verses or more. By the end, I'd at least learned how three chords were played on the mandolin.

I'd loved the instrument ever since.

So when I saw those men sitting in their chairs, exactly as I had hoped they would be, in front of the open garage door, I felt I was truly, finally home. The sunlight raced downward in slants of amber and tan, the cool air seemed like a lens, focusing the image clearer for me.

They saw my truck. In utter silence they watched me park, get out, shut the car door.

There was no leaping, no rushing, no throwing of arms—except in the heart.

Shoo leaned close to Carson and whispered something.

Carson set down his coffee mug. "Is that my boy?"

"Don't look like a boy no more." Shoo stared at me laconically. "But it appears to be Fever, sure enough."

"That you, boy?" Carson called out, still seated.

"You *know* it's him," Hek shook his head. "What did Shoo just tell you?"

Carson waved his massive hand, ignoring Hek. "Come on over here quick, boy."

I couldn't help stepping a little faster. Shoo pushed a dilapidated chair my way with his foot. I took it.

We sat in silence for a moment.

"So," Carson said after I'd settled. "You come back."

"I have," I told him. "But it's not a visit this time. I'm here for good. I've quit university life. I've moved back into the cabin. I've come home."

"I heard." Carson nodded calmly. "That's good."

"It is," I agreed. "It is good. Everything's good."

"Not everything," Hek snorted. "That ain't what we heard."

"You shut up, Hek." Carson turned his head quickly in the direction of Hek's voice.

"We heard," Hek went on, "you was shot dead on your front porch. That's what people was saying yesterday."

"God damn it." Carson's deep voice grew louder. "We know good and well that ain't what happened."

"What do you think happened, Hek?" I asked Hezekiah.

"Never can tell." He looked away. "Up there on that damn Blue Mountain? You can't never tell." I knew he was teasing me.

"You think I might have been killed last night, then?" I glanced at Shoo, who stifled a little laugh. "Think I might not really be here at all right now?"

"How many times," Hek answered, "have I told you about that?" His face was glowing. "How many haints I done told you about?"

"Dozens, Hek," I agreed patiently.

"You know about Lucy," he reminded me. More teasing.

Hek had, perhaps a hundred times or more, told me about a day, long past, when he had gone squirrel hunting up on Blue Mountain.

He came upon a pretty black-haired girl sitting by a clear stream, twirling a daisy in her fingers.

She smiled up at him, so he sat down on the bank to speak with her.

"What's your name?" he wanted to know.

She said, "Lucy."

"Are you lost?"

She said, "No."

"Where do you live?"

"Here," she said at first. Then she shook her head and said, "I mean, up the road just a piece."

"Do you have a beau?" he wanted to know.

She said, "Naw—but *you're* awful pretty. Maybe you could be my beau."

That was enough for Hek. "Do you imagine you'd let me court you?"

She said, "Well, you'll have to ask my papa about that."

Hek was up on his feet so quickly that he forgot his shotgun; left it by the stream.

He carried himself up the road until he came to an unfamiliar house. He went to the door and knocked.

An old man answered, "Who is it?"

"It's Hezekiah Cotage, Mister. I live in town, I make a fair living, and I'd like to come in and talk about your daughter."

There was a long pause, then the door opened, and a sad, bent old figure was displayed before him. "My daughter. Yes. I miss her so."

"Miss her?" Hek said.

"Yes," the old man replied, "she's been gone for some time now."

"She has?" Hek was unable to hide his confusion.

"We used to live down by the stream, years ago, down the road just a piece," the old man told him, "but there come up a terrible lightning storm one night, and the house was struck and set afire."

"My Lord." Hek felt dizzy.

"Didn't mind losing the house," the old man said, "but my little baby girl was inside sick as she could be, and before we could get her out, the fire burned the house to the ground."

"The house burned down?" Hek took ahold of the door frame to steady himself. "What you say happened to the little girl?"

The old man said, "She died in the fire."

"So," Hek began, "you had two daughters."

"No." The old man stared back strangely. "Just the one."

Hek's tongue moved thickly. "One?" His head was swimming. "And what was her name?"

"Her name was Lucy."

Hek ran as fast as he could back to the waterside, and there all he found on the bank of the clear stream was his shotgun, plaited all around with a ring of daisies.

"Yes, Hek," I said, one side of my mouth higher than the other, "I remember your story about Lucy." I never completely knew if he understood that the story of the ghostly Lucy was at least three hundred years old, and had no less than fifty variants in hundreds of folk communities around America.

"Well, then." Hek just nodded. "Good."

"God A'mighty." Carson sat back, irritated with Hezekiah. "If you're all done with teasing him, I'd like to find out how my boy is."

"Never did find that old man's house again—Lucy's father." Hek shifted in his chair, utterly ignoring Carson. "It's like it just disappeared."

"Hek!" Carson had had enough.

Hek knew to stop.

Carson's face turned back my way, and he waited. He seemed to know this was not the ordinary first-visit-back-in-town that we'd had before. "So?"

"So." I gathered my thoughts. "Much as I'd love to spend the rest of the day here, sitting around telling stories, catching up, and perhaps, a little later, picking out a song or two, I can't do that just now. I have some . . . chores first."

"Go on," Carson nodded. His beard was all gray, but I remembered when it was black as coal—just yesterday, it seemed.

"I need to know who's been living in my cabin."

Silence.

"Look," I tried again. "You three know about everything that happens in this county—you had to know that there was a man living in my cabin."

Hek looked away. "We knew."

"Do you know who he was?" I asked him quietly. "Do you know anything about him?"

"Fever." Carson's voice was softer than the felt in Shoo's hat. "You sure you *want* to know this, son?"

"What do you mean?" I looked into Carson's stony face.

"Well," Shoo started slowly, avoiding my gaze, "it's about your mother. I mean, I don't like to talk about your mother this way, Dev—but you *know* how she was?"

"Everybody seems to be asking me that lately," I told him. "I've spent most of my life adjusting to bits of knowledge about my mother."

"Well, then . . ." he hesitated, apparently not certain he understood what I was saying ". . . you know what I mean?"

"I do." I sighed.

"So the point is—not to belabor the issue for too long . . . and to get right to it . . ." deep breath, ". . . you may have one or two older half-brothers somewhere around here." He stared hard at the dirt on the floor.

More silence.

"I'm aware of my possible siblings," I finally insisted. "I've heard the rumors for most of my life."

I decided to hold back, for a moment, the coroner's information from the previous evening. I also held inside the questions I'd always had about my siblings: who those phantoms were, how my mother could have left them—why she'd kept me, why I'd been the only one she'd lived with. Those questions were not for these men.

I only shrugged, and lied. "That information matters *very* little to me."

50

"Unless one of them," Hek said carefully, "has ended up on your front porch, dead."

"That's just what we're saying, son," Carson nodded, his voice rising shrewdly. "That's what we think." He sighed a little breath of air through his nostrils.

"I see." I stared evenly at all three.

"You don't seem all that surprised." Carson's voice was almost amused.

"It's just," I began, "that Skid received some information last night. What you're saying just, I suppose, confirms that information—which I was hoping was, somehow, inaccurate."

No one knew what to say to that.

"That's enough of that." I changed the subject. "So what do you know about the someone who took a few shots at Skidmore and me when we found the body?"

All the men sat straighter.

Shoo managed, "What?" He seemed more startled than the others.

"Well," I gave a curt nod, "Skidmore was able to keep that information silent, and I've just let it out of the bag."

"Somebody shot at you boys?" Hek leaned forward.

"With that body still stretched out on the porch," I affirmed, "someone took shots at us from the woods with a rifle."

"Well, now." Carson's shoulders sank. "Deputy Needle held out on us."

We all let another moment pass. A hawk was circling overhead, and cried out in the clean morning air. The sound seemed to prompt us to speak again.

"What made you all think that man on my porch was really my brother, Carson?" My voice came out a little harder than I'd intended. The coroner might have seen a document as some sort of proof, but I trusted the word of these men more than any piece of paper—if they had reason to actually be informed.

"I believe it was your brother, sure enough," he answered—it seemed to me—a little more quickly than he had meant to.

"How do you know?" My voice was steely.

"Well," Carson's tone lowered. "Your half-brother—his name was Thresher . . ."

"What?"

"He was named Thresher," the old man repeated. Then he tried for a grin. "Your mother surely was a pistol when it come to naming you boys. He surely could sing, though. Had a voice on him—"

"I have to know what he was doing here," I interrupted harshly. "In my house."

"Well, see," Shoo put his hand on my shoulder for a second, "we thought you knew all about him, his living there. I mean—he did appear to have a key." But then he looked away so I couldn't see in his eyes. It struck me, finally, that he was not telling me something.

"Did you all speak with him?" For some reason I was a little wounded by that prospect, once I'd said it out loud. "Did you know him?"

"Didn't know him at all." Carson set my mind at ease. "Hek just seen him up there in the woods when he was rabbit hunting."

"In fact," Hek went on, "I thought it was you when I first seen him. You'uns favor a good bit."

"We do?" I could barely picture him—and then it was only the side of a corpse's face. "Or did?"

"Well," Hek offered, "you know . . . from a distance, anyway. It's hard to miss that snowy hair. I was about to holler out to you when he turned back to the wood side and I could see he weren't you. Then he skittered on in the house—with a key. Unlocked the door just as nice as you please."

"Hek come on back down the mountain," Shoo finished, "and told us you done lent your cabin to your twin brother."

"Only Carson knowed you didn't have no twin," Hek continued. "I guess we all did, you know." Another glance Carson's way. "But it was him that told us about your brother name of Thresher."

"I have to ask again." I looked down at the concrete. "Did you all know him?"

"No." It was Carson's voice. "He didn't live around here, you know."

"Where did he live?" I still didn't look up.

"Blueridge."

"Close to where Shoo's uncle used to live?" My voice was more hollow.

"Naw," Shoo said, "furtherer than that. Over across the big lake. Next county."

Oddly, the fact that my apparent half-brother had lived in another county was comforting. Another county was somehow another reality.

"All right." Carson cleared his throat. "You care to know more about him, then?"

"That's what I'm here for this morning, among other things. Yes." I nodded. "But you haven't said, yet, how *you* actually knew about him."

"Your daddy told me." No hesitation. "When Hek come back and told us what he'd seen, I knew it had to be Thresher. I always heard you two favored that way. Then we found out more about him."

"Wait." I was the one who hesitated. Then: "My father knew?"

"Your mother and father," Carson said slowly, "didn't never have no secrets from one another. Not one."

"Only from me," I said. My voice was bitter as hemlock. "They only had secrets from me."

"That's right." Carson turned his vacant, milky eyes my way, and the hint of a smile touched his lips again. "I can't imagine why they might have held back," he intoned, "seeing how well you're taking all this now."

Even Shoo nodded. He seemed to understand the truth of what Carson was saying with his amused sarcasm. "This ain't something you can tell a boy who's as troubled as you, Dev—as you was back then in the younger days."

"I was *what*? I was troubled?"

"As a summer day's long," Hek answered right back. "You were dark and deep as a sinkhole." Grin. "Hell, Carson put a mandolin in your hands on account of we was all afraid for you to have a hunting gun."

"No you weren't." I couldn't help smiling a little. This was a key ingredient of our brotherhood, this truth-saying wrapped in a comfortable blanket of jocularity.

"Well," Carson laughed a little, too, "we weren't quite that worried about you, but you got to admit you was a strange one."

"How? How was I strange?" I knew we were still playing.

"Well," Hek volunteered. "You used to talk real funny. Still do. You don't talk like nobody else I know."

"Anybody you *know*?" I looked around at the trio, falling into the same taunting-speech. "You don't *know* anybody at all—except our present, ill-spoken company."

"Let me see, that ain't entirely true," Hek leaned back. "I'm kind of friendly with that old boy Skidmore Needle, nowadays." There was something different in his voice.

"I see," I said, ignoring, at that moment, what he might have meant by that comment. I had another question in mind. "I'm glad you brought him up. It's just occurred to me: Why do you think he didn't know who was on my porch when everybody else did?"

"He'd been gone from town," Carson began, "on a job."

"That's right," I nodded. "He said something about being away on business."

"Business. Shoot," Shoo smiled. "He was in a bus for three weeks playing bodyguard to Alan Jackson."

"Who?" I asked.

"You don't know who Alan Jackson is?" Carson shook his head. "All that education and you don't know a damn thing."

"Alan Jackson, Dev." Hek explained it to me as if I were seven. "He's a big star. Born right here in Georgia."

"Oh," I said, rolling my head, "a country singer. A *pop* country singer."

"No need to put on that air, boy. I know you don't have a lick of respect for *any* singer from up in these hills that ain't ignorant, flat, and dead, but—"

"I'm just more interested," I began, "in authentic—"

"If it's good music, it's good music," Carson shot back. "That's all I care about."

"Well," I answered him, "despite the fact that this is not at all what I'm here to discuss, I'd have to say that I find the concept of 'good music' to be one of the most *subjective* in American culture."

Silence

"See?" Shoo spoke up after a moment, grinning. "That kind of sentence right there, that's what makes us all think you talk funny— like we was saying."

I smiled back and assumed a pronunciation even more insufferable to them than my usual diction. "My speech is, to you, somehow aberrant?"

"Always was, boy," Carson intervened. "You care about words the way a miser cares about pennies. But that ain't the point. The point is that you were a trouble-child, and we didn't none of us think twice about telling you all this. We knew you wouldn't take it well—so we just didn't talk about it at all."

Another part of the mountain ethos: If you don't discuss it, it doesn't exist.

I took a second to get back to what he had so correctly indicated as the point. "All right, then, just how many more are there?"

"Brothers?" Hek asked. "Well, of course nobody can say for sure. Thresher lived over in Blueridge—lived with your mama's sister. That is until your daddy died and your mama went to stay with them herself."

I knew my mother had moved in with her sister before she'd died, but there had always been a great air of mystery about the move, and by that time we had grown so estranged that we were barely in touch at all.

"Why didn't they live with us, these brothers, if everybody knew about them?" I'm certain my voice had grown quite thin. "Are they still there now, with the aunt that I barely ever knew—the part of the family that we never talked about?"

"Okay." Carson slapped his knees with his hands. "That's enough. We don't need to talk about this any more right now."

Moses had spoken. There would be no more discussion of the subject at that moment.

"Here's what you need to know right away," he concluded. "Thresher—who is now dead—come up here not quite two weeks ago and commenced to asking all manner or questions about you. Asking all around. That's how we found out more about him. He spoke to June and to me and to Hezekiah. It was like he was writing a book. He wanted to know everything."

My voice came out barely a whisper. "Why?"

"Said he wanted to know as much about you as he could," Hek answered, "before he went to talk to you in the city."

"Came to talk to me?" I tried to steady my voice. "About what? Why was he coming to the city to talk to me?"

"That's why he was here, boy, living up at your place. He was getting ready." Carson leaned forward ever so slightly. "He said he had some kind of a message for you—an important message—from your mother."

I did not move or speak. To the casual observer, my reaction to the possibility of a message from my dead mother might have seemed as calm as my reaction to rifle bullets two nights before. But there's a certain manner of accepting things in the mountains that I'd never quite escaped. Good news, bad news, joy, sorrow, plenty, and pestilence were all received with little or no reaction at all—a casual nod and a comment about the weather.

There was no pouring out the dram of my emotions to these men. The only acceptable catharsis to be had in that circle would come later that night, and would involve string band music and white liquor.

When Andrews had asked me once, in fact, why I'd never gone in for therapy of any sort—something, to him, I'd so obviously needed—my answer had been simple: "I don't need therapy. I play the mandolin."

Still, I did need more information—more than these men would give me. I had the answer I'd been looking for from them, at any rate: The man on the porch was, in fact, my half-brother. The birth certificate was not a faked document set forth to deliberately mislead me.

What I needed next was something from the feminine side—things only June Cotage would tell me. I needed to know how and why a stranger would have anything to give me from a woman who had been dead for over a decade.

My mother had passed away in a strange town, completely alone. I'd gotten the news from June, in a three-line letter, during my first year teaching at the university. The news had produced little effect in me except to wonder at the strangeness of my mother's life.

Still, I began to consider what information the dead man could have had from a person so long deceased. I knew these men would not know, would not have presumed to even ask—so strong was their conviction that such issues were very much none of their business.

So:

"Is June at home, Hek?" I asked him.

"Most likely." He stared at an oil stain on the concrete in front of him.

"Okay, then," I stood. "I think I'll just go on over and pay my respects."

"You'll have to pay more than that," said Carson, grinning, "if you expect Junie to gossip about all this with you. She's a changed woman. She don't gossip no more like she used to."

"Changed?" I glanced at Hek.

"Now my wife," he began, very grandiloquently, "*was* known in five counties as the biggest gossip God ever permitted to give birth to natural children. She can take an ordinary apple pie, and turn it around five ways from Sunday, until it's quinces and blackbirds." This was the *Hek Show*, his bumpkin act, for my benefit, I knew. I also knew he was doing it to distract me from my concern—and maybe to hide something from me. "Do you know that she once ran half a mile in a thunder storm to tell everybody that she saw *you*, Dev, kissing Lucinda Foxe over by the Hearth? That was back one day when she was gathering up blackberries, long time ago. She happened to come across you two—"

"But you say she's changed, now, Hek?" I had to stop him.

"Well, sir," he shifted into the topic with complete ease, "it was last Decoration Day. We was all at the dinner on the grounds, and she come upon these other two people splashing and cavorting in the water over by the Split Creek dam—-in their best Sunday clothes. She run back to the picnic, gathered up ten or twelve other biddies, and they all rushed on to see who it was. What do you think they saw?"

"Hek, I'm in something of a hurry—" I began.

"Minister Greenwire baptizing old Ms. Shump!"

All the men exploded with laughter.

Ida Shump was in the habit of being baptized on the average of twice a month by the Reverend Greenwire. The unkinder members of the congregation whispered that those ablutions constituted the only times that the old woman ever bathed.

Her own explanation for such spiritual diligence was that a per-

son ought to wash her soul at least as often as she washed her windows. The whole matter had become something of an embarrassment for the minister, who had taken to performing the ceremony in private. He admonished the congregation to please allow such a holy transformation the privacy it deserved, away from prying eyes.

"That preacher got hotter than a poker when he seen those women standing on the bank," Hek managed between snorts, then shook his head. "Minister Greenwire give us a two-and-a-half-hour sermon next Meeting on the evils of gossip and what he called 'the jumping to conclusions.' Lord, was Junie's face all kinds of red. She ain't been the same since."

Part of me wanted to give over to that moment—to explore the nature of gossip in the community, and Ida's psychosis, and the minister's embarrassment. That was the work I had come back to the mountains to do—those were the stories I wanted to hear. What pleasant and beautiful work it would be, in the cool September air, sitting back, spending the morning idly talking, moving slowly through ancient ceremonies and loving curiosities.

But that work would have to wait for another day.

"I'll still be going to see her," I told Hek. "I just want to say hello."

"Dev." He looked down. "You want more than that."

"Do you still do a weekday service, Hek?" I asked him, deliberately changing the subject.

"Yes I do. I'll be over there directly." He looked down. "You'd be welcome this morning."

"And will you all be here tonight?" I asked everyone. "I've got a new mandolin—like you all to hear it."

"We'll all be here by seven," Carson nodded, kingly as he was. "There's a new high school boy plays the guitar with us now. You got to hear it to believe it. Faster'n lightning."

"Well, I may have a new lick or two to show you all."

That was it. I turned and walked to my truck without saying good-bye, as was proper, and the men resumed a relaxed discussion about the temperature of the air around them.

Six

Most ghosts appear as they should: after dark, in the moonlight, with the noises of the night all around. But some ghosts come forth, unbidden, even on the brightest of days. These are the most haunting, and the most difficult to dispel, because they are not cowered by the sun, not troubled by standing in the light. Often the person they represent—these spirits abroad in the daylight—is not even dead and haunts the mind of the beholder, not the eye.

Walking with me back to the truck was such a ghost: the form of Lucinda Foxe. Lucinda was, thank God, very much alive. The ghost that was walking with me had been born of recollection and tied to me by memory's thread.

I was thinking about every detail of her face, her walk, her summer dresses, her wheat-colored hair, the way she always smelled vaguely of honeysuckle. We had shared more than a kiss that day up on the Hearth—and many more days like it.

In my mind I saw those long summer days. All across the deep purple bachelor buttons that grew wild for acres down the slopes of Blue Mountain, we had rolled. Arm in arm in the summer grass we'd lie on our backs, watching hawks circle, telling stories, making plans. Her hand fit into mine the way a perfect word ended a poem. I had not known, before I'd met Lucinda, that it was possible to like a girl as much as I liked the air or music or the light of day.

And so, like Hezekiah's ghost of Lucy—perhaps even called forth by the mention of her story—there was Lucinda, walking beside me, climbing into the truck with me, slowly fading beside me on the way to Junie's house.

The Cotage household was centered on as fine a piece of bottom land as Nature had ever gathered together. The earth was black as a rain cloud, rich as an ancient melody. The house was small, white, clean as a pin. The porch was spotless, the rockers both had pillows in them that had been adorned with June's needlepoint. The tin roof seemed polished like armor against the elements. All the windows were open and white curtains billowed out, as if the house were waving at me, welcoming me home.

I pulled into the yard and got out of the truck. I let my eye wander about the yard, up the slopes of the mountains around it. Behind the house the hill rose up like giant arms from the earth, enfolding the house, keeping it safe. The leaves were not yet turning, but there was a hint of color, a dab of yellow here, a smudge of red at the top. I stood by the truck until Lucinda's ghost was completely gone before I called into the house.

"June Cotage?"

Not many people in the mountains still relied on "helloing the house" to announce themselves, but I'd always been nostalgic for a tradition that had, in most realities, died before I was born.

"Who is it?" Her voice rose from the kitchen. "That ain't Fever Devilin out there, is it?"

"Junie."

I could hear a commotion through all the open windows.

"Boy." She appeared in the door, her image exploded through it, down the steps, and before I knew it, my neck was in the crook of her arm.

"Junie." I held her, eyes closed. This was the greeting the men could never give me. "I missed you."

She was rocking me like a little boat on the ocean. "Lord, it's good to see you." She let me go and stood back, examining me. "See you home, sugar."

"Yes." I looked out across her fields again. "It is good to be home."

"Well come on in the house." She wouldn't completely relinquish her hold on me, and took my arm. "Did you have your breakfast?"

"I had coffee," I told her, knowing what her response would be.

"That don't get you through the day." She dragged me back up the porch steps. "Come on in the kitchen and I'll fetch you a little something."

I knew very well what she had in mind: five eggs, bacon, grits and gravy, biscuits and jam, and a gallon of hot, weak coffee.

"Junie, I really came to talk. And actually," I told her, following her into the house "my cholesterol level—"

"—Would not be a problem if you'd do a lick of real work once in a while instead of sitting at your desk at the schoolhouse." She didn't even look back. Resistance was futile.

I followed her through the living room crowded with a hundred pictures of family members and old friends. Everything was exactly as I remembered it: two sofas, three rocking chairs, one coffee table, one book—a battered family bible—and a huge gas space heater in the fireplace. The only difference I could see was in the number of photographs of her family, which had grown to threaten everything else in the room.

Down the hall and into the kitchen I realized how dark the house was, even in the bright sunlight. I'd always thought of a darkened house as a sure sign of aged inhabitants. Light equaled young, dark equaled grandmothers. The dismay was in realizing, in just that moment, that Hek and Junie were growing old.

That gloomy feeling grew as I stepped onto the checkerboard pattern of her linoleum floor. When these people and the others their age were dead, the true Appalachian folklore and folklife would be, for all intents and purposes, gone from the earth. It only lived, almost hiding, in a handful of older folks. Those ways would die a final, irrevocable death when the last of that generation passed away. Junie'd learned her songs from her mother. Junie's children more readily sang television jingles and pop songs from the radio. There was really no untainted spot left in the mountains. And "taint" was the word, in my opinion, for co-opted country music, pop radio and television, the invasion of vicious technology into the hollows of Greenwood County.

Hek's stories, Shoo's chairs, Junie's music—they were all a part of our story as human beings, our unwritten story from the beginning of time, handed down by the spoken word and the observed action, for thousands of centuries.

That story, the very fabric of the world's mythology, had been torn to shreds by the twentieth century and was unsalvageable.

I was reminded, in such moments as that one walking into June's kitchen why my work was so important to me. I labored, I thought honestly, in order that something so important as *that* story—our big, collective story—would not perish from the earth.

"At least have you a biscuit." June's voice roused me from grandiose pretensions of saving the world. "That ain't likely to kill you."

"And some jam," I said. "I could probably live through some of your blackberry jam as well."

She smiled. She knew I was humoring her—but she was a woman who had achieved most of her accomplishments in life by making men believe that they were only humoring her.

The kitchen was warm, and brighter than the hall. Every bit of countertop space was taken, but the stainless steel and linoleum kitchen table, with the pattern of wildflowers on it, was cleaned and cleared. She pointed to the chair where I was to sit. It made a pleasant sound when it scraped the floor as I pulled it out. It was a sound that had always promised me good food and better company.

June's dress was blue, and the collar was white. It was simple and modest, well below the knee and loose but secure around the neck. Her hair was in a tight bun at the back of her head; there was more gray than black.

She clattered and fussed, toasting, in the oven, leftover biscuits from the breakfast that she and Hek had shared, I imagined, hours earlier. They generally rose at four-thirty or five in the morning.

I knew better than to speak before the ceremony of the food had been presented. So I watched her work, hoping that she would begin, as she so often used to when she worked in the kitchen, to absently sing.

She did not.

When all was finally prepared, she set before me a plate of three biscuits, halved and toasted, fresh butter, blackberry jam, a bowl of milk gravy, a small plate of homemade sausage, and a big cup of nearly transparent coffee—into which I had seen her pour two table-spoonsful of white sugar. She had also brought a cup of her own to the table.

"There." She sat beside me. "Eat up."

"You probably know why I'm here." I began to butter a biscuit. "Or you've guessed." She was a bright woman. There was no point in my pretending that I was there on a purely social visit.

"I expect you've already been to see Hek and the rest over at the filling station." No expression, no valuation.

"Yes." Jam. "So, then—are you going to tell me what I want to know?"

That was the trick. Never speak directly. Assume the other person knows what you want, treat them with gruff respect.

"Well, you most likely want to know something about that boy that's been living up at your place."

"That's right." A bite of sausage.

"I guess you know he's your brother." She lifted her cup to her lips and looked into the coffee.

"Half," I insisted.

"That's right." She still had not even exhibited the blink of an eye. "Half-brother."

"Didn't anyone think it was strange, his moving in there?" I took a sip of the awful, sweet concoction.

"He had a key," she answered, steadily. "We thought you give it to him, thought you knew."

"Nobody asked?" My voice rose, though I tried to keep it steady. "Nobody even called me to check?"

Her gaze was very even. "Why would that be any of our business?"

I nodded. I let out a breath. I knew better. *The concept of laissez-faire was invented in mountains like these*, I thought.

There was no place in the world where a person could be so thoroughly discussed and—simultaneously—so completely ignored, as those mountains.

"He's dead now, I hear." June continued to stare. "So there's an end of it. That all you wanted to know?"

"No. That is not all I wanted to know." I set down my cup. I wiped my lips. "I understand you may be reticent to divulge any further information about the man," I couldn't help smiling, then, "given what I've already heard about your *incident* with Ida Shump."

"That woman is crazier than a jaybird." Her face flushed.

"Yes, she probably is, but still," I leaned forward, "you have to make a distinction between gossiping about a woman that insane and giving me *information* that I . . . I need to know everything you can tell me about that man—"

"Your brother," she interrupted. "Half."

"Yes." I sat back.

"All right," she sighed, "in the way of giving out *information*, I'll tell you what I know. Seeing as it's you." She raised up her finger. "But this ain't gossip."

"Right." I leaned back farther and prepared.

"All right." She took another sip of coffee and gathered her thoughts. "Said his name was Thresher Devilin."

"So," I held up my hand. "He used the last name."

Anyone unfamiliar with my family history might have questioned that last name, knowing that my father, Fletcher Devilin, was not the father of the person found dead on my porch.

But the icy fact was that my father and my mother both, prior to marriage—prior to even meeting—had been named Devilin. They were third cousins who had met at a family reunion. They had been distant enough to be legal, but not distant enough to have escaped the name.

I was concerned with why the bastard—simply to use the appropriate technical term—had taken it. He would have subjected himself to the certain ridicule of small-town moralizers. "Why did he take the name?"

"They say he was proud of his mother," she croaked—it was a hard phrase for her to say, "and wanted her name."

"Who says that?" My fingers were tapping on the tabletop and I could not seem to stop them.

"That's the talk," she said, placing her chin in her hand, "over Blueridge way."

"You asked people in Blueridge about this man," I said, my voice narrowing again, "but you never called me about him?"

"No." She shook her head. "I didn't have to ask." Her voice was scolding. "Word just gets around, Dev. You know how that is."

"June." But I sank in my seat, unwilling to let my irritation get the better of me. "I suppose." I let out another short breath. "Go on."

"He was an automobile mechanic, Thresher was, over in Bug Creek. That's where he lived. Grew up with your Aunt Rosie. Kept to himself. Sang in the church choir. Never married, nor had children." She looked away. "Like you."

"Life with my mother," I began, "did little to promote familial yearnings."

"I guess." She looked back at me.

"What I really want to know," I told her slowly, "is something about his reason for being here at all." I looked studiously into the coffee cup. "Carson said it had something to do with a message from . . ." but I had to start the phrase over after a healthy gulp of air. "From mother."

"What makes you think I'd know about that?" I could see her fingers grip the handle of the cup more tightly. Her lips pinched shut.

"Carson said that this man wanted to find out all about me," I answered. "Who knows more about me than you do?"

"You're right there." She nodded once, short, stabbing. "I know all about you."

"Yes, you do," I smiled down into the biscuits. "And besides, Carson told me the man talked to you."

"Oh." She sighed, and her whole face changed. She was blushing, and a little relieved, I thought. "Fever, he swore me to a secret, you know. Your brother did."

"But he's dead now." I hadn't meant it to sound as cold as it did. "So that pledge is dead too."

"I reckon that is true." She caught my eye at last. "You know, sweetheart, that could have been you, shot like that on your own front porch. That's what I've been thinking. He looked an awful lot like you. I've a great mind to worry about that."

"Why would anyone want to shoot me?" I saw no reason to alarm with my own paranoia on the the subject.

"People are crazy." She looked away. "Folks can be so strange these days."

"Deputy Needle's on the case, as they say," I said calmly. "There's nothing to worry about."

"Skidmore's a good boy." She scratched her jaw, her face revealing nothing. "But he don't have your brains."

"June, you're avoiding the issue."

"Yes, I am."

"You know what I want to know. The *real* thing I want to know. The thing that I wouldn't admit to anyone but you."

"I do." She wore the same expressionless face.

"Then why won't you say it?" My voice was tighter, and I could tell she was tensing as well.

"Say *what*?" But she knew I would not even answer that question.

A shot of cold air raced down the mountain behind the house, burst in through the window, and billowed the curtain inward, snapping it like a sheet on the clothesline.

"I don't know what you think you came here for—but you really want to know," she leveled her eyes on mine and said what I could not, "if it's possible that your mama could still be alive. Sending you a message."

The curtain, as if shocked by the statement, froze in midair for a second, and then dropped dead into the window frame and would not move.

"Yes," I admitted before I could stop myself. Then, to deflect the harshness of that idea, I began again slowly. "But I also want to know, regardless of the answer to that question, what message this man could possibly have had that he considered so important he had to come here, invade my home, and stir things up in this community."

"Well," June put her hand on mine. "Let me answer your first question first. I never went to a funeral for your mama. I don't even know for a fact that there ever was one, as such. But I did see the notice of her passing in the paper, like I told you in the letter I wrote you when it happened."

"Yes," I said softly, "I was just thinking of that letter this morning."

"Not to mention that I hear about everything that goes on in this part of the state. You know that."

"Yes," I agreed, wondering where she was going with her thinking.

"And you think about it real good," she continued. "Recall how your mama was, really now." She gave me a moment.

"I *know* how my mother was, yes," I insisted. "Everyone seems intent on reminding me."

"Well then you tell me this: If that woman was still alive, could she keep it secret for ten years? Would it be at all possible for her to keep a thing like that shut up? Wasn't she just plain too loud and wild for that?"

"God." I felt a small weight lift from around my neck. "I suppose you're right." I felt a genuine smile crease my face. "She certainly wasn't capable of that—not the woman I knew. You're right." I reached for her hand, and held it. "I don't know what I was thinking."

"I'll tell you what you might have been thinking," she said quietly. "You might have been thinking, '*How could my mama have done all this to me?*' I believe the rest of whatever is going on in that head of yours is all clouded up with that. That's been your trouble right along through this life, Fever."

"Is that so." I straightened. Her assumption was accurate, of course—I'd been thinking that earlier at Gil's. But I wouldn't admit it. "Does *everyone* believe that I'm an emotional invalid? I *am* a different person, you know, than when I was ten."

"Well, I don't know about your friends in the city," she glared back at me, "but most folks around here have always been right concerned about you." There was the teasing again, a little more loving, but just as the men had done.

"Fine." I relaxed, as she had intended for me to do, and received her words as good-naturedly as they had been given. "You just see if I invite you to my house for dinner this year."

She let go of my hand. "About the other—the part about what Thresher really knew, or wanted to tell you—I've got no idea about that. He did have something stuck in his craw, that boy did. You could see it. He was set on knowing you. And he was set on telling you something." She lowered her voice. "I don't have no call to say this, but I always got the idea he thought his little secret might be worth some money."

"Money?" I leaned my elbows on the table. "He thought I would pay him money for a secret from my mother?"

She nodded. "Or something. I thought he was looking to get something out of it. I felt that."

"Well, he obviously didn't find out enough about me if he thought I would do that."

"I don't know for certain that's what he wanted." She shifted in her place. "Just a guess."

I took a second to further calm myself. Then: "Well, your guesses," I told her, picking up a sausage with my fingers, "are worth most people's two-year research papers."

"Don't eat that sausage with your bare hands." She smacked the tabletop with her palm.

I deliberately picked up two biscuit halves with my fingers, put the sausage between them, and bit.

She slapped my shoulder. Then she got up, as if she had more work to do, and turned her back. "Have you seen Lucinda yet?"

"No." I didn't look up. "Why would I see Lucinda?" Did my voice betray anything about my true thoughts?

"You should visit." June went to the sink and began shuffling plates, looking out the kitchen window. The fact that all the dishes there were clean and dry meant nothing. She could not be looking at me for this part of the conversation. "She's lonesome."

"She is?" I put the biscuit down.

"Right after Hammon died, she still had the two kids to think about. But they've all gone from home now, so she's just got her work at the hospital to keep her mind occupied."

"What does she do there at the hospital?" I asked, mostly to deflect the rest of the conversation. "I know you've told me . . ."

"It's administrative," Junie sighed, lifting a plate into the drainer.

"How long ago was it that her husband died?" I knew, but my mouth would not stop making sounds. "I sent flowers when you wrote me about it, I just don't remember when that was, exactly."

She stopped her faux-work for a moment, staring hard out the window. "I believe it was summer, five years ago."

"I still feel . . . it seems to me that Lucy's still married, in some ways," I said quietly. "What a terrible way for her to lose a husband."

"That tractor, it crushed him right away," she nodded. "He didn't suffer."

"I meant . . ." but I didn't finish my sentence. I had meant that it was a ridiculous, an ignoble way to die for a man like Hammon. He had been the sort of person who should have died saving other men in a war, or rescuing someone from a burning building. So all I said was, "I'm glad he didn't suffer."

"Not from dying, anyways." She resumed her idle noise. "He surely did have a hard life, though. Orphan boy, working a farm, married to a woman who was probably in love with another man." Even though her back was still to me, I knew that her eyebrows were raised at me. I knew it just as surely as I knew the spear of sun that struggled through the window and stabbed the floor beside me. I could see she was finding a way—her way—to make me go to Lucinda. June Cotage was not washing dishes.

She's doing what she considers her real mission on earth, I thought. *She's matchmaking.*

"You know," she began, transparently, "I always thought you two made a nice pair."

"No you didn't." My sausage biscuit was gone, then, in one last bite. I wiped my fingers on the paper-towel napkin she'd placed on the table. "You didn't approve of our . . . of the way we carried on."

"Didn't approve?" She turned quickly, still holding a wet plate, slinging a small spray of water onto the floor.

"June?" I said, startled by the force of her reaction.

"I always had my heart set on the two of you, Fever." Her voice was almost pleading. "The best thing you could have done in this life was to marry that girl and stay right here at home where you belong." Her eyes narrowed. "But I reckon you had to do what you could to get away from that mother of yours." The word "mother" could just as easily have been the word "viper."

Then she turned just as suddenly as she had before, back to the sink, to her misdirecting task.

"Boy." Her voice was very hard. "I want you to go see Lucinda Mae."

I stared at the back of Junie's dress for a full minute before I realized that her vehemence was not borne of her normal desire to see me coupled—she was not playing matchmaker after all, not entirely.

"Does Lucinda have something to do with all this, what we're talking about?" I leaned forward in my chair. "Is that what you're saying?"

"Not exactly." She stopped washing again, but she did not look at me. "It ain't that she's got something to do with all this. It's just that . . . I'm thinking there's so much more that's involved in this sorry business than you might know. So much more. And she could help you to understand it better, is all. A woman can be a comfort, if you let her. I know it's hard for you to believe that." She sniffed, and I could tell she had begun to cry.

"God." I stood and took the four or five steps to the sink beside her. "What is all this, June?"

She finally looked me in the eye again, tears clouding hers. "Some of the things you think you know about yourself—your life up here in these mountains?—maybe you don't know them at all." Her voice was growing angry. "You don't even know what you're doing here. You don't even know your own name."

Seven

There hadn't been many awkward moments between June Cotage and me over the years—and we managed to live through that particular one. She would not say one word more on the subject, nor any other, in that kitchen. She just threw her arm around my neck again and hugged it until I was sore. When she finally released me, she dabbed her eyes with the sleeve of her dress, and shoved me out the kitchen door.

As I stepped off the frame, headed toward my truck, I told her, mostly to dispel the air of discomfort, "I'm going over to the church. Hek has a service this morning."

"You know he does," she said, finally breaking her silence. "It's *every* morning."

"I know." I put my hand on the truck door. "Is it the full service today?"

"Oh," she shook her head. "No, he just does that on Sundays and Wednesdays now."

"All right, one more question." I looked out across her yard again, as I had when I'd come. "What day is it today? I know it's a weekday . . ."

"You're a mess, you know it?" She smiled. I was glad. "Been to college all his adult life and don't even know what day it is."

"And?"

"It's Friday."

"Friday," I repeated. "Now I know."

That was all my farewell to June. She watched my truck pull

around and head out, but she did not wave, nor did I. The last time I glanced in the rearview mirror, she was still watching the truck as it pulled out onto the main road.

To avoid driving immediately to the hospital and confronting Lucinda at her work—which was what every fiber of my body wanted to do—I decided instead to visit Hezekiah's church.

But I also thought I might interest Andrews in joining me—it was the sort of true mountain experience that he would find amusing, so I headed the truck back to my cabin.

The full service included snakes, lye, quaking, speaking in tongues, and an odd variant of Sacred Harp music. We'd have to save that for Sunday. The Friday affair was likely to be short, cordial, and very informal—just the way to introduce Andrews to Hezekiah's church—and for me to show him Dr. Bishop's astonishing discovery. I knew Andrews would be interested in that sort of outing. I'd certainly told him often enough about the church. Perhaps it would even help him to understand a few of my reasons for moving back to the mountains. Or perhaps, I thought, I might clarify those reasons in my own mind.

I was trying not to let the information I had received in my short morning sojourn with the men, and then with Junie, cloud my mind unduly—but images from my past were storming in my mind as I drove back to my cabin.

I was remembering a wild night in North Carolina when some men who had been drinking heavily had come to the show. They were, as so often had been the case, quite agitated by my mother's gyrating performance. By the time my father's magic show had come onto the stage, the noise of those men was deafening, and several of the roustabouts had gathered, preparing for trouble.

I was in a panic, only nine or ten, staring into the tent from behind the stage, terrified that my father would be harmed by these men. And when my mother came on stage as the magician's beautiful assistant, they erupted—laughing, screaming, saying words I mercifully didn't understand. Just as I was about to call for help, my father stepped forward to one of the loudest, largest drunks, and sat down in front of him on the edge of the stage.

"Brother?" He offered the man a cigarette. "Care for a smoke?"

The man, barely able to focus, took the cigarette.

"There." My father lit it for him. "Having a good time?"

The man hooted at the top of his lungs. The other men shoved him. The crowd had grown still as death.

"That's good, that's good," my father said. "Always like to see people having a good time. Look—let me introduce you to my wife, since you seem to like her work." He looked back. "Honey, could you come over here for a second?"

"Okay." My mother smiled and walked very calmly to the edge of the stage, sat beside my father, took his hand, and lay her head on his shoulder.

"So." My father looked at the man, who was temporarily at a loss for words—or any other sound—and said, "This here's Mrs. Devilin, my wife."

"Hi." My mother held out her hand.

The man started to shake it, then wiped his hand on his coveralls, straightened his hair a little, and finally took her hand. "Glad to meet you, ma'am." The crowd was absolutely silent.

"There." My father started to stand. "I just thought you two ought to meet, as I was saying, being that you're a fan of her work."

The man only nodded.

Then—and I was never quite certain exactly how he did this— my father swirled around very suddenly, and there was a loud boom that startled everyone, accompanied by a cloud of blue smoke. The drunk, his friends, and most of the crowd gasped or screamed.

When the smoke cleared a split second later, my mother was gone.

My father's eyes bored into the man in the front row, who was— it would not be an exaggeration to say—stupefied.

"She's vanished, brother," my father said to him. He started to turn, then looked back out over the crowd. "Or was she ever really here at all?"

The rest of the show proceeded as usual, to a very appreciative crowd, without my mother's assistance.

I'd always admired my father for that moment, which had taught me two useful perspectives concerning my mother. The primary lesson was that it would be better for me to think of my mother as the real flesh-and-blood Mrs. Devilin, than to think of her as the naked Eve.

But the other, seemingly contradictory lesson, was that the real flesh-and-blood Mrs. Devilin might not actually have been there at all—ever. It was a fine and expanding thought to try and grasp such complex lessons at the age of nine or ten.

Or in your thirties, for that matter, I was thinking as the truck pulled up to my cabin.

Andrews and Skidmore were sitting on the porch, coffee cups in hand, all four feet up on the railing.

"You've been out early," Andrews called to me as I stepped out of the truck.

"Yes."

Skidmore eyed me wryly. "That's all? Just 'yes'? What you been doing?"

"Well," I said, closing the truck door, "where do you think I've been?"

"Hold on." He barely had to consider his thoughts. "Gil's, I reckon."

"That's right."

"All right." Andrews looked between us. "Who's Gil?"

"He owns the filling station," Skidmore answered, "down at the bottom of the hill."

"Ah," Andrews sipped. "You've mentioned it to me before. The place where you gossip with men and play your mandolin."

"Yes," I stepped up onto the porch.

The morning air was still crisp and clear, and there were little hints of steam rising from the cups. The wind was high in the pines, the sky nearly free of clouds, and a woodpecker dotted the morning with its rhythm.

"So did you gossip?" Andrews wanted to know. "Did you find out everything?"

"In the first place," I told him, standing on the top step, "we don't *gossip*." Then I sighed. "And in the second place, I found as many questions as I did answers."

"That's always the way, at first," Skidmore said, looking away, "when you're on a homicide investigation."

Andrews and I both stopped moving at all for a moment. Both of us flared at the deputy.

"One seldom has such a clear example," I began, "of what we might refer to as a collision between gestalt perceptual fields."

74

He didn't even bother to look at me. "I hate it when you talk like that." He looked over at Andrews. "What's he saying to me?"

"You're absolutely on your own." Andrews set his coffee mug down on the floor of the porch.

"Skidmore's perception of the moment is clearly that of a policeman," I explained slowly, "so he has assumed that my morning's task had concerned a homicide investigation—though how he would know anything about the subject is unclear to me."

"I watch a lot of television on the subject," Skidmore mumbled.

"And the perspective that Andrews holds," I continued, "is that of a visitor to a foreign land who has no real comprehension of what is happening here."

"Your point is . . . ?" Andrews intoned.

"That all reality," I answered, "is a point of view, isn't it?"

"What point of whose view?" Andrews managed.

" *'There is nothing either good or bad'* " I told him, " *'but thinking makes it so.'* "

"Wait." Andrews took a moment, and I could almost see him running through the catalog of Shakespearean quotations he kept in his brain. Then he broke into a smile. "I see what you mean. *'To* me *it is a prison.'* "

Skidmore looked back and forth between Andrews and me several times before he asked, "What in the hell are you two talking about?"

"Hamlet," Andrews said.

"Oh, Hamlet," Skidmore nodded. "The one that can't make up his mind."

"Right," Andrews seemed surprised, or impressed, I thought. I could tell he was about to ask Skidmore something further, but before he could I interrupted.

"I'm going to Hezekiah's church service." I glanced at Skidmore. "He still starts at nine in the morning?"

"Yup."

"Would either of you care to go?"

"He's just being polite including me," Skid said to Andrews. "He knows me and Girlinda goes over to the Baptist."

"You could still come," I told him, "for the experience."

"I've had enough experience with Hek Cotage recently." Skid

tossed out the rest of his coffee, over the porch rail in front of us, and stood.

"Yes," I said, "he told me this morning that he was getting friendlier with you, but I didn't know what he meant."

"He meant that I've arrested him twice in the past three months—and I've been gone a good bit during that time too."

"Arrested him?" I tried not to be as surprised as I was. "Why?"

"Incident at his church." Skidmore stared out into the pines.

"What kind of incident?" I couldn't imagine anything that happened in a church that would be cause for being arrested.

He set his jaw, clicked the fingernails of his left hand, about to tell me something, then shook his head. "If you want to get over there to the service, you'd best get on. This'll keep. I've got some work to do, anyway—but we'll catch up at dinnertime."

"Dinner?" I was hoping that meant an invitation.

"You come to my house for dinner." He smiled at me, finally. "Girlinda wants to see you, and the boy is feeling much better." He turned to Andrews. "We had a sick boy."

"I'm sorry to hear that." Andrews looked to me, then back at Skidmore. "Dinner?"

"Around six?" Skid turned to go inside. "I'll lock up here. You all go on."

Andrews looked about, momentarily at a loss, then set his cup down on the porch rail. "So I'm going to church?"

"Not just any church," I reminded him. "This is the place that Bishop wrote about, the snake-handling group I've been telling you about."

"Oh, my God," he said, and his steps grew quicker, off the porch and into the yard. "I don't want to miss this."

"Don't get too excited." I turned toward my truck. "It won't be the snake-handling service this morning, it's just—"

"Sod the snakes. I want to see the *bowl*."

"Well. Yes. The Serpent Bowl." I followed back into my truck. We climbed in. I turned the key in the ignition. "It's there, all right."

Eight

The road to Hezekiah's church was even worse than the one to my house. We forded a small stream, dodged rocks the size of hunting dogs, and had to stop twice to move large fallen pine limbs from the road. Most people who went to Hek's house of worship walked there, and the road was a back road that few people ever took.

When we got there, we saw only eight or nine of the faithful, men and women, gathered together outside Brother Cotage's tabernacle. The exterior of the building was very simple, whitewashed wood; white-painted rocks outlined a path to the door. Nearly hidden by loblolly pines: four walls and a roof. Plain windows, no stained glass, no steeple—only an old rugged, life-sized cross nailed to the wall beside the door to identify it as a house of God.

The place could seat about forty comfortably, but I'd been there when a hundred or more had crammed in. Hek was seated by the only door, reading something in his bible, in a chair Shoo Walters had made for him. The rest were standing, not speaking, waiting to go in. Everyone was dressed in plain dark colors, so Andrews turned heads with his wild Hawaiian shirt the minute we got out of the truck. The shirt, a different one from the day before but just as insane, was purple with green palm fronds and dotted here and there with well-tanned hula girls. It was quite a contrast to my black cloth jacket, and people stared openly.

Andrews barely noticed. He was looking at the church. The building had been built there by Hek's predecessor, the Reverend Coombs.

The story went that Coombs had been called to that exact spot by God, in order to build a temple-house for the Serpent Bowl, the sacred, secret relic that he had carried—in his arms—from Scotland in the early 1920s. It was a well-guarded holy sanctuary until Dr. Bishop "discovered" the object on one of his first trips to the mountains. There had been almost no folklore research at all in that part of Georgia before he came to visit, and so to Bishop it had been like stumbling across the Holy Grail.

I'd seen old photographs of the Reverend Coombs. He hadn't looked like the sort of person who would carry a heavy stone object across a room, let alone across an ocean. Still, the story was a good one, and often told. *Our people came to these hills from Scotland and from Ireland, and here is a reminder of our ancient heritage.*

Hek nodded when he saw us coming toward him, but there was no other acknowledgment. No talking was allowed before one entered into his sanctum. We were supposed to be taking a moment of quiet reflection, preparing ourselves for the experience. Even the wind silenced itself in that part of the woods out of respect for Hek's power. The elements were complicit in his pact with God and Nature, and there was a palpable air of *otherness* surrounding the nondescript building and the silent, staring mountain people—a moment out of time, a place with no reference to any other place on the earth.

When Andrews and I arrived Hek stood, as if he'd only been waiting for us to show up, and opened the door. Everyone went in, Hek first. Andrews and I followed.

The inside of the room was no less austere than the outside. Benches with no backs, white walls with no adornment. The exposed beams above our heads were spotlessly free of cobwebs or dust. The windows, despite being clean and clear, seemed somehow capable of keeping out light—and prying eyes.

Andrews and I took seats in the front row, despite what appeared to be his growing discomfort. The rest were scattered here and there, mostly over eighty years old, and barely awake, it seemed to me.

The only place in the room with artificial light was the spot up front where the altar might have been in another church. There, bathed in the light of a single bare bulb, sat a large boulder with a flat top. It must have taken ten men to muscle into the room.

Placed securely in a hollowed-out spot atop that rock was the sacred object from the old country: the Serpent Bowl.

Difficult to see even from where we were sitting, the motif of the bowl was etched in my mind from childhood memories, and the countless pictures of it that I had seen in Bishop's old office— the articles I'd read years before. Two snakes twined upward along a central axial post (some said the snakes were copulating) and on either side were griffins, or two winged lions flanking the serpents. Of course this symbol, minus the griffins, had survived millennia. First as the staff of the classical Hermes—who was the guide of the soul into its eternal life—and today as the Hippocratic symbol still used to represent modern medical doctors: the twining snakes.

It was an astonishing thing to find anywhere in the world. It could be thousands of years old. It was entirely unbelievable that it had been a secret in the north Georgia hills. Dr. Bishop's papers and experiments had proved to everyone in the academic community that it was genuine. The only thing that made colleagues skeptical was the thing for which I admired him most: He had steadfastly refused to divulge the exact location of the bowl in his general papers—or to the occasional inquiring newspaper reporter—out of respect for the church's privacy.

The bowl served as a sort of cistern, and was always filled with fresh spring water. This was important in Hezekiah's ceremony. Each person who wished to take up a snake in the Sunday service would first touch fingers to the water in this Serpent Bowl, dab a bit on his lips, rubbing the rest into the hands. The claim was that this alone prevented the poisonous viper from proving fatal to the true believer.

Hek stood beside the bowl, closed his eyes, and spoke.

"Friends? 'As Moses lifted up the serpent in the wilderness, so must the Son of Man be lifted up.' John 3:14. Moses lifted up the serpent, brothers and sisters, and that's a fact. It was a sign of things to come, that we ought to lift up the Son of Man. Why do I say this? In Numbers we find that God sent fiery serpents among the people of Israel, and the serpents bit the people, so that many died. And the people came to Moses and said, 'We have sinned, for we have spoken against God and against you. Pray to God that He take away the serpents from us.' So Moses prayed, and God said, 'Make you a fiery serpent and set it high on a pole and everyone who is bitten, when he sees it, shall live.' And Moses did this thing, and the miracle was accomplished: Everyone who looked upon the serpent upraised was saved from death. This was a sign of the Living Christ to come. Do you see that children? Everyone who looks on Jesus up there, lifted up on the Cross, *will* have everlasting life."

There was a rustling in the congregation, heads nodding, looks exchanged.

"Now, we also find in Exodus," the preacher continued, "when Moses went to frighten Pharaoh, that Moses turned his own staff into a snake. And we find in Numbers again, that Moses struck a rock with that very staff, and water, the element of the serpent, came forth and restored life."

A soft mumbling began in the congregation—people saying "Amen" or repeating what the man had said.

"We therefore take up snakes not to tempt God, nor to try our own faith. God has given us faith—we do not need to test it. We bring forth this symbol of the serpents from its sacred resting place, the *cista mystica*—we summon the serpent from its cave—in order to do as we have been instructed, to lift up the Son of Man. Jesus was, praise God, likewise reborn from His own cave: the tomb of Joseph of Arimathea. He rose out of his cave and shed his earthly skin and was born anew in the spirit and would not die!"

The group began to stir, mumbling words I could not understand.

"And so I say to you this morning, 'As Moses lifted up the serpent in the wilderness, so must the Son of Man be lifted up—that whosoever believes in him may have eternal life.' In Jesus Christ's name we pray: Father of Eternal Life, grant us that when our time has come to die, we shed this earthly skin, and fly to that Everlasting Light."

The congregation repeated, in perfect unison, the prayer.

Hek waved both hands, as if dispelling smoke, and whispered, "Amen."

That was the service.

The faithful began to stand and leave as soundlessly as they had entered.

"That's all?" Andrews whispered. "That's it?"

"For today," I answered.

"Well, that's no good. It was like a . . . a teaser for a film. Now I have to see the whole thing. I'm coming back on Sunday."

"Hope you do." Hek had overheard. "You'd be welcome."

"Brother Cotage," I stood, "meet Dr. Andrews."

"Dr. Andrews?" Hek smiled and stuck out his hand. "I've heard quite a lot about you."

"Likewise," Andrews answered, taking Hek's hand. "Listen, would it be all right if I took a closer look at the bowl?"

"Surely." Hek was used to academics examining his prize.

The three of us moved respectfully to the front of the room.

Andrews leaned over and stared at the stone relief of the griffins and snakes.

"Oh, my God," he whispered.

"Watch the language, boy," Hek reminded him politely.

"This is absolutely remarkable." Andrews looked up at me, his voice tense. "Has it ever been exactly dated—I mean by any sort of lab . . . ?"

"No," I told him, "Hezekiah, and Reverend Coombs before him, would never allow any testing whatsoever to be done to the stone."

"It's a holy relic." Hek made no apologies. "It's not a classroom show-and-tell."

"No, but I mean," Andrews began, straightening up, face oddly flushed, "you do realize that this image is exactly the same as the one on the Libation Cup of King Gudea of Lagish."

Hek and I stared back.

"It dates to something like 2500 B.C.," Andrews insisted. "In Sumer."

"Sumer?" I managed.

"That's right." Andrews went back to examining the bowl.

"In the first place," I asked him, "how on earth would *you* know a thing like that?"

"For God's sake, Dev." His tone seemed to indicate that I was an imbecile.

"What did I just say about that kind of talk in this place?" Hek said a little louder.

"Sorry," Andrews told Hek quickly, then turned to me. "I've only taught Gilgamesh about a hundred times. Don't you think I do just a *little* research into the culture before I start mouthing off to the students?"

"Well then, in the second place: *Gilgamesh?*" I stared down at the bowl. "Sumer? This was a design of *Celtic* origin, an artifact that the Reverend Coombs found or stole—pardon me, Hek—from some churchyard in Scotland."

"That may be," Andrews said absently, not looking up, "but it's also an ancient Sumerian image."

"Wait," I said, rubbing my forehead. "I think I remember something from one of Bishop's articles . . ."

"I'm shocked you wouldn't already know this, Dr. Devilin," Andrews chided.

"I know," I agreed. "I'm trying to remember. It certainly seems something I would have discussed with Bishop—although you know I've always found this material culture business, in general, a terrific bore."

"But when it's something of this magnitude—"

"Which, I'm remembering, is why this was such a stir in the early sixties when he was writing about it." I was crashing through my memory, trying to retrieve conversations from years before with a man who was now long-dead. "Bishop's first articles said something about the relationship between ancient figures—that is, prehistoric pictures—of coiling snakes and Celtic interlocking line patterns. That's how he explained it. Then most of his articles were about the bowl's effect on Coombs's parishioners—the anthropological approach. He always seemed to me a little reticent to make too much of the actual symbol." I squinted. "Or was it that I—was *I* reticent to leap to such a conclusion about the connection between Celtic patterns and these snakes?"

"With your famous argument in favor of 'not knowing'?" Andrews said absently, staring at the bowl again. "I wouldn't be surprised if it were you."

"An argument in favor of *not* knowing?" Hek repeated, very surprised. "From *this* boy?"

I thought, then, how remarkable it was to experience two such rare moments as I'd had in such a short time. The first was my earlier realization about perceptual realities—and then this sudden, forced examination of my so-called "famous argument."

"All of human thinking," I explained to Hezekiah, "has historically been divided into times when it was better to have knowledge, and times when it was better not to have knowledge. In the European Middle Ages—the so-called Dark Ages—for example, seeking after self-knowledge, aspiring to knowledge of God, lusting after academic knowledge outside of the Church, these were all considered direct sins against God. God had knowledge. Who was man, that he dare aspire to such an estate? How like Satan that aspiration seemed. This was a period in human history when it was better *not to know.*"

"Now you've got him wound up," Andrews said to Hek. "Make him stop."

"Then came the Renaissance," I went on to the preacher, ignoring Andrews, "and suddenly it was more important to have knowledge than anything else—self-knowledge, knowledge of history, of technology, of science, of biology, of art, of letters, of music. It was far better *to know.*"

"The problem," Andrews interrupted impatiently, "that I often argue, only half in jest, is that the latter decades of the twentieth century were times when it often seemed better, once again, *not* to know."

"I did not really care to know, for example," I agreed, "that the nation of Iran had achieved nuclear technology to aid its concept of *jihad.* Of what use is that knowledge, other than to terrorize my dreams at night and prevent my peaceful slumber?"

"I have to admit," Hek said, an amused grin splashed across his face, "that it's hard to believe the most educated man I know wants *less* knowledge. Where did you ever get that?"

"I've held this opinion since my early days here in grammar school," I answered. "It was revealed to me, at age ten or so, that my examination scores were higher than ever before recorded at my school."

"It was the county school," Hek mumbled to Andrews. "They were always amazed that any of the students could add two and five and come up with seven."

"I also discovered that my IQ surpassed all known tests," I continued, "and that my aptitude was, in the sixth grade, at the doctoral level—in language, math, and science."

"I'm sure we're impressed," Andrews said, struggling for my point.

"This knowledge had forced me to examine myself," I explained, "and to discover that there was something wrong with me."

"Wrong?" Andrews said, quieter.

The whole church, in fact, seemed to grow more still. The lightbulb dimmed a little, and there was no noise of wind or birds at all.

"They had told me I was extraordinary," I concluded. "I hated that knowledge. I did not wish to be extraordinary. I wanted to be like everyone else. I wanted to feel comfortable. I feared the responsibility of this knowledge—and I still do."

"But—" Andrews began.

"When other people discovered my secret," I interrupted, "my friends, the other students—they only proved my worst fears: I was set apart. I was out of the ordinary. I was strange."

The two men stood silently. There was no argument from them. They knew me. They knew I was strange.

"So there I have remained," I said finally, "on the precipice between a keen ability to *know* and a terrible fear of *knowing*."

What I did not say aloud was that I was possessed of an almost supernatural ambivalence that had prevented me from taking some of the important actions in my life. Wanting to ask questions and being afraid of the answers had kept me from truly understanding Dr. Bishop's remarkable work in my own academic life and the same fears had kept me from ever learning the truth about my childhood and my parents. My ambivalence toward *knowledge* had actually prevented my *knowing*.

In addition to being plagued by that ridiculous intellectual conundrum, I discovered that, in trying to remember what Bishop had told me years earlier about the bowl, I had released another unwanted torrent of memories from my youth.

Among them I found one both especially puzzling and astonishingly situationally significant: I saw my mother twining her snake in her hands and placing it back into its box with a light, musical laughter. I remembered then that she always referred to the box where the snake lived—joking in a singsong manner—as her *cista mystica*.

Something of my thoughts was betrayed on my face. Hek and Andrews were staring at me as if I were in a hospital.

"You okay, boy?" Hek said, trying to see into my eyes. "You don't look so good."

"Do you want to sit down?" Andrews said.

"I'm all right." I felt my forehead. "I seem to have a little temperature. It's a little close in here, don't you think?" I rubbed my eyes.

"Let's step outside," Hek said to Andrews as if I couldn't hear.

"I was just thinking," I told them both, "how funny it was that you were talking about the snakes with such reverence when it was the biblical Hezekiah, in Second Kings, who destroyed the bronze serpent Moses had made."

They both looked at each other and then each took one of my arms and hustled me down the aisle and out the door.

"That was a strange thing to say," Andrews told me once we were outside the church, into the cooler air.

"You got a temperature," Hek confirmed, standing over me and fanning my face with his handkerchief.

"I'm all right." But I did feel dizzy and oddly disconnected from things.

"Are you certain?" Andrews peered into my eyes.

"Well, maybe it's just—I mean, it's still morning," I told him, leaning over, "and I've already received far too much information for one day."

I sat in the chair outside Hek's church, my face flushed, my temperature high—as it had so often been when I was a boy.

"What are you talking about? This information about the bowl, do you mean?" Andrews wanted to know. "That's just amateur archaeology—I was playing."

"Idiot." I looked up. "I don't care about that."

"Well, what is it then?" he shot back, his voice rising.

"Quiet now." Hek had his hand on my shoulder. It was very comforting. He smiled at Andrews. "You hadn't never seen him have one of these spells?"

"Is he sick?" Andrews stared at me.

"Not sick. He just gets like this sometimes," Hek said.

"Hence his given name," Andrews smiled, relaxing a little.

"That's right," I ground out mockingly. "That helps, making fun of my name—that's bound to help me feel better."

"Well, what do you think it is," Andrews insisted, "that's brought this on?"

"Nothing. I just got a little hot inside, that's all. I hate this. I thought these were gone, these little spells. I haven't had one in so long. I hate being treated like a sick person." I tried once again to sit straight. "And these stupid memories of my mother."

"Your mother?" Andrews pulled back a little.

"Hek?" I turned his way.

"Yes?"

"What made you say *cista mystica* just now?" I asked him. "In your sermon."

"Is that what I said?" He stared vacantly. "That's just what Coombs used to call it—the box we keep the snakes in. Got it from him, I reckon."

"Coombs called it that?" I asked, wiping my brow.

"It's Latin," the preacher said.

"I *know* it's Latin, Hek."

"Means 'magic basket,' " he went on to Andrews, "or something like that, I think."

"Please stop talking," I insisted.

"Okay." He patted my shoulder where his hand was.

There was a slight breeze that stirred up the branches of the pine and filled the air with their scent. All around me the world did its best to reassure me: grass stayed green, but it was the dying green at the end of the summer. Trees rustled, but it was an autumnal sound—the sound of leaves aware enough to rejoice in their home because they knew that soon they would decorate the cold, cold ground. Across the sky, behind the pines, an arrow-point of geese called out, but they were leaving the mountains for a warmer place to spend the rest of the year. The sound echoed in the darker part of the woods, a lament for anything left behind when the time had come to go.

Reassurance migrated with them.

"All I'm saying," I managed to tell them both, "is that my mother called her snake box that: *cista mystica*. That's the memory I was talking about." I finally stood and looked directly into Hezekiah's eyes. "Did the Reverend Coombs ever meet my parents? My mother, I mean? That's not an ordinary phrase for people up here to toss around." I turned to Andrews. "I mean, for one thing . . . it's in Latin . . ."

"We all knew the Reverend Coombs." Hek's gaze was steady, and betrayed nothing.

"You know what I mean, Hek," I spoke carefully. "Did my mother know him *well*?"

"Now how would I be party," he answered, disgusted, "to a thing like that?"

"I'll just go back and talk to June if you won't tell me." I hadn't meant for my voice to sound like a twelve-year-old's.

"She won't tell you neither." He looked down. "She won't tell you that."

"Tell you what?" Andrews looked between us. "What is this about?" He took my arm and shook it, but I don't think he was entirely aware that he was doing it. "What are you saying?"

"I don't know what I'm saying," I told him. "Not really." I took a deep breath. "Hek, will you at least hand me your bible? Let me check my memory on this other thing—before I forget it. I don't know why—maybe I just don't trust my memory. But why would I have said anything about Second Kings?"

"Yeah." He rolled out the sound. "I didn't never think of you as one to know your bible quite that well. I kind of wondered where you got that from."

He reached into his breast coat pocket and handed me his book. My head was still swimming a little. I found Second Kings, chapter 18, and read it aloud to them both.

"Here it is. 'In the third year of Hosheason of Elah, the king of Israel, Hezekiah . . . began to reign.' Skipping. 'He removed the high places and broke the pillars . . . and he broke in pieces the bronze serpent that Moses had made, for until those days the people of Israel had burned incense to it; it was called Nehushtan.' That's what I thought—but why on earth would I know it?"

"Nehushtan. Is that saying that the Jews worshiped a snake god?"

Andrews blinked at me, and seemed more confused than ever. "What's that got to do with anything?"

"Nothing!" Hek suddenly glanced toward the woods, took in a breath, then drew the bible out of my hands, and, without looking, paraphrased a later chapter. "It was also that Hezekiah in the bible, boys—my namesake—who showed the envoys from the king of Babylon all the treasures of Israel. The prophet Isaiah asked him what he had done, and he said, 'They have seen all that is in my house; there is nothing in my storehouses that I did not show them.' And Isaiah said, 'The days are coming when all that is in your house shall be carried to Babylon; nothing shall be left.' So. Because of that other Hezekiah's foolishness in *revealing* all his treasures at the wrong time, the Israelites suffered slavery in Babylon. And then in Egypt, for a thousand years." Hek closed the book, put it back in his pocket, and stepped back from us. "I won't make *that* mistake again. That's why it's important to keep secret things to yourself!"

Before Andrews or I could even understand exactly what he had said, Hek was gone down the path and into that greener cathedral—and the black shadows of the trees.

We watched him go in silence, and in the darkest place in the path, I could see several other figures—could have been the Deveroe boys from the way they were laughing when they greeted Hek. Then the whole group walked away together.

"Well." Finally Andrews found his wits. "What the hell was that about?"

I looked at him. "I really don't know."

"So," he said as he watched Brother Cotage and his entourage disappear into the woods, "at least tell me what you meant when you said you'd had too much information for one day. I'll let the bible quotations go for the moment."

"For one thing," I answered, "I am certain, now, that the dead man on my porch was, in fact, my half-brother."

I nodded in the direction of my truck and we both began walking toward it.

"Someone," he responded, "that you never even knew existed until yesterday—or today."

"Not positively," I told him. "What's more, I may even have several other older half-siblings wandering about these hills."

"I suppose that is quite a lot to hear in one morning." His voice was deep and sympathetic—I felt babied and hated the sound.

"There's more to it than that," I snapped.

"Oh?" He remained calm.

"Some sort of strange message from my dead mother," I said evenly, "that the corpse wanted to deliver to me before he became a corpse—on my porch."

"I know which corpse you mean," he interrupted wryly.

"Déjà vu—that's what I said to Skid—"

"The message," Andrews insisted. "Not the digression."

"I don't know what the message was." We had reached the truck, and I put my hand on the driver's-side door. "But now I have in mind that there might be some connection between them."

"Between which *them*?" Andrews asked, amused.

"These half-relatives and the late Reverend Coombs." I opened the door. "That, in fact, Coombs might be the father of one or more of these . . ." I couldn't bring myself to finish the sentence.

"Well, yes," Andrews grimaced and got into the truck. "That is a good morning's work, I'll grant you."

"And as long as you're taking notes on my psychological status," I said, starting the truck, "I've got another flash for you. You do know the book, *Man and His Symbols?*"

"Jung," he affirmed.

"I have an image from that book in my head. Something that was drawn by a patient of Jung's. Just popped into my mind." I turned to him. "Why is that image in my head? Does that ever happen to you?"

"Do the strange images from a book by Carl Jung—and drawn by a mental patient—ever pop into my head?" He buckled his seat belt. "No. That only happens to you."

"Fine," I muttered. "It's probably something I used in a class. I've only been through that book about a thousand times."

"What's the image?" he prompted impatiently.

"A single eye," I said instantly, "at the surface of shaded water, and on either side of the eye there is a snake."

"More snakes." He rolled down the window exactly as he rolled his eyes.

"What else? Jung's interpretation was that the woman—a woman drew the picture—was struggling for spiritual development. The eye

represented the birth of a new insight from the depths of the unconscious . . ."

"Which would be the sea, the water," he nodded.

"Yes. And the snakes represented the reborn soul or spirit."

"Because the snake is the natural symbol of rebirth, shedding old
skin and acquiring new." He pulled on his earlobe. "Doesn't seem
such a mystery to me why you'd have that in your head. You're finding new emerging selves, you're awakening to some new knowledge—that sort of thing."

"That's right." I turned to him. "Andrews?"

"Hm?" He was staring out the window, obviously thinking.

"Have I ever told you," I began, my voice flooded with a warmth
I hadn't known I could muster, "what a joy it is to be able to have a
conversation with someone who understands even half of what I'm
saying?"

"No." He looked over at me. "And I'd imagine I'm one of few in
that number."

"Exactly."

"Well." He sat back in his seat and stared out the window. "Same
here."

We rode a little way in silence. The rush of the road and the tires
made a white-water sound, and the truck poured on down the
mountain. The trees and rocks and golden wildflowers all flew by,
blurred Monet, and the sun crashed through the clouds with such a
blinding force that it seemed to make a sound in the mind.

"How did Hezekiah inherit his church from this Coombs person?" Andrews finally asked, still staring out the window.

"Hek was just a farmer like everyone else around here," I told
him. "He and Junie were only married a year when something com-
plicated happened with her first pregnancy. I don't know what, but
it was apparently life threatening. She was in bed for her last three
months. Everyone in the community helped out, made meals, did
chores—my father even did a little plowing. I remember helping
him. I was seven or eight. The tragedy was that when the baby came,
not only was it stillborn, but June died—clinically died during the
birth. She stopped breathing; her heart stopped. She was pronounced dead."

"Jesus." He turned to stare at my profile.

"Coombs was well established in the community by then," I went on, "and was, of course, in the room when she died—lots of people were in the room helping, praying, watching."

"She was having a baby with the entire community in her room?"

"Anyway," I forged ahead, "the people there asked Coombs to do something. So he laid his hands on June's head, prayed in a language no one had ever heard before, and June opened her eyes. She smiled at everyone, and she recovered."

"Oh," he said, leaning my way, "there's more to it than that."

"Of course the story's grown since the actual incident," I agreed. "Now people will tell you that there was a strange light coming from his hands, or an odd humming sound in the room. Whatever happened, the important thing is June started breathing again—she'd only been out for a minute or so."

"And she was all right," Andrews pressed.

"She was. No damage—except that she could not have children after that."

"And this incident had such a profound effect on Hezekiah," Andrews concluded, "that he became an apostle?"

"Not exactly," I wrinkled my brow. "It would seem that the Reverend Coombs actually left town almost immediately after that incident. Vanished. Everyone said he'd been called away—by God."

"Well." Andrews was trying his best to absorb the story.

"June insisted that Hek take over the church," I said, "and assume stewardship of the relic. That was important to everyone here about. The artifact was somehow—it somehow connected the community, gave it a sense of being unique. Being chosen."

"And because his almost-dead wife told him to," Andrews asked, "Hek agreed?"

"He was reluctant at first, I'm sure," I answered. "But he's taken to it quite well now, don't you think?"

"Had Hek ever handled snakes before, that sort of thing?"

"Yes, he grew up in the tradition," I said. "We all did."

"Mm." He looked back out the window. "Whatever became of Coombs, then, really?"

"Don't know."

"And what," Andrews began, with, I thought, very pointed diction, "was Bishop's part in all this?"

"What? Bishop's part?" The truck slowed. My attention was on Andrews. "Dr. Bishop?"

"Was Bishop here when all this transpired?" he wanted to know.

"Jesus," I had to think for a second. "I suppose he was." I absently chewed on my lower lip. "He never really talked to me about that period of time, much. He always concentrated on his *work* up here. I never really knew him then, he visited so infrequently after I was born—although, of course, his presence certainly influenced my choice of university and my path of study." I was seeing Dr. Bishop in my mind's eye, bent over the bowl in the church, oblivious to his surroundings, making furious notes. What a mysterious figure he had been to me then, when I was young. He represented everything I longed for: the city, the university, the larger world. "You have to understand—Dr. Bishop was so good at finding and explaining material folk culture because he was more interested in things than in people. Still is, in fact. It's his one failing, I think. I probably know more about Shoo's chair-making, for example, than Bishop does—even though Bishop is the expert—because I don't just look at the chairs, I talk to Shoo. I listen to him while he works; I pay attention to his stories. That's what's interesting to me. The chairs are only the end product of that work. I'm more interested in the work itself."

"The process," Andrews said.

"Exactly."

"I'm not surprised." Andrews breathed in the sweet, sweeping air. "You like a question more than an answer, you've always said— and what is an answer but the end product of the process of the question. You like the question; you don't care much about the answer."

"With a question," I started slowly, "you can *travel*. An answer is the end of the journey. Nothing more left." I glanced his way, then back at the road. "What, exactly, is your point about Dr. Bishop?"

"I don't know that I have a point," he said. "Except that it seems to me, at least in this case, you might be a little uncomfortable with some of the answers you find. So that, given all these philosophical underpinnings we've just been tossing about, you might just try and avoid important answers—out of your fear."

"Fear?" Irritated, I tightened my grip on the steering wheel and stared at his profile.

"That's right. You might just try using your 'existential quest' argument, I'm saying, to keep yourself from finding out some things that you *need* to know—but that you don't really *want* to know."

"For God's sake!" My voice rose a good bit more. "Once and for all: I am *not* the emotional cripple everyone seems to think I am."

In my insistence that I was a whole and secure person I lost sight of the fact that I was also the person driving. The truck swerved dizzily across the road to our left, toward the granite cliffs at the side of the pavement.

Andrews lurched and grabbed the steering wheel. "Watch where you're going!"

I turned my eyes back to the front of the truck just in time to see a sheer wall of the mountain flying toward us at the speed of sound.

The sound, in that case, was the squeal of the brakes, like a peacock screaming at midnight intruders, and the truck scrapped wildly along the blacktop, barely avoiding a collision with the rock wall—our looming tombstone.

There was a second of breathless silence while the truck righted itself and we continued down the highway.

Then Andrews burst into laughter.

"Yes," he managed between uncontrollable bursts of relieved laughter, "you're in great shape."

"Well," I told him, my heart still pounding from the confrontation with stone, "I can only concentrate on one thing at a time. What do you want, emotional stability or good driving?"

"At the moment? Drive. You can see an analyst later."

I was even able to muster a little smile myself.

Curiously, the event had made me feel better. The laughter helped. Andrews helped.

And I couldn't keep from noticing that the day was growing more beautiful by the moment. The air was clear and cool, the ageratum and goldenrod painted mauve and sunlight even in the darkest shadows.

I felt as if the strangeness of the morning were being washed away by the air streaming in through the windows of the truck. It blew my hair in wild, cold fire around my head—and in that juxtaposition of flame and ice, some alchemy was born: I was soothed, and my mind was calm.

Nine

We pulled up to the house and saw an extra car in the yard. The blue lights on top caught the sunlight just right and sent an azure pall over everything else in the yard. The silver star on the door glared in that light like a genuine threat. Sheriff Maddox was on my front porch, seated in one of my chairs.

I got out of the truck carefully. Maddox was a short, round little man with a hat too big for his head and a belt too small for his pants. His left cheek always looked as if he had a golf ball in his mouth: Cheap, brown chewing tobacco had stained his lips, his chin, and almost always his uniform shirt. We had a history; he was a person I didn't like. The reasons were legion. He treated Skidmore like an errand boy, for one. He took money from men who paid him to arrest other men—and sometimes paid him not to arrest other men—so that a question of guilt or innocence was often irrelevant on Blue Mountain. I had absolutely no respect for the man, and less trust.

But I would have to admit that a portion of my opinion of him had to do with the fact that he had arrested me—twice, when I was a teenager—for being a minor out after curfew. Since the arrests, harmless boyhood incidents, he had thought of me as a vandal and a troublemaker. I had thought of him as a corrupt gnome. As with any generalization of that sort, there was a grain of truth in the stereotype—both his and mine.

So the mood of calm repair fled quickly. A sheriff on the front porch never means good news.

"This might not be a good thing," I whispered to Andrews as we got out of the cab.

"Devilin." He touched the front of his hat briefly.

"Sheriff." I slammed the door shut.

He glowered at Andrews.

"This is Dr. Andrews," I said, as if it were an introduction at a church social, "from the university where I work."

"Worked," Maddox corrected.

"Well," Andrews grinned, immediately sussing my opinion of the man, it seemed, from the tone of my voice, "he still works there in something of a consulting capacity. That's why I'm here, in fact. I'm consulting with him."

Maddox spit out a stream of brown tobacco juice. It arched in the air and stained the lawn with a sickening pat.

"Crap." He stared at Andrews without expression. "You're here because your buddy got shot at, and he got scared so he called you." He turned to me. "Dev's here because he was about to lose his job from the college so he quit to come running on home." He stood. The rocker moved back and forth, trying to shake off the smell of the man. "But I don't care about any of that. What I care about is your messing up this case I got. I can't have that, Dev."

"Case?" Andrews said calmly.

"Shut up," the sheriff answered back.

"I don't know how to tell you this, Sheriff." The screen door opened and Skidmore stepped out on the porch. "Dr. Devilin is just helping me here at his house. He answered a few questions and offered a few opinions, as he has done in the past when I've asked him—"

"Don't you piss me off too, Deputy," the sheriff snapped back.

"Based on previous case studies," Skidmore went on, as if his boss hadn't even spoken, "Dr. Devilin's advice has resulted in a significant positive conclusion to every case he's ever advised me on—"

"I said shut up!" Maddox snarled at Skid, then spat again. "You have a *significant positive conclusion* right up your wife's fat ass."

"Let me see." Skidmore did not look the sheriff in the eye. "I could tell her you said *hey*, but I believe that's as far as it'll go."

"Uh huh." The sheriff's face was red as wild strawberries. "Well, if you get in my way on *this* thing, or Devilin or his homo friend, here, I'll put you all back in the jailhouse." His insect eyes bore down on me. "Like I done to you before."

He lumbered off the porch, clomping and waddling past Andrews and me, toward his car. Without turning to look at me, he said, "I mean it, Dev. I don't want you to have a thing in this world to do with this case. You hear me? You got nothing to do with it."

"As always," I answered, "a pleasure to see you, Sheriff."

He made a guttural noise that I thought might be some sort of carnal description, and then his voice rose. "Do you understand me when I say you have nothing further to do on this case?"

"I understand what you're saying," I told him as innocently as I could manage.

He grunted, threw himself into his car, which sagged as he sat. He cranked the ignition, ground the gears, and roared off down the mountain, red dust and foul fumes in his wake.

"Lovely." Andrews watched him speed away. "Why did he call me a 'homo,' exactly?"

"It's the Hawaiian shirt, most likely," Skidmore said calmly. "He hates anything that ain't brown and polyester."

"My students love this shirt." Andrews stared down at it, baffled. "I love this shirt."

"So." My eyes followed the dust of the sheriff's car down the hill for a moment, then I turned to the best deputy in the county. "What's the next thing for us to do—on our case?"

"So you don't find yourself intimidated by the sheriff?" Skid said, electricity in his voice.

"I just don't want him to spit on me," Andrews said. "What the hell was that?"

"Chew tobacco," Skid answered. "I believe it is the most disgusting habit that a man can acquire."

"We have news," I suggested.

"Maybe we should go on over to my house," Skidmore said sweetly, "and plan a little strategy. Then Linda'll make us an early dinner."

"There's an invitation too fine to pass up," I told Andrews immediately. "Girlinda Needle's company special: chicken livers, fried okra, field peas, cold tomatoes, cornbread, sweet tea—"

"And banana pudding for dessert," Skid concluded proudly.

"I don't think," Andrews began slowly, "that I've ever had a single item you've mentioned. I mean, I only drink milk in my tea."

"It's not even your kind of tea," I told him, grinning from ear to ear at the mere thought of Linda's meal. "It's cold and amber and half of it's sugar."

"You want to go in the squad car?" Skid asked.

"No," I told him. "I should follow you in the truck so that you won't have to take us back home later. You've been away from your wife on my account just a little too much lately. The last thing I need in this world is to have Girlinda Needle mad at me."

"Okay." He didn't look back, just got in his car and started it up.

"Wait," Andrews commanded. "House key." He held out his hand.

I gave it to him and he ran into the cabin. Short moments later he emerged. He had changed out of his gaudy flowered Hawaiian and into a gray sweatshirt. The front said, in small letters, "Rugby Players Eat Their Dead." The back said, "Captain Andrews." I was still in my black cloth jacket.

"Am I going to be able to eat any of that?" Andrews whispered to me confidentially as we climbed back into the truck.

"The question, I think you will find," I answered, cranking the engine, "is: 'Will you be able to stop eating?' You're about to have one of the finest meals of your life."

"I doubt that," he sneered.

The drive to the Needle household was fairly brief: down the mountain, up the highway, and past a series of small farms. The air was warming, and the sun ladled its gold over the pine and cedar trees in the distance. The fields were all in various stages of harvest, some rolls of hay, the occasional tent of corn sheaves, but peas and beans were still green and blooming. In one small patch of land we saw an acre or two of pumpkins that dotted the otherwise tan and jade patchwork of fields with a kind of round fire. Cows watched our truck pass, passively observing, majestically evaluating.

"Hey." Andrews, utterly betraying his urban affiliations, saw them and turned to me, delighted. "Cows!"

"Yes," I agreed. "Those are cows." It was a little like a person from the country marveling at all the pigeons on a city street, but I saw no reason to deflect his joy.

The Needle household was settled at the end of a long dirt driveway in between two giant rhododendrons. Behind the house a small hill rose up, and became a sheer cliff, rocky and gray.

The house itself was plain enough, a white, wooden house with attic dormers and a central stone chimney crowning the roof. It was made remarkable by the presence of every imaginable flower that could possibly bloom in the fall. There was a curving shape of pansies outlining a path that wound to the porch. Guarding the house were tall autumn flox, purple lantana, smoky sprays of muhly grass, fall-flowering crocus, salmon mums, red dwarf sunflowers, all anchored by lace-cap hydrangeas on both sides of the flower bed. Hanging from the rafters of the porch were dozens of baskets filled with all manner of cascading flora: purple fuchsia, variegated ivy, spider plants, shower roses, and creeping fig.

"I see that this Girlinda," Andrews said as we pulled up to the house, "has something of a green thumb as well as a talent with food."

"Actually," I answered, unbuckling my seat belt, "all of this is Skidmore's work. Gardening makes him calmer, he says."

"Calmer than what?" Andrews responded, sliding out of the truck.

"Dev?" Girlinda's voice from inside the house curtailed further exploration of Skidmore's agrarian habits. "Is that you out there?"

She appeared on the porch. Her face was even more beautiful than I had remembered it, filled with overwhelming love, flushed and rosy, beaming and beatific. Her hair was the burnished color of certain autumn leaves, and her eyes were so blue they were almost black. She was wearing black jeans and a charcoal T-shirt. She stood little more than five and a half feet tall and weighed more than a hundred and eighty pounds, but her size and weight were irrelevant. It was my belief that any person on the planet would find her one of the most attractive women they'd ever seen. This was primarily as a result of a supernatural ability to make her spirit shine through her flesh. Everyone was attracted to that astonishing light. I, personally, could not move quickly enough out of the truck, up the steps, and into her arms.

After an embrace that lasted hours—and not nearly long enough at that—I turned and waved in the general direction of Andrews, who had lingered on the steps a few feet from us.

"This is Dr. Andrews," I said, still holding onto Linda. "He's looking forward to your dinner."

"Good," she drawled, holding out her right hand. "I already set some of it on the stove—it'll be cooked real good by the time you all are ready to eat it."

"A pleasure meeting you," Andrews said, taking her hand. His voice was soft and low, a tone he generally reserved for attractive graduate students.

"Come on in the house," she told us both.

She finally let go of me and pushed the door open. The living room was cluttered but clean, the furniture was well made but modestly designed. The walls were decorated with pictures of children, and drawings by them. Toys and clothes were scattered randomly about the room, but the general appearance was welcoming and peaceful. The fireplace, central to the room, was surrounded by indoor plants, ferns, and potted mums.

To our right was the kitchen, and there was a pleasant, familiar clatter of pots and pans. Through another archway—in a room I knew to be the den—we could hear children talking and playing.

Skid appeared in the doorway to the kitchen.

"Hey." He was wiping his hands on a dish towel. "Come on in the kitchen. I put on some more coffee and I thought we might talk some of this out while Linda keeps the kids in the den."

"I have to go say hello to them," I objected.

"They're not allowed in the kitchen," Linda explained to Andrews. Then to me, whispering: "I wish you wouldn't do that right now, hon. I'm trying to keep them calmed down . . . this talk about dead bodies and all."

"I understand," I told her. My disappointment must have registered in my voice.

"I had no idea you would be at all interested in children," Andrews muttered, amused.

"He's like an uncle to the kids," Skid said.

"You have . . . how many?" Andrews looked between them.

"Three boys and a girl," Skid told him plainly. "Linda wants more but that's enough for me."

"You'uns just sit down at the table, now—I'll hand over the coffee." Girlinda pointed to our seats: bent-wood chairs that had been painted white in 1914 and used every day since. The table was likewise white and worn, but the effect was more inviting than June's chrome and Formica kitchen set. The kitchen had all-white appliances as well, and two huge windows over the sink that looked out on fields and woods. A pantry large enough to rent as an apartment in New York was open and stocked for the end of the world. Aside from the kitchen table and chairs, the only piece of furniture in the room was a wooden stepladder used for fetching essential items from the higher shelves: pickled okra, dried purple hull peas, large green mixing bowls.

We sat, the shuffling of the chairs and our feet the only sound for a moment. Even the children in the other room seemed silent.

"Who goes first?" Skidmore finally said, leaning forward on his elbows and clicking his fingernails together.

There was a long pause. Then Girlinda set a mug of coffee in front of her husband and said, "Why don't you start with what you know, like make a list, and then use that to move you on to what you want to know."

"Christ," Andrews said, drawing a treacherous grin across his lips, "have you been studying with Dr. Devilin?"

"She simply recognized the proper course of action," I defended her—and myself, "that any sane person would take under the circumstances."

"Okay," Skid sighed. He pulled a small spiral notebook out of his shirt pocket and a stubby, eraserless pencil. "What *do* we know?"

For the rest of the afternoon we talked, shared ideas, made jokes, picked on each other, and generally came to no conclusion whatsoever.

Just before sunset, Girlinda called the children to wash up, I finally got my moment of reunion with them, and we ate in almost total chaos. Andrews could not stop talking about what a miraculous find fried okra was. The boys were full of questions about the body. And Becky, the little girl, wanted to know if Andrews was married.

"I am not," he announced, flashing the most winning smile in the world.

"Okay, then," Becky said, satisfied, and squirmed in her seat.

The boys made fun, Linda swatted Andrews, and the flood of

warmth and well being I experienced at that table sufficed as my dessert.

Andrews, on the other hand, ate three bowls of banana pudding.

Toward the end of the debacle, when things began to quiet down and the boys excused themselves from the table, Girlinda leaned in toward my ear and said, "This ain't none of my business, but it's my opinion that you ought to try and discover—what would you say?— the *nature* of the message that your brother, the dead man, was trying to bring you."

The three men left at the table looked at each other in ridiculous simplicity.

"Good one, hon," Skid told her, patting her hand.

"Of course that's what I ought to do." I sat back. "And I'll do that tomorrow. But what I need tonight is a therapy session."

"Therapy session?" Andrews asked. "Is that what you said?"

"Let's go," I told him, standing. "You need it too." I turned to our hostess. "Best meal ever," I assured her.

"Shoot," she grinned, "you say that every time."

"Gets better every time," I insisted.

"Where are we going?" Andrews whined. "I was going to have another bowl of that pudding."

"I believe," Skid told him, stretching in his chair, "you're going down to Gil's store."

Ten

That evening was cool and clear, the air was crisp, and Gil's garage was filled with the men I loved. Andrews had come along. Skid had encouraged him to go because he knew how good the music would be, but Andrews had been convinced when we promised him a taste of genuine moonshine. He made his musical reluctance all too clear as we pulled up in front of the place.

"Let me remind you," he told me, getting out of the truck, "that I prefer my *folk* music strained through the classical filter of Percy Granger. And I generally prefer my casual social encounters to be conducted standing up, cocktail in hand."

The men from my home had gathered, sitting in a crescent of chairs underneath the blue neon glow of the night sign GIL'S GAS AND GO, and barely took notice of the truck as we pulled up.

"Let's see how you feel after a shot of corn liquor," I whispered to Andrews, "and an hour or two of this music."

Without another word, I went to sit next to Carson and unpacked my new mandolin, forgetting everything else in my life. The musicians looked, nodded approvingly, and then we all started playing the old-timey version of "Cotton-Eyed Joe" in honor, I knew, of my return. We were five pieces, but we sounded like fifty.

When the time came for the mandolin to take a chorus, my fingers seemed to move by themselves, without any meddlesome intervention from my brain. The notes were clean and silver, punching holes in the air all around us. Some of the men were smiling to themselves, and I took the compliment: My playing was still accept-able. Then it was Carson's turn to play.

I was still in a strange mood from the events of the day, and his playing had a profound effect on me. He started off slowly at first, making mournful sounds, scraping the strings near the bridge, white rosin flying up from the bow like fog or steam. Then the notes got higher and sweeter, and I felt I could hear the man's soul rising up from the depths of some awful despair. As his solo gained momen-tum, I could actually see, with my eyes closed, the images that his music wanted me to see: Carson running through a field, running so fast he thought he could fly. Even though he was running wildly, he never stumbled. He played faster and faster, I could barely keep up. I had the sensation that we were all running toward the edge of a cliff, a tall one, overlooking a ranging valley with a roiling river below. But Carson didn't slow his pace, and I knew he was running to the edge.

Bowing the fiddle more furiously, as if he were kicking back his boots in the dirt, arms thrown out wide, heart pounding, breath like a bellows, pushing himself forward, trying to fly—praying to fly. The edge of the cliff grew ever nearer. And just as we reached the edge, his fiddle gave a horrible, heavenly swell of complete surren-der: Fall or fly, the die was cast. Fall or fly, he leapt into the open air with nothing below him but raging water, and nothing above but the gathering clouds.

Then, in the highest, sweetest musical note ever played on a fid-dle, he rose up—up into the air, not down. Floating, flying, soaring, piercing, rising—body and soul—upward into the sunlight of eter-nal day. And he was taking all of us with him on this flight of notes, because his soul was so purified and filled with heavenly grace by the music he was playing that he could not bear to leave anyone, any liv-ing soul, behind on the lonely planet.

We played that way nonstop for an hour before we took our first break.

Andrews was beside himself, he couldn't stop talking about the music.

"That was *fantastic*." His face was flushed from the corn liquor he'd consumed. "I knew you played the mandolin, but I had no idea you could play like *that*. And this Carson. He's a *genius*. He's a monster. Why didn't you ever tell me about *that?*"

"You've had too much to drink." I smiled at him, my hand on his shoulder.

"Yes. But I'd still have to say that the music was unbelievable."

"Fine," I nodded. "You can say that, but I think you've had quite enough to drink."

"You may be right about that," he nodded, staring at his glass. "This is lethal."

"Literally." I took the glass from him. "Care to meet Carson?"

"Absolutely." He meant to move forward but took two steps sideways instead.

I helped him, mandolin in my right hand, Andrews's elbow in my left, out into the night air. Carson was standing all by himself in front of the garage, out of the glare of the sign, in the cool of the evening. He had filled up a large tumbler with ice and poured straight bourbon over it, all the way to the rim, and was gulping it down. He always called it simply "iced tea"—which it looked like—and he felt it was a more polite thing to say than "liquor." I knew from many nights like that one, the drink would barely affect him at all.

"Carson," I said softly, "I want you to meet my friend Andrews."

Carson turned toward the sound of my voice and held out his hand. "Dr. Andrews, Dev's told us all about you."

"I hope not *all*." Andrews took his hand and shook it vigorously.

"Well," Carson smiled, "I guess everybody ought to have a few secrets."

It seemed, to me, an odd thing to say.

"I mean, Jesus." Andrews just kept pumping Carson's arm. "Your playing is the most fantastic thing I've ever heard." He was searching, I could tell, for the best way to simultaneously compliment and also prove that the compliment was worth something. "And I've heard Perlman live in concert."

"That cripple Jew boy?" Carson nodded. "He plays pretty good."

I looked at Andrews, who was absolutely at a loss for a response. I'd seen Carson do exactly that sort of thing a hundred times before. He so loathed the idolatry that his phenomenal artistry often engendered, that he would immediately do what he could to destroy his standing in the eyes of any new and ardent fan. This was a crude litmus test for Andrews. Would he be offended? Would he laugh? Would he go away? Would he change his mind about the playing? Carson didn't want the casual admiration of strangers. He just wanted to play.

Andrews looked to me for help, but I was concentrating very studiously, pretending to tune my E strings.

"Well," Andrews said as he turned back to Carson. "Far be it from me to impose my own philosophical shite on anyone at all, but once you've heard Perlman play live, you really don't think of him as a cripple or a Jew, and certainly not as a boy. You only think of him as one of the singularly exquisite instruments of God."

"Well said." Carson smiled, face to the ground.

But Andrews didn't hear him, and wouldn't let it go. "I mean, if you'd ever heard the man in person—"

"Andrews," I tried to intervene.

"No. I'm sorry. That's what's wrong with you people in this part of America, anyway. That kind of bigotry just demeans this great music you've been playing." He turned to Carson again, more flushed, filled with corn-liquor ire. "I was saying that if you'd ever heard him play—"

"Stop!" I told him firmly. "They've met. They've played together."

"What?" Andrews was at a loss. "This man and Itzhak Perlman . . ."

"That's kind of an exaggeration," Carson spoke softly. "We were at the Kennedy Center. He was getting his UNICEF award."

"Carson was performing that night," I explained.

"And we just kind of noodled around for a minute backstage before the ceremonies got underway. Would you believe that he knows 'Cotton-Eyed Joe'? That tune we started with tonight? Played ten or twelve variations on it." Sip of *tea*. "Played rings around me. I was right disheartened."

"Surely did make you play up a storm that night, though," I told him, then stared at Andrews. "He received a ten-minute standing ovation from the president. At the Kennedy Center. In Washington . . ."

"I know where the Kennedy Center is," Andrews gurgled at me under his breath.

"Yeah," Carson agreed with me, "that cripple Jew boy certainly did light a fire under me that night. I believe it did me some good to get whupped on."

"I see." Andrews finally seemed to clear his mind enough to understand. "You're baiting me, both of you."

"After a fashion," I said, "he was."

"Well, I deserved it." He turned to Carson. "And I've learned my lesson. I hope you'll believe that I'm actually not that much of a sycophant, usually."

"I don't know what that word is," Carson said, and took another sip.

"Somebody who seeks favor by flattery," Andrews told him, "and I don't usually do it."

"That corn liquor you've been drinking," Carson took another sip of his own drink, "*will* take care of you, won't it?"

Andrews looked at me, then at Carson's vacant eyes. "How did he know . . ."

"I think there may be people in Pittsburgh," I answered, "who can smell what you've been drinking."

"Oh." Andrews smiled and turned back to Carson. "Yes, this moonshine is good—but that's not what made me appreciate your playing. Honestly. You're a genius."

Before either man could be further embarrassed by that comment, the road in front of the filling station exploded with the roar of a familiar rusty red hot rod rounding the corner and barreling through town. Hanging all around the vehicle and flailing wildly within it were the Deveroe boys—sneering, tossing beer cans, and generally destroying the peace of the evening. In the blink of an eye, they were gone again, and the road was silent.

"What the hell was *that*?" Andrews stared in the direction of the vanished distraction.

"That," Carson said, finishing his tumbler, "was the Deveroe boys. They don't mean a thing by that behavior. Just hellion kids, having a good time. Excuse me." And he moved away, toward the place where he had stashed his bottle of bourbon.

"I think those are the boys we saw with Hek today, in the woods," I said to Andrews, my voice lowered, "in the shadows, remember?"

"Yes." He was still glaring at the last of the dust that the hot rod had kicked up. "At the church. I remember."

"I should have told Skidmore about seeing them," I said, nearly to myself.

"That new mandolin plays real pretty, Dev," Carson called out, heading back in our direction, ignoring the previous scene completely. When he got closer to us, his voice got softer. "And I hear you made the rounds after you left us: June's house, Hek's church . . ."

"I did."

"A visit from the sheriff," he went on.

"That too," I assured him.

"Find out all you wanted to?"

"Not really," I started in. "Hek wouldn't tell me what I wanted to know about my mother and the Reverend Coombs, for example."

"Mm hmm," Carson intoned, sipping his *tea*, "that's what he told me."

"So why don't you?" I asked nonchalantly.

"Why don't I what?" He was doing his impersonation of a goat, I thought—stubborn and unmoving.

"Why don't you tell me what I want to know, Carson." My voice was a little more sharp than I'd intended.

"Shh." He sniffed. "Your old teacher and the Reverend Coombs were tight as ticks in the old days."

"My old teacher?" I leaned closer to him. "Bishop, do you mean?"

"Yes." He took another long gulp.

"Hardly," I told him. "Coombs was sort of an odd folk informant; Bishop was on a research mission. They might have *seemed* close, but it was all work for Dr. Bishop."

"Maybe it started that way," Carson said, a little gravelly, "but they surely got thick fast."

I glanced at Andrews, who nodded a little, staring at the blind man, obviously as curious as I.

"What makes you say this, Carson?" I asked him.

"They slipped around together all the time," he said, expressionlessly, "went fishing nearly every day, ate dinner at Miss Etta's every night. They always had their heads together about something."

"Like what?" I squinted.

"Oh, this and that," he offered. "First one thing, then another."

"For *example*?" My voice was hard. "What did they have their 'heads together' about?"

"For example," Carson shot back hard, his face directly in mine, his blank gray eyes looking, it seemed, right into me, "they went into business together just before you was born."

Before I could even completely understand the words of that sentence, our peaceful night was shattered again by the sound of squealing tires, but it wasn't the Deveroes this time—the racket was topped by the blare of a police siren.

Skidmore's squad car was careening toward us with such speed that I was afraid he would not be able to stop, and would plow right through the small crowd in the garage.

But just as he was about to spin out of control, he hit the brakes and turned, moving toward us in a graceful, if ear-splitting, power glide that ended only four feet short of Carson, who had not moved during the entire, chaotic matter.

"Get in!" Skidmore said to me. His face was frantic. "Girlinda's been shot!"

"What?" was all I could manage.

"Shot! Get in the car."

"Of course." Without thinking any further, I moved immediately toward the car. "Where is she now?"

"On her way to the hospital," he let out, urgently. "Get in the car."

"You go on." Carson reached out and squeezed my shoulder. "We'll put up your new mandolin." He ducked his head a little and spoke to Skid. "You need anything right now?"

"I need Dev to get in the car!" Skid raced the engine.

"Wait." Andrews, seeming to sober up quickly at that point, lurched toward the car too. "I'm coming along."

"Jesus." Skidmore rocked frantically back and forth in his seat. "Just hurry."

We both got in. Before our doors were even closed, the car was off again, down the center of town toward the hospital, siren blasting.

"What happened?" I asked him over the incredible din.

"You all hadn't been gone from our house but twenty minutes or so," he began, struggling to maintain police department composure, "when we heard somebody pull up out front. Girlinda thought it was you all coming back for something, but it sounded more like a car to me."

"Car?" Andrews was impatient. "How was she shot?"

"All hell broke loose." Skid's control was nearly at an end. "I got no idea what really happened. The windows started popping, and it was like lightning outside."

"Like automatic weapons?" Andrews couldn't believe it.

"No. Christ." He had no patience. "Not automatic weapons. All I know is that my kids was all screaming, and Linda was scooping them up to take them into the pantry when she got hit. I had my pistol out, but it was all over in five seconds and they was gone like smoke. Jesus God."

"Linda—will be fine." I put my hand on Skidmore's shoulder. "I don't know a person in this world who's tougher than your wife."

"There's not many, brother." His eyes were wet.

"Where was she hit?" Andrews voice was insistent and irritated.

"Shoulder," Skid mumbled, "I think. I don't even know what all happened next." His voice was wild.

"You saw her shoulder. You called the ambulance. You called the boys at the police station—got somebody to take care of your children." I tried to sound calm, going through a routine for Skidmore, to make his mind focus on business instead of fear. "And then you came to get us."

"No." His pause was filled with sudden surprise. "Wait a second, here." He shot a sideways glance at me. "I didn't call nobody."

"What?" Andrews and I called out at the same time, still over the incredible howling of the siren.

"The ambulance was there on top of the gunfire. I was holding Linda and trying to stop the bleeding, when I heard the sirens."

"Maybe one of the kids called," Andrews offered. "Every pre-schooler in the world knows how to dial 911 these days."

"Maybe." But Skid was already trying to think of other explanations.

Eleven

The hospital was schizophrenically busy—people were everywhere, and everyone seemed in need of immediate help. Skidmore had to remind me that the entire county was served by this one medical establishment. The emergency room was crowded with people. Some were small children in dirty yellow pajamas, some had bleeding wounds that they soaked up with hotel towels, some were old people with their heads bowed and their hands quaking. It could have been the emergency room at Grady Hospital in Atlanta, where I had gone once with a friend—a numbing nightmare of pain, panic, and barely contained desperation.

Andrews and I made it past the wounded and dying, and found seats in the waiting area.

Skid confronted the nurse at the emergency desk, and was told that his wife was already in surgery.

He came to the place where we were sitting.

Andrews was searching in his pockets and I was distracted by it, irritated with him.

"At least they got her here fast," Skidmore said, sitting down. "Got her into the operating room right away."

"You want some mechanical coffee?" Andrews offered, eyeing the vending machine a few steps away. "I'm buying."

"Okay," was all Skid could manage.

I let him settle into his seat before I launched into my theories. "This is too close to what happened at my house to be coincidental, wouldn't you agree?"

"You think?" He stared. "Your idea is that this has something to do with you?"

"Isn't it obvious?"

"Well, Dev," he took a deep breath, "I do know a few other people up here besides you. I have arrested a few hundred kick-ass rednecks, and any one of them would be perfectly happy to get all liquored-up and spray my house—they call it 'police pesticide.' I even know some kids that would do it just because there's nothing else to do on a Friday night around here."

"When is the last time this happened to you?" I asked him quietly.

"All right, never, but that don't prove—"

"Regardless of what it proves," I interrupted, "I have to assume this is my fault, and I have to do something about it."

"Your fault?" He stared at me. "Man, do you have some troubles that need fixing."

Just as I was about to explain to him what I thought needed *fixing*, I saw her out of the corner of my eye: the ghost.

She was standing stock still in a blue dress, hair still sunny, face still filled with wonder. She seemed like a patch of clear sky.

Instantly I was fifteen years old, lying on the hillside half a mile from my house, gazing out across the field of wildflowers that appeared every spring in a circle of sunlight at the junction of two mountains. I was propped on my elbow, and she was reciting the names of the flowers: "foxglove, bachelor button, forget-me-not, dianthus, sweet william, zinnia, salvia, joepye weed, creeping flox, hollyhock, nasturtium, yarrow, wild mountain thyme." The sound of her voice was a song.

"Fever?" She said, shaking me from the vision of our past. Her voice was just the same.

"Lucinda." I stood. "Don't you realize that the laws of our physical universe actually compel a person to *age* over the course of ten years?"

"God Almighty." She smiled. "Don't you realize that sweet talk won't get you anywhere at your age?"

"My age?" I held out my hand.

"You heard me." She took my hand in hers and held it tightly, not letting go. "You surely are a sight. I heard you were in town. Look at your hair. Just like snow."

"I'm not just in town," I said very softly. "I'm home."

"Really?" She matched my volume, but her voice was gently mocking. "We'll see about that."

"I've had it foremost in my mind," I began clumsily, "to come here and see you, but there's actually been a fair amount of bizarre—"

"I've talked to June," she told me. "I've heard all about the rest. A lot's going on."

"Yes," I agreed, "I think you could say that."

She turned to Skidmore. "I checked for you, sugar. It's Dr. Osaka that's working on Linda. She's the best there is." She leaned closer to Skid. "Plus, they think there's not even a bullet in her. They think it went clean through."

"If there's no bone damage," Skid said, mostly to himself, "this could all be all right."

Lucinda touched his shoulder. "She'll be fine, Skid."

"She'll be fine," he repeated, but his expression betrayed a complete lack of conviction.

"Good." Lucinda turned back to me. I realized then that I had not let go of her hand, and tried to release my hold, but she just squeezed tighter. "Let's take a little walk, Fever."

"I feel I ought to stay." I looked at Skidmore.

"Go on." He shook his head. "It'll be a while before we find out anything, you know."

Andrews returned with three cups of coffee.

"Andrews?" I said, declining the coffee. "This is Lucinda Davis—you've heard me speak of her."

"So *this* is Lucinda," he said, looking her up and down. The sentence was too rife with suggestion.

"I'm going to take a moment with her," I told him, holding her hand tightly again, "would that be all right with you?

"The moonshine and these odd events—and this bad coffee—I don't think I'd have the first idea *what* would be all right with me at the moment." Andrews closed his eyes. "But sitting here and being quiet would be very good right now it seems to me, so I'm saying: Please, take a moment."

"All right, but don't wander off." I smiled at him.

Lucinda and I walked, still holding hands a little awkwardly, down toward the atrium at the other end of the long hallway. The lights there were dimmed and the room was lush with potted palms and ficus trees.

We found two seats in a corner, out of sight from the only other occupant of the room, a young pregnant woman who was reading a magazine.

We sat in silence a moment, each of us watching the other's face.

"You really haven't changed," I opened.

"You need glasses, sweetheart," she chided softly. "I have a face made out of care and worry." She finally let go of my hand.

"What are you talking about?" There was not a single visible wrinkle on her face. "Are all women your age so self-critical?" I smiled.

"Oh, now it's your turn to use that 'my age' language?" She shoved my shoulder gently.

"You started it." I felt, for a moment, we were fifteen again.

"I'm self-aware," she told me, "not self-critical."

"What kind of care and worry could you have up here?" I finally looked away. Suddenly, it seemed, looking at her face only hurt something in the corner of my eye, or a lesser room in my mind.

"I had a really hard time about Hammon." She folded her hands.

"Yes." What else was there to say? "I sent flowers, you know."

"Did you?" She looked out the window, her voice a little weaker for a moment. "I wasn't really myself for a while there." She took in a shallow breath. "I didn't know the human heart was capable of bearing that kind of sadness."

I had no idea what to do, so I just sat there until she spoke to me again.

"Some days I still feel like I'm married to him." Her voice was like smoke.

"I know." I hoped the odd bitterness that I was feeling hadn't shown through in my voice. "I feel that too."

"Still," she finally went on, "there comes a day when the winter is over and the spring comes back—without your having to do a single thing about it. Spring just comes." She shifted. "And I have enjoyed all your letters, and phone calls, and this *E-mail* business, now."

Her smile—that smile, that moment—doubled the ambient light in the entire room. I believed that she was, indeed, over her sorrow or loss or whatever it was she had felt when her husband had died.

Still uncertain, however, what to tell her about it, I turned the conversation back to the more pressing matter of Girlinda Needle.

"Will Linda really be all right?" I asked her.

"You know how tough she is," Lucinda reminded me.

"Yes," I told her. "Once, in high school, I saw her slap a half-grown male bear on the snout and chase it off when it came into her backyard."

She laughed. "That's Girlinda."

"She didn't seem to think a thing about it, either. Just went right on with her perennial rant about how much better the world would be if horses replaced all cars and trucks."

"Yup." Lucinda nodded once. "Still goes on about that."

"Who's this Dr. Osaka?"

"Fine Japanese-American woman from Chicago. Best ER doctor we ever had. Takes a lot of guff around here, as you might imagine."

"I'd imagine," I concurred, "that some of the good old boys around here would barely be able to believe she *is* a doctor."

"That's right. But you just give her five minutes with any one of those boys, and they'd pick up their own truck if she told them to."

"So Girlinda's in good hands, you're saying."

"Yes, hon." She looked at me gently. "I believe that is what I'm saying."

"Then," I started, a little confused about my intentions myself, "would it be too odd if I asked you a few questions of my own?"

"Like what?" Her voice was still very gentle, I was glad to hear.

"Well—June Cotage," I said, as if it were an entire explanation. "It's her supposition that you might shed some light on this business with my half-brother—the one that was found murdered at my place a few nights ago—or was it a hundred years ago? Quite a lot's happened—"

"I've been thinking about it already, Fever," she interrupted, stopping me before I could go on babbling.

"You have?"

She sighed, folded her hands, and cocked her head almost imperceptibly to the left, the way she always did when she was on the verge of telling a story of some length.

"You left here—you left this town and your family . . . and me—

when you were still young. You started college when you were young too, and so, in a way, you grew up in the city. Partly."

"I don't know about that."

"You're more worldly," she went on. "I grew up entirely here. I lived here. I got married and got widowed here."

"Lucinda . . ." I began.

"Still," she went on, "in some odd way, you know these hills better than I do."

"I don't know what you mean," I told her. "You mean because of my studies?"

"You can see the forest; all I see are the trees," she agreed. "While I've been living here, you've been studying it, thinking about it, writing your articles—those fine articles. It's different when you live here like I do. You don't think about it so much."

"I can see that," I admitted slowly. "Still, I don't know the day-to-day events the way you do."

"Those are what you might call the 'trees.' "

"I suppose," I agreed.

"Well, that's what June and I were talking about."

"What?" I asked. "The day-to-day things?"

"Sort of." Her eyes darted suddenly for a second, but I saw them. "I don't know where to start."

"Okay." I kept a steady gaze on her. "Why couldn't you start with June's strange supposition that there are 'things' I don't know about myself and my life to which everyone else seems to be privy."

"A lot of it's just talk." She wouldn't look me in the eye. "You know how *that* is up here."

"I do. I understand the nature of gossip." I turned to look directly at her. "I just don't know the specifics. What is the talk? What don't I know? What's the big secret?"

"Big secret?" She put her hand up close to her face, almost trying to keep the words from coming out of her mouth. "Well, you know how your mama was."

"Does everyone have to say that?" I tried to keep my voice down, but the pregnant woman looked up from her magazine. "Did everyone get together before I arrived and write the script for this? I know how my mother was, and who she was, for God's sake."

"All right," she said patiently, encouraging me to be a little calmer. "Maybe you do know who your mama was. I'll just go on then." She thinned her lips a moment. "It's just that—maybe you don't know your daddy as well as you think."

"My father?" I leaned forward. "What about him?"

"He might not have been the man you always thought he was."

"You mean there's something about him I don't know?" I looked into her eyes.

"No," she shook her head. "I mean, that man—Fletcher Devilin—might not actually have been your father—your real father—at all."

"There you are!" Before Lucinda's suggestion could even sink into my mind, Andrews had rushed into the atrium with news of his own. "That damned Sheriff Maddox is here. He's taking Skidmore off the case. Off *our* case."

"He's what?" I stood.

"He says it's for his own good, for Girlinda's safety," Andrews was very wound up, "but it's a clear case of professional jealousy if you ask me."

"Professional jealousy?" I glanced at Lucinda.

"Isn't it obvious? Skidmore's clearly the better man, and it rankles Maddox." Andrews momentarily stalled. Then: "Because Maddox is an idiot."

"You've had words with Maddox." It wasn't much of a guess on my part. Andrews was much more animated than he ought to have been, and his face was flushed.

"Well, as a matter of fact . . ." but he trailed off when Maddox himself came barreling in.

"Don't you walk away from me when I'm talking to you, boy," he growled at Andrews, stopping inches from the much taller man.

"Sheriff Maddox," I smiled at him, then turned to Lucinda. "You've taken Officer Needle off the case of the man murdered at my house, I'm told." My voice was so polite that I felt it was a clear insult.

"I've seen to it that Needle," he answered, spitting, "nor you, nor your foreign, sissy-ass friend here can have anything to do with my case."

"And how have you done that?" I was still smiling.

"With a wave of my hand, brother." Just to make certain I understood, he waved his hand. "That's all it takes. What I say goes around here. What you say is absolutely nothing."

"No," I corrected him, "I mean what have you done that can compel the three of us from—"

"Official police documents," Maddox blustered. "A form five-oh-three and a restraining order with everyone's name on it just waiting for trouble."

"Ah," I said, "a form five-oh-three." I had no idea what it was, of course.

"You bet your ass."

"And why, may I ask, have you done this thing?" I wouldn't let him go. "Could you tell me? It wouldn't seem to make much sense, as Skidmore's pointed out, he and I have always—"

"I don't give a frog's dick what you always do!" he screamed "He's out, you hear me?"

"I'd imagine," Andrews tried to copy my tone, "that everyone on this wing of the hospital could hear you. Deputy Needle's off the case. Is that what you're trying to say?"

Maddox screeched a vile Germanic-sounding obscenity at the top of his lungs, spun, and crashed out of the atrium.

When he was completely gone, Lucinda touched my arm. "He was pretty mad, Fever. I know he's an idiot, but you ought not to mess with him just the same. He can be a dangerous man. Maybe you'd better clear out."

"Not likely," Andrews snorted.

"All this means," I assured him, "is that Skidmore needs me—and Dr. Andrews—now more than ever. He'll have a great deal of trouble moving about without incurring further ire from 'the boss,' but I'm less visible, at least to the offices of the police up here. I can maneuver more easily."

"I was just wondering," she continued, "why Maddox would be so upset about all this business, and why, sure enough, he would want to keep Skid away from it—when he really needs help."

"Good point," Andrews allowed.

"I have to spend a few quiet moments to myself," I began, "to think out several of these bombshells of information I've just received. When my mind is clearer, I'd like for you to ask me that question again, Lucinda. But Andrews's supposition about professional jealousy seems accurate enough, doesn't it?"

"I've had a thought in Atlanta, just this week," Andrews said then, his voice taking an odd downward turn, "that somehow pertains. Maybe this is another bombshell, Dev, but the thought was that Bishop, by proxy, was having you removed from your position at the university—for exactly the same motive."

Indeed, there was a third bombshell. It exploded in silence because I could find no words to use for a response.

"Why are you saying that?" Lucinda asked. "Dr. Bishop was Fever's teacher."

"I've been thinking it all out," Andrews said to me, "and the only thing I can see is that for some reason Bishop was jealous of your work and wanted you out of the folklore program. He was willing, in fact, to go so far as to close down the entire program."

"Why?" was all I could ask.

"Because you were eclipsing his former fame in the same arena?"

"What possible evidence could you have for such a fantastic accusation?" I began.

"Oh, there were plenty of rumors at the university." He shoved his hands into his pockets. "I kept them from you because I knew you wouldn't believe them."

"And I don't believe them *now*," I insisted.

"It came clearer into focus," Andrews went on, ignoring me, "when I thought about this Skidmore/Maddox friction, you see?"

"Jesus." I sat down suddenly. It must have been obvious how stunned I was.

"Are you all right, Fever?" Lucinda sat beside me again.

"No. I just remembered." I blinked. "Carson told me, immediately before Skid came to get us and bring us here—so I couldn't pursue it with him—that Bishop and Coombs were working together . . ."

"The business deal he mentioned," Andrews finished. "I nearly forgot about that in all this other mess."

"And then," I went on, staring at him, "Lucinda tells me that the man I've always believed to be my father might *not* have been my father . . ."

"Fever . . ." she tried to stop me.

"What are you talking about?" Andrews eyed Lucinda.

"And now you," I pointed at Andrews accusingly, "suggest that the man I've always thought of as a surrogate parent, a second father, Dr. Bishop, is the one responsible for the hellish conditions at the university. It's too much, Andrews. That part is too much, honestly."

Again, silence.

"Well." Lucinda put her hand on my forearm. "It's nice to see you're just as big a mess as you ever were." She looked up at Andrews. "Some things don't change."

"It's comforting when that happens." He smiled back.

"I can't digest it all." I was staring blankly.

"I can see that," Andrews said.

"Why don't you just go on down to where Skid is," Lucinda suggested, "and see can you help him stay calm. I'll go get the update on Girlinda. That's the most important thing here and now. The rest of it—you can sit around and talk that out amongst yourselves." She nodded a very feminine punctuation to her pronouncement, then she headed, all business, straight down the hall.

Andrews watched her leave, then raised his eyebrows in my direction. "I can see why you still think about that one—even after all this time."

"Yes." But those thoughts were the farthest from my mind. "Andrews? I've just now come to the conclusion that you were right. I agree."

"About my suppositions concerning Bishop?"

"No, that part is ridiculous." I stood, shaking my head. "I'm talking about the earlier estimation of these events." I looked out the window at the night. "Someone *is* trying to kill me."

"Unaccustomed as I am to hearing the words 'you're right' come out of *your* mouth—"

"There's more." I started out of the atrium and down the hall to where Skid sat with his head in his hands. "All of these events actually *are* my fault."

"All of what events?" He was staring at the floor as we walked.

"Let's start back at the university," I said, almost to myself. "Obviously Bishop's not behind the attempt to close down the folklore department, but someone is. And I've been too caught up in the matter personally to take a step back and ask myself the primary question."

"What question?" He'd fallen into step beside me.

"Why?"

"Why would someone be trying to shut down the department?" He nodded. "You don't buy my 'professional jealousy' theory?"

"I know that those feelings exist, but they hardly motivate someone strongly enough to work so hard at closing down an entire department. I think that there must be something more important at stake. I think I've somehow, inadvertently, threatened something bigger: someone's professional existence, perhaps—something that big, of that order. That's the only thing that would make sense of this much violence and insanity."

"And it's followed you, if that really is what this is all about, all the way up here? A dead body on your doorstep," Andrews recounted, "shots fired at you and Skidmore, threats from the sheriff, and now Girlinda." He smiled at me. "These people must be really happy you've come home."

"That's what I've got to get straight. How my university problems could be tied with my . . . personal historical matters." I felt uncomfortable even mentioning the bulk of the other problems out loud.

"Such as?" Andrews was apparently less shy about enumerating them. "Your father wasn't really your father, your half-brother had a message from your strange, dead mother." He smiled slyly. "Not to mention, by the way, that the ghost of your first love still seems more than a little interested—"

"You may now shut up," I finished for him.

We had come to the waiting area. The place seemed a little calmer than it had a few moments before, and quieter.

Skidmore didn't lift his head, and his voice was very tired. "If you two are planning on talking like that for very long, go somewhere else."

"Lucinda's gone for an update." I moved to sit beside him. "But the word is that Girlinda's fine."

He looked up. "As fine as she can be with a bullet through her shoulder, you mean?"

"As fine as she can be under the circumstances," I told him firmly, "and I'll admit that the circumstances are revolting." I lowered my voice. "I'm sorry it's not me in that hospital bed."

"What?" His discomfort with my suggestion was etched into his face. "How the hell would that make me feel any better?" He looked down. "I'll tell you what's the real problem: I'm a sorry excuse for a law man."

Again I was struck by the collision of perspectives. All I'd been thinking was that it was my fault Girlinda'd been shot. Obviously Skid blamed himself. It was time, I thought, to get us all out of that mire.

"You know," I said to Skidmore, "I blame myself for Girlinda's condition. You seem to feel you're to blame. Neither opinion will help. The shooting was a phenomenon. That's all. We give it value. We impart meaning to it." I looked up at Andrews. "Let's all suspend the interpretations of this particular event for the moment, shall we? You have work to do. You have to find the person who shot the man on my front steps—and probably shot your wife—the person who's doing all this. That's your task."

"Despite," Andrews interjected seriously, "the fact that Maddox has removed you from our case."

I only smiled a little at Andrews's including himself. "Right," I said. "All that means is that we have the opportunity now of working without having to observe some of the official niceties that we might have had to previously," I smiled. "Maddox has actually made your job easier."

I watched Skid's face adjust to the idea that he had wallowed in the mess of the moment long enough, and then saw the resolve on his face. "You're right, Dev." He sat straighter, staring down the hall toward Girlinda's room. "I need to get me somebody and put them in the jailhouse. That's what'll make me feel a whole lot better."

"So," Andrews folded his arms and furrowed his brow, "what's our first move?"

"I'm going to watch Shoo Walters make a chair," I said very cheerily.

Both men looked at me for a long moment.

"How on earth will that help us?" Andrews shook his head.

"If you buy the basic Freudian context of folklore research," I began, and saw both men steal a glance at one another, "then you have to agree that my work is a kind of psychological archaeology. Instead of digging up pyramids, I dig up human minds: the wealth of stories, folkways, abilities, songs—memories in general—of an entire people. It's unimaginable that I would let these stories and abilities disappear from our planet without at least recording them, if the people and ways *themselves* can't be saved from extinction."

Both men still glared at me, so I pressed on.

"In mining this metaphysical gold," I explained, "I also discover myself. We all investigate the world, don't you think, to discover ourselves? I'm going to talk to Shoo Walters, for example, in part to find out what there is about me that would make someone keep trying to kill me."

Andrews was genuinely at a loss for words, and dropped his hands to his side, still trying to think of a response.

But Skidmore smiled, and it was good to see. "You think that Shoo," he said slowly, "knows more than he's been telling us about your dead brother. You're going to get him talking about his chairs so that he won't know that you're really asking him about something else entirely."

"Yes, I am," I admitted, smiling back at him.

"What?" Andrews looked between us.

"Dev used to do it all the time," Skidmore answered. "Shoo's easy to get secrets out of. Easier than those others, anyway."

"It's just something about yesterday when I first saw him," I confirmed. "I thought it wasn't just that he didn't want to hurt my feelings about my brother; he avoided looking at me most of the morning. I think he knows more than he's saying."

"People tell things to Shoo," Skidmore told Andrews, "because they rely on the fact that he doesn't generally know what the hell they're talking about. And he don't usually remember what they've said ten minutes later anyway." He shot a glance my way. "But Dev always had a way of getting things out of Shoo."

"Just good field research technique, really," I said plainly.

"Well what am I going to do?" Andrews whined, cocking his head in my direction. "I don't want to sit around while the two of you—"

"You'll have to try Carson," I interrupted.

"No," Andrews complained immediately.

"He likes you," I insisted.

"He does not. He thinks I'm an idiot."

"But he likes you anyway," I reiterated, "and he'll tell you things he wouldn't tell me because he doesn't think you'll understand them, and because it's not personal with you—or he won't think it is."

"What are you talking about?" Andrews took a step closer to me.

"Since Carson thinks there was some kind of business deal between Coombs and Bishop . . ."

"Right, right." Andrews nodded. "I think I see where you're going with this."

"I'd like to know if there's anything at all to that notion, if the 'deal' might be somehow connected to the shooting of my half-brother—and the rest of the shootings too."

"What makes you think it would be?" Andrews's voice was still a little belligerent.

"Because Carson wouldn't have brought it up otherwise," I said, a little as if I were explaining something to one of my students, I'm afraid.

But Andrews wasn't offended. What I'd said had taken him aback. "You mean Carson brought that up to you on *purpose*? Because of all this other mess, you think?"

"Yes, Andrews," I nodded, wearily. "You're not yet convinced that these people up here in the mountains know *much* more than they ever say?"

"What?"

"In the mountains," I said patiently, "you're always taught to have big ears and a little mouth."

" '*Give every man thy ear, but few thy voice,*' " he said, almost absently.

"Thank you, Polonius," I agreed.

"So you mean," I could see he was beginning to understand, and he folded his arms again, this time to ward off a chill that his understanding was bringing, "that they know who killed your brother?"

"I think they certainly have an idea," I nodded. "And they know who my real father was—they probably know your aunt's maiden name, somehow." I looked him squarely in the eye. "This very mountain we're standing on now? Nearly eighty percent of it is underground. The same thing goes, metaphorically speaking, for the people who live on it."

"I see what you're saying." He shook his head ruefully. "I won't underestimate them again."

God smiled, then, somewhere close by, as evidenced by the sudden appearance of Lucinda, coming down the hall from one of the closed consulting rooms.

"Girlinda's awake, Skid," she announced softly. "She wants to see you." She looked at me. "They already told her she had to stay here for a couple of days, of course, but by the time she got through with the doctors, they were all willing to walk her out to the car and let her drive herself home tonight."

"That's my girl." Skidmore's face lit up.

"You go on in." Lucinda patted his arm.

"Dev," he said, standing, "I don't know how long this'll take, or whatever . . ."

"We came here with Skid in the squad car," I explained to Lucinda.

"Don't you worry about Fever and Dr. Andrews," she said to Skidmore. "I'll get them home tonight." She darted a glance at me.

I nodded. I liked the idea very much of an excuse to see more of her right away.

Skid started down the hall, then turned back to me. "By the way, I've got my work set too." He lowered his voice. "I'm going to speak with Hek."

I nodded, and he hurried off to be with his wife.

Lucinda handed me her car keys. "It's the '57 Chevy out in the front lot. It was Hammon's. You all take it and drive yourselves home. I got lots of work to do, and someone can give me a ride home later. But this means," she said slowly, taking my elbow in her right hand, "that you'll have to come pick me up and take me to work in the morning."

"I can do better than that." I squeezed her hand to my side, pressing it with my elbow. "Let's have lunch tomorrow—we have a lot of catching up to do. And maybe you could call June and see if we could go over there tomorrow night together. I want to record her and she usually does better if there's a woman with her in the kitchen. Would that be all right?"

"It would be all right." There was just the whisper of a smile on her face. "But it's a sorry way to ask a girl for a date." She turned and went back down the hall, around a corner, and vanished—just like a ghost.

"I guess you'll have to pick her up and take her to work in the morning," Andrews repeated, mockingly.

"Didn't I tell you to shut up just a minute ago?"

"Why is our deputy going to visit Hek?" he countered.

"Well," I headed for the exit door of the hospital, "Hek took over the church business from Coombs, as we were discussing last night. Maybe he knows more about all that." Then I frowned. "There's something going on between the two of them—between Hek and Skidmore—that we don't know about. Bad blood of some sort."

"Is that a part of all this too? Do you really think all this is tied together?" Andrews kept up, following me out the door.

"We don't live in a random universe," I told him certainly.

"Oh, yes we do," he said, just as surely.

"Then how about this?" We stepped out into the crisp night. "I know that everything in this entire affair is tied together because I believe that it all has to do with me, and I just got here, just arrived back here in the mountains."

"Yes?" He wasn't following me.

"I mean that I haven't personally been here long enough to set all this in motion myself, but set in motion it has been. Ergo, if it all does have to do with me, it must have been set in motion, around me, for some purpose. Which is what makes it my fault: because I'm at the center of it, do you at least see that?"

"You're not making any sense." Big sigh. "Are you going in for some sort of Atlas complex?"

"That's not what I'm saying at all," I told him, zipping my jacket against a sudden, chill wind. "I said that I really *was* to blame."

"Like saying you're not paranoid if they really *are* all out to get you."

"Exactly."

"I'm just going along with all this to humor you, you realize." He glanced around the parking lot. "An old Chevy?"

"There it is." I pointed.

The car was two-toned: white and lemon-green. I remembered it when I saw it, and approached it trying hard not to think about it too much—whose car it had been. I unlocked the door and felt an odd tug, once more, of days long past.

"You know, Andrews," I said, opening the door of a dead man's car, "we have to be careful in what we're about to do. The person we're looking for has killed someone, and tried to kill others."

"Hurry up, can you?" Andrews growled, shaking the passenger-side door handle. "I'm really beginning to sober up now. Under the circumstances it's a much more frightening prospect than a little thing like death."

Twelve

Shoo Walters's house was nearly invisible to the casual visitor, hidden by a tangle of ancient muscadine and honeysuckle vines, thick wild privet and holly hedges. The place was much more overgrown that it had ever been when I was a boy—years of yard neglect seemed a certain affirmation of the age of the occupant.

I had gotten up at five-thirty that morning to go to Lucinda's house and take her to work. I had made a very grumbling Andrews follow me in my truck. We'd left Lucinda, and her car, at the hospital, with a promise of lunch later that day. Then he and I had gone in my truck to Gil's garage, where I'd dropped Andrews off with an admonition not to be tempted that early in the morning by any further offers of corn liquor.

I'd only gotten a little lost because time had drastically altered the dirt paths that passed for roads on the backside of the mountain where Shoo lived.

As I pulled up in his side yard and turned off my engine, I heard the grandfather clock that he owned crashing out the time: seven o'clock. It could have been heard a mile away. The silence that followed it was unearthly.

I got out of the truck and yelled into the house.

"Shoo!"

"Who is that?" I knew that he called from the kitchen without even getting up from where he was sitting at the table.

"Fever Devilin."

"Hey." He was calm, almost as if he were expecting me. "Come on in the house."

I slammed the driver's-side door behind me and it seemed another rude noise in the middle of all the morning's silence.

Shoo lived all alone and always had. Nothing about his home was marred by normal domestic convention.

I pushed my way through the stubborn front door and took in the place. A single bed and a small wooden table took up most of the room in the kitchen, beside the black woodstove.

The living room was nearly bare except for a knotted spiral rug that covered most of the wooden floor, an imposing grandfather clock, and a laughably incongruous blue 1920s sofa that looked as if it had never been touched by human hands.

The only other room in the house, the bedroom, was filled with Shoo's chairs—so crowded that I didn't understand how the chairs had gotten so packed in, nor how they could ever be extracted.

There was a pump in the kitchen area that passed for running water. Through the bedroom window I could barely see the out-house. From the kitchen the work shed could be seen, the really important building where Shoo made his chairs.

The woodstove in the kitchen was burning so hot that I could barely stand to be in the room. Shoo was in his long johns at the kitchen table with a pot of coffee in front of him.

"Coffee?"

"Yes." I went and fetched myself a coffee cup.

I held it out. He poured. I sat. We listened to the clock's loud ticking.

"So," he said after a long silence, not looking at me, "you reckon it to rain today?"

"Might," I nodded and sipped coffee.

Another long minute or two went by. This was as good a practice with an old friend as it was with a new field informant: Don't push the river. Let the river take its own sweet time. We'd get to the purpose of my visit soon enough.

"You go on to the hospital last night?" he asked me, clearing his throat.

"Yes."

"Girlinda's okay?"

"You know Girlinda."

He gave a curt, sober nod. "Take more'n a slug of lead to keep her out of the kitchen when she wants to eat—or feed them kids."

"That's right." I sat back. "I think she went home last night."

"They couldn't even convince her to spend one night there?" He was clearly impressed.

"No."

"That's one fine woman." He took a big gulp of coffee. "You want you some breakfast? Got some jerky biscuits."

"No." I'd only made the mistake of eating breakfast with Shoo once in my life. He made biscuits that could be thrown, unharmed and intact, entirely through a plate glass window. Then he used the horrible things to make a sandwich with some kind of leather. He'd told me that the substance was his own venison jerky, but I'd always been absolutely convinced he'd gotten confused and chopped up part of his own belt instead.

And to make matters worse, the only thing he ever had on hand with which to wash down these abominations was thick, chunky buttermilk.

"I've already eaten," I told him.

"Suit yourself."

We finished our cups, poured two more, and watched the sun creep across the windowsill.

"Nice of you to visit," he finally said.

"Happy to. Thought I might get to watch you make a chair."

"Oh." He sat perfectly still for a moment, still not looking at me, then quickly tossed back the last of his coffee, pulled on the flannel shirt that had been hanging on the back of his chair, and stood. "Time for work, then."

I stood too, and in seconds we were out of the kitchen and headed toward his work shed.

That very shed was one of the primary reasons I'd moved back home. It was small—only ten feet square—but it was still sturdier and much more meticulously kept than the house. It smelled like cedar, and inside it was as silent as a church. Not a cobweb nor a scrap of dust was in evidence; the floors were scrubbed spotlessly free of wood shavings and bark chips. There was a huge window in each of the four walls, and the light poured in from all directions and seemed to converge directly on the work area in the middle of the room.

The implements—all the tools he used to make his chairs—had been personally handmade by Shoo himself, and not significantly altered in design or function from chair-making tools of the Middle Ages in England. Illustrations from as early as 1120 A.D. showed men using the same lathe, the exact hammer—even the same oak-split cane bottoms.

The lathe was the most interesting and ingenious of all the instruments to me. It consisted first of a stout, tapered tree limb, wedged immovably into the roof beams of the shed, with the smaller end free. That end extended four feet out and three feet above our heads. To that tapered end, a thin, taught, hemp rope was tied and reached almost to the floor. There the rope was attached to a board that was six inches wide by two feet long. A hole was cut in one end of the board and the rope had been pulled through and knotted. The upper end—where it was connected to the rope—hung almost a foot from the dirt floor. The lower end rested on the dirt, making the board rest at a forty-five-degree angle.

Situated around the rope at a height of about three feet was a cut-away table, the empty space about the size of a small dinner plate, and on the table on either side of the rope were two miniature pillories that held the ends of a small branch on both sides.

This whole apparatus was used to round the rough pieces of wood. Wrapping the rope once around a crude tree limb, then securing it in the pillories, Shoo used the footboard as a treadle, and worked the wood back and forth, making it spin with miraculous speed and force, while holding a very sharp wood chisel to it. The first time I'd seen him operate it, I couldn't believe my eyes—that something so crude could, in the hands of this master, be so efficient, so quick, and so precise. In a matter of minutes, the crude branch was a smooth, perfectly round chair leg.

The lathe was exactly the kind that had been used in 1120, as evidenced by European drawings from that date of similar devices. The rest of the place was just as much a museum, and staring, in fascination, at everything in the room, I nearly lost interest in all of my own troubles.

"Shoo," I said slowly, staring up at the the ceiling, "would you mind very much if I got my video camera and recorded your making a chair again?"

"What for?" He was irritated by the prospect, it seemed. "Don't you have about twenty of them things by now?"

"I think it's important to have a record of your work now—the work you do now."

"I don't know." He scratched himself. "It's more important to have a good chair, don't you think?"

"Yes," I agreed. "No one will ever be able to sit down comfortably on my videotape, but you know the kind of work I do, and it's important to have some kind of reference to your work." I caught his eye. "After you're gone."

"That's right." He lit up. "All that damn video that you done took over all these years, it'll be there when I'm dead and gone, won't it?"

"Yes." I waited while he considered.

"Could you show it at my funeral?"

"Yes, I could, if that's what you want." I tried not to sound amused. "But more importantly, people years and years from now will be able to see you building a chair."

"Yup." He looked around the shed. "That's a neat trick."

I took that as an affirmation, and ran to my car to get the camera. I always kept a video camera and a fresh tape in the truck hidden under blankets behind the driver's seat. Dr. Bishop had told me that a good folklorist would always be prepared to make a record of anything important.

By the time I got back to the shed, Shoo was prepared. Even given my views on the generally boring nature of material folk culture, I was quite excited, and I always had been, by the prospect of recording what might have been the last traditional chair maker of his sort on the planet.

"Well," he began, very stiffly, and aware of the camera, "this here's the workshop, folks."

I lowered the camera and paused it. "Shoo. Just talk to me. I'm the only one here now."

"Oh," he nodded nervously, "okay."

I turned the camera back on.

"Well," just as self-consciously, "this here's the workshop . . . Dev."

I let his continuing awkwardness go, and began interviewing. I was watching his world through the camera. I tried to keep it steady, and let his images and words speak for themselves.

"How do you start to make a chair?"

"Start?" He looked around. "Well, I go out into the woods and I gather me up a bunch of branches, like. Mostly oak. I take this ax," he hefted his homemade tool, "and chop off branches, oh . . . about this big around." He made a circle with his thumb and first finger.

"Where'd you buy that ax?" I knew the answer. I was asking for the audience.

"You know good and well I made this, Dev." He was relaxing. "Made it with my own two hands. This here handle? It's oak. The blade I taken over to the blacksmith back in . . . I believe it was the year you left for college, that's . . . ten years ago? No. More. So . . . but, anyway, this is the new blade. I had the one before it for about twenty years. That one was give to me by my uncle. This one I hammered it out my own self. Doubled it over one hundred times exactly. I could chop a Ford engine block in half with it if I wanted."

"But you don't use it for that?"

"Naw." He laughed. "I just chop the branches."

"So you gather them up—where, from right around your house?"

"Well, sometimes I have to go a good ways away to get what I want."

"Up to the Hearth?" I knew what his answer to that would be too. I was asking because I knew that I would include shots of the Hearth in the tape as a link to some of the local stories about the place. It always made a much more exciting tape to show the Devil's Hearth, and to hear the local stories about it.

"You know my feelings about that place, Dev. I don't never like to go up there." He blinked at the camera. "Too slippery, on that moss. I'm afraid I'd hurt my back."

"All right, so you gather up the branches—how many at a time?"

"About . . ." he made a big circle with both his arms in front of him, glad to change the subject, ". . . as many as I can carry."

"And how long do you spend doing that?" I asked him. "How long does it take?"

"Gather up all the wood branches?" He looked out the window and thought. "That takes about . . . a day."

"So can we go out into the woods now and get some branches?"

He stared into the camera. "What'd we do that for? I got me a big stack here." He pointed. "I did all that yesterday."

"I see." I panned over to the pile of raw tree limbs. It looked like a bunch of larger kindling even though they'd been trimmed and cut to a more or less uniform length. I panned back to Shoo. "Then what?"

"I brought them back here." He shifted his weight.

"Sorry, I mean now what do you do?"

"Oh, well." He looked around at everything. "I round the branches."

"Could we see?"

"Sure." He reached for one, wrapped it in the rope of the lathe, and began without any ado.

"Whoa," I told him. "You've got to explain this lathe you've got here." I moved around him, getting a better shot.

"Oh," he stopped working. "This? My uncle invented this over in Blue Ridge many years ago. I made this one, of course. I used to do stone work—carving and masonry—before that. Then he showed me how to make one of these, and I've been making chairs ever since."

"Your uncle invented this lathe?" I knew his answer to this conundrum, too—but having it on tape was irresistible.

"Now, I know you done showed me them pictures, Dev," he said, ignoring the camera finally, "but that was back in the old country. How in this world would Uncle Shellnut have known about that? He was born right here in America."

"Never mind now," I told him, lowering the camera again, unwilling to argue with that logic, "just tell me about it."

"Okay," he told me, as if I were the most ignorant person in the county.

I resumed taping, and he spent nearly half an hour explaining the intricacies of the instrument. Then he began to use it and stopped talking, and I taped for a while longer, watching the rough limb shed its bark and turn smooth and white before my eyes—and on the tape.

He stood over the work, dressed in his long johns and flannel shirt and battered construction boots, like any artist from any time: rapt, absorbed, trancelike. Everything else on the planet fell away, and the only thing that existed in the universe was the tree limb, growing increasingly more beautiful with each beat of the manual treadle. It seemed he was tapping his foot to a song that only he could hear. And the sun only existed to provide him with enough light to see his glorious work. Every once in a while a woodpecker, close by in a tree outside, would rattle the stillness with his own woodwork. The sound seemed to urge the lathe to turn faster, in perfect harmony with the music of the wind and the bees and the tree branches high above the tiny workshop swaying and clicking in time to Shoo's work.

"Once I get to rounding?" he finally said, "I like to round a whole bunch, keep them in stock." He was completely at ease in front of the camera—virtually unaware of its existence.

"I see. How long do you spend with that?"

"Time spent rounding?" He stopped what he was doing and looked around the room, as if the answer might be written on the table or the floor. "Round a whole bunch? That takes . . . about a day."

"All right."

He went back to work, again completely silent, and I bided my time. When he seemed thoroughly absorbed, I asked him the real questions I had come to ask.

"What do you think," I began, using the same tone of voice as in all the other sentences, "the message from my brother was, Shoo?"

"What message?" he asked me, without looking up, bent over the lathe, eyes wide, hands sure.

"The message that Thresher wanted to tell me—from my mother."

"Oh, I expect it was something about her and the Reverend Coombs, don't you think? She always told us, your mama always used to say she thought Coombs might be your real daddy."

I nearly dropped the video camera, but the lathe was making enough noise and Shoo was so absorbed that he didn't notice. Not that I hadn't been partly prepared to hear a statement like that, but the offhanded manner with which it had been said had quite startled me

"Coombs." My voice was steady. "You think?"

"I don't know," he sighed, "I didn't much take to the idea when I first heard it—although the Reverend Coombs was a good man. I just happened to like Fletcher better. No judgment, just a personal preference." He stopped the treadle a moment, ran his hand along the white pole in the braces, then started up again.

"And you think," I managed to continue, "that's what Thresher's message was for me?"

"Well," he began, shifting the treadle from his right foot to his left, "I know it was something about Coombs. He told me that much."

The camera jerked visibly at that.

"He did?" I said, a little hoarsely.

"Yup." He stopped turning the pole, took it out, examined it—perfectly round. He nodded, set it aside, and picked up a new rough branch. "Reverend Coombs was a good man. I liked working for him."

"You *worked* for him?" I couldn't help it. I turned the camera off.

"Oh, now and again." He stopped, looked up at me, and grinned. "He had your same interest in my tools, my work. He said they was God's work, and you couldn't tell my tools from the tools of yesteryear, just like you say." He looked back down at his work. "I always thought he got that from Bishop though—your friend Bishop." He looked up again. "You know he come up here many years ago, Bishop did, to the workshop, and taken pictures of this, of me making chairs. Not this video—he taken just pictures, you know, with a camera."

"Yes, I knew that."

"But he weren't as interesting to talk to as you are." He looked back down at his work. "You're a good boy, Dev."

Finally I set the camera down. "Could we take a break for a second, Shoo?"

He looked up. "Sorry, Dev. When I get to doing this, I get all wrapped up. Same with making the seat weaves. Once I get started on a pattern I can make a hundred of the things and not get tired of them. You okay? It is kind of cold out here."

"No," I said, "it's not that."

"Oh, I see." He finally nodded slowly. "You want to know was Coombs really your father?"

"Is that the message Thresher was bringing me?"

"I don't know."

I thought about what I'd told Andrews the night before about these people, how what they showed was only a small percentage of what they knew. And how secrets were power, and once you told a secret, you lost the power—so some secrets were held onto for years. And after all, I thought, what's a century or two to a mountain? These people wouldn't talk if they didn't want to, wouldn't tell a secret if there wasn't some reason for it, and time meant little to them. It made them simultaneously the most admirable and the most maddening people on the face of the earth.

And just as I was thinking that, Shoo leaned forward casually, elbows on his worktable and said, "You could just get it directly from your mother in person." He shrugged. "Seems like that would answer your question once and for all, wouldn't it?"

I had been hoping for information from Shoo Walters, and I had been clever about it: distracting him with his own work and at the same time continuing some professional research. But as I stood there staring back at him in his workshop, I had a momentary glance at what might really have been the case: Perhaps he had been the one using the excuse of research to tell me something he'd wanted to tell me for a long time.

"My mother," I began weakly, "is dead."

"Well, now," he answered me, in what seemed a kind of lampoon of his own stereotype, "there's dead and then there's dead."

"Since when," I said, trying to get a little control over the fire in my brain, "have you become inscrutable?"

"Have no idea what that means," he waved his hand dismissively, "but here's what I'm talking about: Your mama kept a diary."

"A diary?" When stunned, the bewildered will often resort to merely repeating what they've been told.

"I believe that is what your brother was bringing you." He took his foot off the treadle. "Your mama's diary."

"And that," I sighed, relaxing, "is what you mean by 'asking her personally.' "

"Yes."

"Not that she was physically still alive." I lowered my head.

"I guess." He sniffed.

"Then I guess I'd have to say," I accused him, "that it was an odd way of putting it, what you just said."

"My mother wrote in our family bible nearly every day." He only sounded a little defensive. "The margins are filled up with her little sayings. When I pick it up at night, I can hear her voice just as clear—it's just like she's right there beside me. That diary of your mama's, it would be just like her voice to you."

"There's dead and then there's dead." I let out a final breath.

"That's what I said." He blinked. "What the hell did you think I meant?"

"Well, what am I supposed to believe?" My voice was a little hot. "And, by the way, as long as we've stopped the tape, what exactly is all this about Coombs being my father?"

"It's all in the diary," he matched my tone, "I would reckon."

"Well where is this diary?" I took a step toward him and got louder.

"I don't know," he raised his voice back.

"You don't know?"

"How the hell would I know where the damn thing is?" His voice made the sawdust on the table quake.

We were practically shouting at one another, but I couldn't quite have explained why we were doing it, not to any rational person who might have happened along at that moment.

"And how do you even know that there *is* a diary?" I upped the volume even more.

"Because I *saw* it the night Thresher was killed!"

In the silence that followed that sentence, I took a step away from Shoo and tried to read his face. It wasn't out of the realm of possibility, I thought, that he could have killed Thresher. He was, after all, a crazy old man living all by himself in a cabin with no electricity or running water, talking to himself and his dead mother. It was the perfect profile of the backwoods loner—one of three or four favorite portraits of the mass murderer. How much farther would he have to go to kill a strange trespasser in the middle of the night?

Shoo took in, then blew out, a long breath.

"Okay, here's the story," he said, resigned. "Hek come back from hunting one day . . . what was that, about two weeks ago? Sometime when Skidmore was gone with Alan Jackson. They know each other, you know, Skid and Alan—"

"Would you please go on?"

"So anyway," he continued hastily, "Hek come back—over at Gil's—and told us he seen you up at your place, only we knew it wouldn't be you on account of we'd have know if it had been you . . . on account of you would have come to say hey to us like you done when you actually did come to stay at your place."

All I could do was nod at his convoluted diction.

"So," he went on, "I knew, we all knew, it wasn't you. So I was just curious, you know, about who it was, and just went on up there myself to see." His face twisted a second from the strain of thought. "Come to think of it, could even have been the night right before you come back. Just the night before. Huh. You got a smoke? I need one."

"I don't smoke anymore."

"Too bad." He looked around the workshop. "I got some in here somewhere."

"I'll buy you a carton," I told him, tapping the tabletop impatiently, "if you'll just go on with this now."

"Oh. A carton?" He smiled and resumed very rapidly. "Okay. So I went up there, you know, to your place and it was your brother and he showed me your mama's diary. The end. Let's go get them smokes."

He started for the door.

"Wait!" I held up my hand. "We're not going anywhere."

"Damn it." He proffered a heavy sigh. "What more do you want to know?"

I watched his face, and decided, once again, to change my assessment of the situation: He really was just a harmless, none-too-bright old man—however strange he might also be. He wasn't hiding anything, and he didn't seem to understand the significance of the things he knew. Sometimes the most mysterious thing about a human being is that they have no mystery. It can be deceptive—one imagines depth where there is only, really, vacancy. My notion that he might have been using my own work to distract me—and worse, that he could be some ominous demon—was like the clouds that passed over the mountains: dark, quick, odd, then suddenly gone.

"I want to know a few more details," I said in my most scholarly voice, "about your conversation with the dead man."

"Dev." He leaned against the door frame. "He wasn't dead when I was talking with him, he was just nervous."

"Nervous?" There was that bewildered repeating response again.

"Nervous about meeting you, is what he said." His eyes lit up as he stared at the pile of rounds he'd been working. "Hey. Smokes!" His took three lightning steps to the pile and his hand darted into the maze of wood. He retrieved a pack of unfiltered Camels, his familiar, perennial brand.

"Good." I tapped the table again. "Go on."

He held up the pack for me to see. "Even got matches."

There was a box of kitchen matches jammed tightly into the cellophane around the pack, distorting it.

"Great. Go *on*."

"Right." He drew a bent cigarette from the pack, lit it, and inhaled. "I caught him just about sunset, and he was cracking into your house. I'd been waiting on the side of the house, you know over there where you got those big old rhododendrons? I pops out and says, 'Hold up there. You know whose house that is?' And he says, 'It's my brother's.' So I got a good look at him and sure enough he did look like you. Good bit. He says, 'Who are you?' And we begun to talk."

Shoo rested against the windowsill, and the light streaming in behind him made his face impossible to see, and the smoke all around him gave him something of a mystical air.

"We just sat down on the stairs there on your porch, shared a smoke, and talked. He was hungry for some talk, you could see that.

So he says, 'I got something here. It's from my mama, and I got to show it to my brother, Fever. It was her last request.' That's what he told me. Said that showing you the diary was his dying mother's last request. I tell you what, Dev, I was right touched."

"You're *touched* all right." I shook my head. "Is that all?"

"About. He was tired, and he didn't invite me in. Showed me the cover of the diary, though. It was right pretty, one of those kind that they have a leather strap and a lock? You seen those?"

"Yes."

"I says, 'You got the key?' And he just told me good night and got up and went inside so I went home."

He offered up a slow, rolling shrug. End of story.

"He didn't ask you who you were?" I asked suspiciously. You never could tell what Shoo might make up.

"Oh, yeah. He did that. Says, 'Did you know my brother, Fever?' And I says, 'I practically raised him.' And I told him about it. Then he says, 'Well don't say anything about my visit if you happen to talk to him before I do. I'm going on down to Atlanta after a while, and I kind of want it to be just between me and him, you understand.' And I told him I did understand, because it was a family matter, and *then* I took off."

"June said he was in my house, and around these parts in general, because he wanted to get a certain familiarity with me." I was only repeating what June had said.

"That's what I got out of him." He took another deep drag. "That's what Carson and them thought, anyway."

"And then someone killed him."

"Well, yeah," he argued reasonably, "but be fair: They thought they was killing you. That's what everybody says now."

"That does seem to be the consensus." I sighed as heavily as I ever had in my life. I had to find that diary, if, in fact, it existed—but I had to get my mind clear before I could proceed. So: "Ready to finish the video?"

"What?" He held his cigarette in midair.

"Let's continue," I nodded.

"You're going to go on with this video now?" His chin jutted out.

"That's what I'm here for."

He dropped what was left of the cigarette on the floor and crushed it out, stepping away from the window so I could see his face more clearly. "That ain't what you're here for."

"But it's what I'm doing now." That was all I could say.

I think he might have even understood, a little, that I needed something to distract my mind for a moment so that I could digest the story he'd given me—before I could act on it. And too, I needed to separate what might be considered facts from what were certainly Shoo's own odd speculations or even fictions.

"Okay." He looked around, trying to decide what to do.

"So," I pointed the camera at him again, "you've got your rounds. What's next?"

"Okay." He picked one up. "You chunk out some holes in the rounds so you can pound them together."

He deftly stepped to the side of the worktable, picked up a rounding chisel and a hammer, and pounded a hole into one of the rounds.

"What's that tool?" I asked, steadying the camera again.

"A hammer."

"The other one, Shoo."

"Oh." He held it up. "This is something else my uncle invented. Don't have a name."

I zoomed in on it. The chisel had a short wooden handle attached to an inch-long tapered iron blade, but there was a smaller flat, thornlike protuberance coming out from the middle of the sharpened edge of the chisel blade. He pounded that part into the round, then began turning the whole tool like a screwdriver, and I could see that the sides of the chisel blade were also razor sharp. He was using the tool to make a tapered hole about the size of a quarter near the top of the round.

I suspected that the tool actually did have a name, and was probably a standard woodworking tool of some sort, but I was content just to train the camera on Shoo's work for a moment.

"You make holes like that in all the rounds . . ."

"That's right," he finished for me, "some like this for the other rounds, like for the seat, then some holes are smaller for the braces."

"All right," I said. "And how long does it take to put all these holes in the rounds?"

"All these holes?" He stopped working to think. "Let's see, four . . . eight . . ." he looked at the camera. "To do it all, all the holes, it takes a day."

I looked at him from around the camera's viewfinder. "A day?"

He nodded.

"Can I ask you, Shoo, how long the whole process takes? Start to finish, walking in the woods to collect the raw materials to sitting down in the finished product."

"Whole thing?" He squinted. "Let me see. Got to pound it all together and split the oak for the seat . . ." He took a long pause, "The whole thing?"

"Yes."

"Make a chair?"

"Make a chair, Shoo." I looked at him through the camera once more.

"Start to finish?" He scratched his forearm.

"That's right." I tried to encourage him.

"That takes . . ." he closed his eyes, earnestly calculating. "Takes about a day."

As much as I genuinely admired the concept of everything happening in the grand, eternal *now*—that *now* being encompassed by Shoo's notion of the never-ending day, a simple good day's work—I turned off the camera.

"That's enough for now." I held up the camera. "We'll finish up another time soon."

"Okay," he told me. He turned back to the table and went right on working. "You still gonna get me a carton of smokes."

"I'm going to pick up my friend Andrews at Gil's," I said, ignoring his request, "and then have lunch with Lucinda."

"Lucinda," he lilted, teasing.

"Just to catch up," I assured him.

"Good." He didn't look up. "It's good to catch up."

I let a moment of silence press between us. Once again the woodpecker dotted the air.

"You really don't know," I said softly, "where that diary is now?"

"Nope." He stopped, then, and looked me in the eye. "But if I was that boy Thresher, I'd have hid it in the house somewheres where nobody could find it, don't you think?"

"I guess that's possible."

"Worth a look." He held my gaze for a pointed second, and then went back to work.

"Thanks for letting me tape you." I held up the camera. "When I get it together, I'll show you."

"Just have me a copy for my funeral."

"Yes," I told him, looking down at the floor, trying not to smile too hard. "I will."

"Well," he said, almost as if I had already gone, "see you."

I headed out the door.

Thirteen

I decided to stop back by the house for a short look around, thinking about where I might hide something if I were a stranger. I convinced myself that the diary was not simply important to my own personal history, but also a vital clue in the investigation of my half-brother's murder. I was beginning to formulate some new conclusions about that murder, and to understand that I was not, perhaps, the intended victim after all. I even had an intuition that there might have been something in the diary that was the cause of the crime.

It only took me thirty minutes or so to get back home. I was happy to see that there was no one around my house. I made some espresso in my little pot in the kitchen and poured the whole carafe into a mug. I took a deep breath and cast an eye about the place. It was still a mess, we hadn't cleaned up since the local police had made their investigation. Everything was an anarchy of papers and clothes and towels and books and plates.

My first thought was that Thresher might have been clever enough to hide the thing in plain sight, somewhere in all the mess: Poe's *Purloined Letter*. Further consideration of the general intelligence of my family convinced me that Thresher was probably the hide-it-under-a-loose-floorboard type—more *The Telltale Heart*.

I was considering ripping up a plank or two myself when I suddenly remembered my mother's secret hiding place.

In her room—my parents had always had separate rooms as far as

I knew—there was a loose windowsill. I knew because I'd seen her hide things there when I was little—when I'd been spying on her.

On so many nights when she'd come home late, and my father and I were already asleep in our own rooms, I would awaken to the sound of her humming—sweet melodies. I would, on those occasions, slip out of bed and down the hall, hiding in the shadows. Those moments, in fact, were some of my favorite memories of my mother, watching her when she didn't know I was there. Sometimes I would see her pick up the board of the windowsill and put something in the hiding place there in the hollow under the window frame.

And sometimes—an even more difficult confession—during those long periods when both parents were gone, I would steal into my mother's room to see what she had hidden there—what she felt she needed to hide, in short, from me.

I only looked in the spot three times, then I stopped because I was always perplexed by what I found. I'd also like to believe that I matured, but the truth is more likely based in my fear of getting caught. Whatever the true reasons, I stopped raiding my mother's secret place after only three assaults.

The first time I found an old love letter from my father to her. It was creased and barely readable—something he'd written her in high school, it seemed.

The second time I'd found a small plastic bag with a white powder in it. I didn't know what it was at the time. I think I believed it was some sort of condiment, or perhaps a medicine—though it was almost certainly cocaine.

The third time I found a loaded gun, an older pistol of some sort, and the beginnings of a note to me and my father telling us how sorry she was about something, and asking our forgiveness. The note was unfinished, and so I never learned what she had done that so required our forgiveness.

Perhaps that experience, the last raid, was sufficiently strange to keep me from looking in her hiding place again.

I'd forgotten about the place until I stood there in the shambles of my home. I didn't for a moment believe that Thresher would know about the hiding place—or perhaps I only hoped he would not. I certainly didn't expect to find the diary there.

Still, I remembered June had told me that Thresher was proud of his mother. I reasoned that perhaps she had also been proud of him, and confided her secret place . . . shared it with him. The fact that she had never shared it with me but might have done so with him was irrelevant to my investigation. It was wild guesswork, anyway. I would never have admitted to Andrews or to Skidmore that I had sometimes used intuition with good result in my fieldwork.

I gulped back my espresso. It burned my esophagus. Without another thought—or before another thought could pry its way into my mind—I bounded up the stairs, down the hall, and into my mother's room—for the first time in many years.

The room seemed eerily unchanged. The bed was made, the walls were clean, the pictures were still hung with gentle care. But I could not look around.

I didn't want to reminisce. I didn't want to see the ghosts that live in that room: the little boy hiding in the shadows and praying that his mother would see him, come to him, hold him; the mother who never noticed him at all.

I charged straight for the window. I drew it upward, and pulled on the loose sill. It was stuck and took some working back and forth, but the secret panel finally came up.

There, perfectly preserved, were the petrified remains of a clutch of Cherokee roses. I did not understand on any conscious level what they meant, but for some reason I found myself sitting on my mother's bed and doing everything I could to keep myself from crying like a nine-year-old boy.

Fourteen

Andrews was waiting by the side of the road when I pulled up to fetch him. Gil's place was utterly deserted. The lights inside were off, the doors were closed tightly, the garage was sealed, and a rag of newspaper even danced in the corner, blown by the chilled wind.

I hadn't even stopped the engine completely when Andrews pulled on the door.

"Thank God you're here." He slammed himself into his seat, tragically dismayed.

"What is it?" I feared more awful news.

"I'll tell you what it is," he snarled. "I've been standing around this goddamned place all morning and *no* one's been here. At *all.*"

"No one?" I looked all around.

"I thought you said," he managed, grinding his teeth, "that they all come here every morning, those men."

"They do." I fought down a burgeoning panic. "They've come here every morning, some of them, for fifty years. No one's been here at all since you arrived?"

"What did I just say?" He was cold, mad, and, I remembered, just as likely to be hung over as well.

"How about some breakfast?" I suggested.

"I don't think so." He looked at his watch. "We'll be having lunch in an hour or so with Lucinda, won't we?"

"Yes, that was the plan," I answered him, "but you need something besides coffee in your stomach right now. It'll help your hangover. Besides, I have some interesting information, and if you get food you'll be in a better mood when I tell you about it."

I pulled the truck out of Gil's slowly, and headed down the street. The sky was beginning to darken, and rain seemed likely. With a turn of the clouds, the world had gone from copper and auburn sunlight to steel-gray fog.

He shifted in the seat. "Information?"

"It would appear that my half-brother was in possession of a diary, something that my mother kept." My hands were glued to the steering wheel. I did my best to keep my voice even, my manner matter-of-fact. "That's what he was bringing me, I'm told. It wasn't just a message, apparently, it was the diary he wanted to give me. Does that seem important?"

"I guess it does," he shifted back and looked out the window. He was still in a mood to complain.

"I think there's something," I went on slowly, "in the diary that someone doesn't want revealed, I think that's why someone shot Thresher. Did I ever tell you that was his name? I can't remember—"

"You're saying," Andrews butted in, "that someone shot your half-brother for a *diary*?"

"I think it's a possibility." I wouldn't look at him. "I don't think the murderer thought Thresher was me at all."

"Hold on, hold on." Andrews was rubbing his forehead. "What makes you think all this?"

"I had a very interesting interview with Shoo Walters," I began again. "Aside from making the first part of a very nice documentary for the folklore archives, I think I may have come across some clearer ideas about this murder."

"Such as?" He was sounding only slightly less irritated than when he'd first gotten into the truck.

"We'll all agree that Shoo is not the brightest penny in the bank."

"To coin a phrase," Andrews responded dryly.

"And he knew," I continued, "that I was not the person living in the cabin last week. He knew this, as it turns out, from a brief conversation that he had, in fact, with Thresher, himself. He learned then that Thresher was my half-brother. And I'm certain he didn't keep that news to himself."

"I know what you mean," he nodded. "Word seems to get around in these parts fairly quickly. I was impressed with how much your friend Lucinda knew about everything."

"Exactly. I think, in fact, that gossip may actually travel all by itself in this community, like spores through the *air* . . ."

"Or like a virus . . ."

"So it's at least plausible, then . . ." I went on.

"That most people would know that you were not the man living at your cabin." Andrews finished for me then blew out a breath. "Meaning the murderer would not mistake him for you."

"Let's say that the killer knew Thresher was Thresher," I agreed, "killed him, and is still around . . ."

"Lurking around looking for this diary?" Andrews snorted. "Not really."

"Or lurking around waiting to kill me." I kept my eyes on the road.

"What on earth for?" Andrews turned his body my way. "I thought you were just saying that the murder had to do with the diary."

"The gossip was that Thresher was in town to talk to me. What if he had already communicated his information to me, especially if the killer didn't find this diary? Maybe the killer even thought Thresher had already given it to me somehow. Mailed it, or . . ."

"As wild a theory as I've ever heard." He shook his head. "We don't even know for certain there was a diary."

"Shoo told me he saw it." I tried to sound certain. "Why would he do that if it didn't exist?"

"He saw it?" Andrews mimicked.

A fine example of the repeating response again, I thought.

"Yes," I said aloud. "And my next question, the real question, is: Why wouldn't Shoo have spread *that* interesting bit of gossip around, particularly to the men at Gil's, the way he always did with everything else?"

"Good." Andrews sat back, thinking. "Could it have been something like what happened to me the other night—was that just last night?—with Carson? When there's a stranger around do they swap information as easily as they do when they're only among themselves? And isn't it interesting what they'll gossip about and what they'll take to the grave."

"A visitor?" I slowed the truck. "I think that's only on your mind because of your own experience with Carson."

"But I did notice how those men were when I was around them. They don't reveal a thing." He turned my way again. "I assume it's not just me; they're that way around strangers in general."

"Yes," I told him dryly, "it *is* just you."

"And speaking of those men," he said, ignoring my dig, and dismissing his own theory, "where *are* they, exactly?"

I gnawed on my lower lip. "I was trying not to think about that too much. I'm telling you it was eerie to pull up and see Gil's just closed like that. It's like a science fiction movie."

"My God." Andrews looked around. "And the rest of the town is deserted too!"

We were next to a vacant lot.

"Shut up." I thought for a second. "Maybe they're all up at Skid's looking in on Linda. That's where I ought to be, actually."

"Now that you mention it," he agreed, "that did cross my mind—as I sat there in the cold for the last thirty hours."

"The important thing," I opined, "is that you're not still upset about having to wait there."

"I wouldn't mind seeing how Linda is myself," he admitted. "Would you?"

"Then we'll get you something to eat," I agreed.

He only grunted.

I slowed even more, turned the truck around in the vacant lot, and headed back up the mountain.

The beginnings of a mist ran blue dots down the windshield, too light for the wipers, and made everything outside of the windows turn into Monet.

We drove in silence; the sound of the tires on the wet road and the blur of new autumn colors seemed to encourage it. A trance of conflicting images and wild speculations churned in our minds, I thought, and an air of melancholy, primarily engendered by the quality of the light, settled over us. Only when we turned into the drive at the Needle residence did Andrews break the spell.

"You know, Dev," he began, "all these things that people keep saying about your mother and your father—along with your own mental peculiarities . . . I mean . . . you know it's going to affect your perception of these events, and your ability to deal with them. Your gestalt . . ."

"Let's endeavor," I insisted as I turned the wheel slowly to miss a lazy chicken in the yard, "not to use very many German words from now on, shall we?"

"You see how touchy you are." He watched the chicken, white with a stubby brown tail and a strange feathery topknot. "I mean, this diary—even if it does exist—what would it have to do with men being murdered, or your being shot at? Doesn't make sense, except in some personal construction you've devised in your own head. Your Atlas complex, maybe."

"You still don't understand." I pulled the truck close to the house and turned off the ignition. "None of this is haphazard—all of this is related. These people up here—you don't know the lengths to which they'll go in order *not* to talk about something important."

"I know," he sighed wearily, " 'they're like the mountain, eighty percent of them is subterranean.' Get some new material."

As anticipated, there were dozens of other cars surrounding the house. I had to park my truck uncustomarily far away from the house. I shut off the engine, and the silence was wool on our ears.

"You don't know the secrets that are hidden up here." I watched the house. "Unmarked graves, buried lives, shadow worlds." I turned to Andrews, my eyes burrowed into his to drive my point home. "And the reason that I think the strange events are all related is that these people are telling me, in their own strange way, that they are. They're telling me things and then standing back to watch me—to see what I'll do."

"Why would they do that?" Andrews was watching me the way he might guard himself against a psychotic.

"Because they have some other agenda, of which we are not yet aware," I whispered, "and they believe that I might take care of it for them."

"I see." Andrews folded his arms and didn't make a move to get out of the truck.

"So you believe me," I said.

"Everything you've told me just now," he unwound slowly, "only enforces my perception of your behavior."

"And that concern is . . . ?" I asked.

"That you're a completely paranoid personality," he exploded. "I don't know how you even *function*. You don't need to work on this so-called case. You need *therapy*." He looked at the house. "I mean, for Christ's sake, Dev, these people are your friends, your oldest friends. You know them better than anyone; you should trust them. And you think they've got unmarked graves and buried secrets and you think they're messing with your mind or something so that you'll do their surreal bidding? God!" He started out of the truck.

"Wait." My eyes followed his to the house. "Would you like to try an experiment in that regard? Right now?"

"What are you talking about?" His face betrayed a considerable amount of alarm.

"Let's walk around the side of the house," I offered, "and listen in at the parlor window."

"What?"

"To see if we can hear the topic of conversation," I said quickly. "And I will pay you one hundred dollars if it doesn't have something to do with me."

"No," Andrews didn't budge. "That's mad."

" 'There are more things in heaven and earth than are dreamed of in your philosophy, Horatio.' "

"That may well be," he said, softening a bit in the face of my *Hamlet* quotation. "But you're still mad."

"Just walk around the side of the house with me," I begged. "I only want to hear what they're talking about. Then we'll go on into the house through the back door, through the kitchen. I've done it so many times no one will think twice about it. Indulge me."

"I'd rather have you committed," he said with firm conviction—but he grabbed the handle and slid out of the seat and into the yard. "On the other hand, I could use a hundred dollars."

The cars were crowded around the front garden and the huge shrubs. We wound our way through their maze, past the corner of the house, before Andrews froze. I nearly tumbled into him from behind.

Coming through the parlor window was—as he told me later—

the eeriest, most unearthly sound he had ever heard in his life. It was, in fact, a noise like no other—a cold wind howling through high black tree limbs, a moan that a mountain might make, a whine so elegant and unearthly that it seemed to come from an impossible instrument of God.

But it came, I knew, from unaccompanied human voices.

"What the hell is that?" he whispered. "Is it some kind of chant?" Even softer: "Is it some kind of ungodly ritual?" His eyes were wide. "Is that Sacred Harp?"

I shook my head. The wind blew and coaxed an easy whir from the pines and the shrubs, a softer percussion to the sound that we heard. It was cold, and we both shivered a little.

I too was transfixed by the tune, but for different reasons.

"Mouth music," I whispered back.

"What?" He was growing more disconcerted. "And do you know that the color has drained from your face?"

"It has?" I said. I leaned against the side of the building. "Isn't it astonishing—the music?"

"What *is* it?" He was actually afraid.

"Listen!"

The song they were singing was called "The Great High Wind That Blew the Low Post Down." After a very short verse, sung by one person, the entire room joined in with a chorus of nonsense syllables—the so-called "mouth music"—in minor-keyed, modal, near-Gregorian harmonies. There was no other sound on earth like it.

"That's my song," I told him. "Everybody knows it's my song."

"What song?" His alarm was reaching dangerous proportions.

"When I was nine," I began, transfixed, "I was outdoors with a group of other children playing hide-and-seek. I found a hiding place near an open window and the adults in the parlor began to sing this song. I'd never heard anything like it in my life. It affected me then the way it's affecting you now. I left my hiding place and wandered into the house, unable to speak. My father saw me standing in the doorway, crying. I didn't even know why I was there. He just motioned me in with his hand, and kept right on singing. I came and sat on his lap. For the rest of the night, I stayed in with the adults learning these songs, hearing their stories—mesmerized by something that was at once so completely strange and so thoroughly human. My father told me that the music had called me." I took a little breath. "I never went outside to play hide-and-seek, not ever again. It was the last day of my childhood."

"At age nine?" Andrews's whispering was growing shrill.

"Well, *listen* to the song."

We just stood there and let the sound pour over us like icy water. It was shrill and lonesome, a train in the distance. The melody was colder than wet granite, and the harmonies were strings of a creaking, ancient wind harp—not sung so much as exhaled. Lungs were bellows, wheezing out the icy air. Men's voices scratched the air, women's keening pierced it. I could have heard it for the rest of the day, and far into the night, without growing tired of it.

But the singing was interrupted, at last, by the announcement of lunch. There was low laughter, some compliments from one person to another about this or that, and I roused myself.

"Let's go in." I marched toward the back door.

"Don't you want to eavesdrop anymore?" Andrews sneered, following.

"I have to see who's in there. I'm certain I heard Carson's voice."

"If all the men are here . . ."

"Exactly. At least the deserted filling station wouldn't be a complete mystery." I glanced back at him. "And you could still do your research."

"I see," he said dryly, following me into the kitchen. "*My* research."

Some of the women were in the kitchen cooking. June Cotage, for one, came to me immediately and hugged my neck.

"Hello, Fever," she said, stepping back and looking at me. "I'm so glad you're all right."

"All right?" I held on to her.

"All this shooting." But she stopped short when she saw Andrews behind me, and her face became more formal—not impolite, just the face reserved for strangers.

"This is my friend Dr. Andrews," I began.

She took his hand. "Hey, there. I'm so glad you could be with us. Skidmore's already real taken with you. Says you're a good boy."

"High praise," Andrews told her genuinely. "How is Girlinda?"

"Yes," I said quickly, "that's what we're here for."

"She's resting," June sighed, "but it wasn't easy for us to get her to stick to bed. You know her."

"I do indeed," I answered. "Everyone else is . . . ?"

June only inclined her head toward the parlor.

"I'll see you tonight then?"

"Tonight?" She seemed genuinely confused.

"Didn't Lucinda call you? She and I were coming to your house tonight to tape some of your—"

"Oh, yes. My God. In all this mess I completely forgot. Yes. We said seven." She even managed a smile. "You and Lucinda."

"Well that's enough of that," I told her. "Would you mind just seeing that Dr. Andrews gets a little something in his stomach? He had some of our local corn liquor last night at Gil's."

"Lord." She glared at Andrews, completely understanding, if not approving. "You'll want some cornbread right away." She lowered her voice and put her head close to his. "Sop up what's left of the brew."

She handed him a plate of golden squares: salty cornbread as thick as cake, as light as clouds, filled with whole kernels of corn, crisp on the edges and heaven in the middle. He took a smaller one, bit into it, and immediately took a larger piece in his other hand.

"God," was all he could say.

"It's good," she agreed.

Then she went back to the stove to continue her work with Carson's wife and several other younger women. I guessed that they were wives of some of the other deputies with whom Skidmore worked.

We moved to the parlor. As we had surmised, all the men from the gas station were there, as well as several others. Notably absent: Hezekiah Cotage and, of course, Shoo, whom I'd just left working at his trade. Carson had his fiddle out, but it was cradled in his lap. Skidmore was nowhere to be seen.

Carson turned his head when we came through the doorway. "Fever?"

"Yes, Carson," I answered. "I'm here."

"Thought I heard your voice out in the kitchen. Got that English boy with you?"

"Hello," Andrews answered, smiling.

"Come on in here and sit down." He motioned for us to come to him, and the men began to move about, making room for two more.

"I can't stay, Carson," I told him quickly. "I have to meet Lucinda for lunch. But Andrews would like to join you, if that would be all right."

There was no warm welcome, as there might have been in the flat southern part of Georgia. There was only a nod here and there to give Andrews a clue that his presence would be tolerated. It was as much as could be expected.

"Good," I said. "I'll just go look in on Linda and be on my way. Would one of you mind seeing that Andrews gets back to my place sometime today?"

More nodding. Andrews, mouth filled with cornbread, shot me a stabbing look, but refrained from speaking—or perhaps the cornbread made it impossible to speak.

"By the way," I said as I turned to leave the room, "was that my song you all were singing when we drove up?"

"That's right," Carson said steadily. "The one that called you in from play when you was little."

By the way he'd said it, I think even Andrews realized there was something more than coincidence that had made them sing that particular song as we'd arrived. I could see my truck through the parlor window, the window beside which Carson was seated.

So the song had been sung deliberately, I thought, when they had seen me coming—a way of seeing if I even remembered my original awe at the power of that music. And if I remembered it, did I still have it in my heart. It was, in short, a test of some kind.

I tried to restrain myself, but I couldn't help giving Andrews an "I told you so" glare. It seemed proof of my theory that this coven was planning worlds within worlds around me. Or at least it justified sneaking around the house and coming in the back door.

"I thought that's what it was," I told Carson innocently as I turned to leave the room. "Still makes me cry like a child, I'm embarrassed to say."

A few of the men exchanged glances. Carson's face betrayed the hint of a smile.

"See you," he intoned. "We'll take care of Dr. Andrews."

I felt a little badly leaving Andrews to fend for himself, especially now that we were more certain that the waters were dark and deep. He seemed a forlorn figure in that parlor in his second rugby sweat-shirt, the only blond in the room, crumbs of cornbread on his chin to match the color of his hair. But I had to move quickly, and he was quite capable of taking care of himself. He was more likely to find out some things that I could not, as we had discussed.

Best to stick to our original plan, I thought. *Divide and conquer.*

And there was June's cooking in his immediate future—an enviable notion.

I headed down the hall toward the master bedroom. Skidmore must have heard me coming, he appeared in the doorway holding a finger to his lips.

I nodded, and he motioned me back down the hall and into the front room, which might have been called the living room in another house, though at the Needle household none of the actual living ever took place in it. This was a room for company, cleaner than the rest of the house and more likely to seem austere—except for the presence of children's toys here and there. In general, however, the room was pristine, and gave no evidence that anything in it had ever been touched by human hands.

"I just got her to sleep," he told me in a hushed voice.

"I understand completely," I told him, matching his tone. "I just wanted to come by and see how she was."

"She'll be fine," he said, but he still sounded worried.

"I wanted you to know what I found out from Shoo," I went on, looking down. "He said that Thresher was bringing me my mother's diary, and that it contained some sort of important information."

"A diary?" Skid was suddenly all business. "*That* was the message he was bringing you?"

"That's the idea Shoo had, anyway." I lowered my voice further. "The implication seemed to be that the diary got Thresher killed."

"Which means, if there's anything to this idea at all," he sighed, staring out the large bay window beside the door, "that this diary could be what's getting us all shot at."

"Especially," I agreed, "since it doesn't seem to have been found yet."

"Right," he said. "But somebody might believe that *you* have it, and you're keeping it hid."

"That's what I thought too. I even looked for it, a little, over at my house a moment ago—thinking that I might actually have it and not know."

"Your mama's secret hiding place." He rummaged in his shirt pocket for a cigarette.

"So you remember about that." I smiled.

"Sure." He seemed irritated, almost insulted by the implication that he might forget something so shared between the best of friends at so early an age.

"But there was nothing there," I went on. "Not really."

"What do you mean, 'not really'? Was there something there or not?"

"Just some old Cherokee roses. They were very dried out."

"Huh." He pulled a cigarette from his pack. "Didn't that kind of surprise you?"

"No," I said. "Why should it have?"

"You think a loose board in a windowsill, where all kinds of rain and cold and heat can get in, is a good place to preserve something like Cherokee roses?"

In the silence between us I could hear the women bringing plates of food into the parlor.

"What are you saying?" I finally asked him.

"Well, those roses haven't been hiding there," he mumbled, his voice gaining a little in volume, "since your mama run off."

Brought face-to-face with the prospect that roses could still be preserved after eighteen years, I had to admit that I didn't know what I thought about them.

"I don't know," I told him. "Don't dried flowers keep forever? Aren't they like mummies? Isn't that why people dry them in the first place?"

"I'm just saying." He looked at the cigarette as if it had just appeared there in his hand.

"Point taken," I nodded. "I won't dismiss them. Still, I have to get on. I'm seeing Lucinda for lunch. Then, tonight, I'm taping Junie."

"You're still doing your *folklore* work," he said, jutting out his chin at me, "with all this going on?"

"Are you still working on this *murder* investigation," I returned, "with your wife in bed from a bullet wound?"

He stared.

"Not to mention that your boss," I insisted, driving the point home, "officially removed you from the case."

"Okay," he responded, too exhausted to do anything but acquiesce, and stole a look back toward the bedroom where his wife lay sleeping.

"Linda's fine." I put my hand on his shoulder. "She'll be all right."

"I know," he said weakly, "but I can't help blaming myself for her getting shot up in the first place."

"What?" I was genuinely surprised. "That's ridiculous. I thought we agreed that I'm the one to blame."

"God Almighty." He laughed out loud. "Your friend Andrews was right about you. You really do think the world revolves around you."

"I don't." I stepped toward the front door. "I'm well aware . . . in fact I was just thinking the other night about the nature of our individual perceptoral fields, and how each of us has a worldview so subjective that we think all the rest of the random events of the world are ordered because of that quite subjective—"

"Fever," he interrupted. "I'm not in the mood for one of your college lectures."

"The thing is," I said, grabbing the door handle and pulling the door open, "that in this particular case, I believe that I'm not just helping you solve another mystery—like we did when we were boys. I'm afraid that I actually *am* the mystery."

"Uh huh." Skidmore eyed me in a very odd fashion. "Wasn't that your song they was singing just now, 'The Great High Wind,' the one that made you quit hide-and-seek when you was a young'un?"

I stopped but didn't turn. "Yes."

"Still make you cry?"

"Not really," I said, still turned away from him, "but it still gives me an eerie feeling."

"Right," he answered in what I took to be triumph. "That's where the mystery is. It's not in *you*. It's somewhere in *there*—that sound, and what it means to you. It's in these hills, and everything there is here."

"Incorrect." I turned around in the doorway. "Wrong. You've

160

just proved my point. That feeling, that eerie feeling? *That's* in me. It's not inherent in the notes of that song."

"It's not?"

"No." My voice rose. "The phenomenon, any phenomenon, is devoid of valuation. Completely. We impart meaning and value."

"Is that so?" His volume increased as well.

"That's what I believe." I nodded certainly.

"Then I guess the mystery would be," he shot back, "why do you give *that* particular meaning to that special tune?"

"What?"

"Why does that song," he said, resting his hand on the door to close it, "give you the willies?"

"The 'willies'? That's your term for how the song—"

"Tell Lucinda I said 'hey.' " And he shooed me backward with one hand and closed the door in my face with the other.

"The 'willies'?" I said louder, knowing he could still hear me on the other side of the door. I stared at it for a moment, but there was no further comment.

I turned and started toward my truck. Before I had even reached it, the group in the parlor started up what was left of "The Great High Wind That Blew the Low Post Down," as if on cue, from right where they'd stopped a few moments before. In my mind's eye I could see them all seated, plates of food on their laps, eyes closed, finishing the song as if it were grace before lunch.

This time Carson played the fiddle, and the silver of it was dominant. I imagined that Skidmore had gone into the parlor and told them to start up the way they had, just to prove his point, knowing that I'd hear the song as I was leaving.

I stood for a second with my hand on the door of the truck when an icy breeze blew up out of the black shadows, a chill creased my face, and I was suddenly possessed by an unnameable, indefinable dread, just as the wordless chorus began.

Fifteen

Why, I thought, climbing into the truck, *does that song give you these alleged willies, Dr. Devilin?*

I glared at myself in the rearview mirror. My father told me, those many years ago, that the song called me because it was in my blood; that the spirits of all the Devilins before me cried out when they'd heard the familiar tune. He said that he'd always known I was a sensitive boy, and he wasn't surprised that I heard the call.

Even at age nine I thought that was a healthy dollop of manure.

The melody was simple enough, and the words could not possibly have engendered the sort of awe I felt. The words were, in fact, ridiculous: "It blew away the dirt from a row of sweet potatoes, and it blew away the skin from a flock of alligators, and it blew away the kiss from a pair of osculators. It's a great high wind that blew the low post down." They never failed to make me laugh as a child.

As I backed the truck out onto the dirt road and headed for the highway, I settled on the harmonies. The strange, unearthly sound—like a night wind through lonely rocks and high trees—was surely the source of my odd feeling.

I drove down the mountain and onto the highway singing the melody softly to myself.

By the time I pulled into the hospital parking lot, the melody had the nagging quality of a tune that wouldn't leave my mind no matter what I did, and it was only irritating. I found a parking spot and made my way toward Lucinda's office.

The hospital waiting room was still crowded, but seemed calm compared to the last time I'd been there. Still, the smell of antiseptic alcohol pervaded the senses—with the same persistent effect as the song that would not leave my brain.

Lucinda's office was down the hall on the first floor and to the right. On the door it only said ADMINISTRATION.

Lucinda was behind her desk, dressed in a dark gray business suit, her hair up in a bun, busily working on her computer. She didn't notice, for the moment, that I'd come in. The office was stark, industrially painted, furnished with standard chrome and laminated wood. In the corner of the room, shoved together in a very unappealing jam of fake-mahogany legs, were two brown, well worn chairs. The vase of wildflowers on her desk, mostly forget-me-nots, was the only object in the room that gave any hint of human warmth.

"Hello," I said softly.

"Oh, my God." She jumped as if I'd shouted.

"Sorry." I took a step toward her. "I thought you heard me come in."

"Fever." She glanced quickly at her computer screen. "I was just thinking about you."

"I'm so sorry I startled you . . ."

"No, no, no." She twitched her head. "Come have a look at this."

"What?" I said, moving around the desk toward her.

"This stuff I found on the computer," she said, once again absorbed by whatever it was on the screen.

I stood behind her and stared at a form which I took to be some sort of hospital administrative form.

"What am I looking at?" I couldn't make it out.

"Here." She pointed to a section marked "Cause of Wound." In the space below it were written the words "gunshot, pistol."

"I see." I glanced at her profile. "Is this the autopsy report or something on Thresher?" It was still hard, I noticed as I said it, to speak his name without a small catch in my voice. I determined to do something about that.

"No," she said firmly, pulling me out of my self-examination. "This is an old form." She looked up. "I was just checking something after I saw this same form for your brother." She stared into my eyes for quite some time, and I could not read what was going on in her mind. Finally she sighed a little and said, "Look, do you want to talk about this here and then go to lunch, or would you rather talk about it over food?"

"I guess it depends," I began slowly, "on what it is we're talking about."

She considered something for a moment, then lifted a finger in the direction of the brown chairs. "Maybe you'd better sit down, hon."

I took a second myself, then got one of the chairs and dragged it, with attendant scraping, to the side of her desk.

"Oh, by the way," she said, more brightly, "because of the fact that the sheriff says Skid's off the case, I checked with the official police records—"

"Wait," I interrupted. "How?"

"On the computer," she told me, as if it were self-evident. "Anyway, he's still listed as the officer in charge of the investigation, on account of he's the one that found the body and all . . ."

"Lucy," I told her firmly, "I'm certain you made me sit down here for more than a chat about who's in charge of the investigation."

"That's right." She leaned back, and her face changed. "I just don't know how to start talking to you about the other."

"The other *what*?"

"The other . . . death." She stood very deliberately, walked around the desk, closed the door to her little office, and sat in the chair beside me.

"There aren't ten people that know all this what I'm about to tell you." Her voice was barely above a whisper. "Reverend Coombs didn't leave town like everybody says. He died. In his church, they say." She looked down at her hands. "There's some that thought it was murder—some that said your daddy did it."

"My father?" I shook my head. "Wait. Weren't you just telling me last night that Fletcher Devilin might not have been my father at all?" I leaned in toward her. "So just exactly who are you talking about?"

"I know it's a lot to think about all at once." She studied her hands, as if the words she searched for might be written there. She didn't look up. "I knew you would take it hard."

"Anybody would!" I hadn't meant my voice to be so shrill.

"Yes, I know," she said hastily, to keep me quiet. "It's just that you're more sensitive . . ."

"More sensitive to *what*?"

"Just listen." She tried again to hush me. "Hear me what I was checking on when you came in—could you just do that and not ask me anything else right now? It's important."

I took in a deep breath through my nose and blew it out through pursed lips.

"It looks to me," she went on when I was silent, "like the same pistol that killed Coombs all those years ago also killed Thresher Devilin a few nights ago."

"All right," I told her, slouching back in my chair, "that's it."

"One Too Many Ghosts," she said sweetly.

Our first date, twenty years ago: a drive to the movie theater in Willet, more than thirty miles south. We hadn't even known what was playing. It didn't matter. Sitting in the dark, holding hands with each other—that's what mattered.

"Not the movie." I relaxed a little. "But the sentiment of the title applies. I've had it with this propensity for holding back secrets for years only to reveal them without the slightest fanfare—and at the strangest possible times."

"This is *my* . . . propensity?" She crossed her arms. She was angry that she'd struggled with the word.

"Not just you," I dug my fingers into my temples. "Everyone up here in these mountains—my home. Hide a secret, never tell—then, suddenly, one afternoon: boom. Out it comes."

"Well would you rather I'd not told you at all?" Her voice rose in anger.

"No," I matched her tone, "I'd rather have known about it from the beginning! This is a very weird thing you're suggesting and it would have been nice to know it back when, don't you think?"

"Fever!" she yelled back. Then she shook her head. "Everybody thought that you couldn't deal with this when you were younger. I had the idea that you might be a grown man by now, and maybe you could take it—especially in light of your brother, Thresher, and all. But maybe we were wrong."

She said "we," I thought. And her idea was an echo of what the men had said at the gas station. "You mean I was too *unstable* to know about all this before now," I asked, "is that what you mean?"

"You were a mess." She folded her hands in her lap and looked up at me.

"But everyone's decided that it's somehow all right, all of a sudden, to let me in on my past *now*?" *She used the word "we."* My brain would not be still.

"Some of us got together to talk about you," she managed in a decent imitation of casual conversation, "at Junie's after church one night when we heard you were coming home. Then there was the strange news about Thresher living at your house. We didn't know what to make of that. We all thought it was time to tell you more about your past. This was before there was any murder, or any shooting." She attempted a smile. "It wasn't like it was in the paper or at a town meeting at City Hall." She offered up a little sigh—the ghost of an apology. "It was just your friends."

What a rage of conflicting thoughts that last sentence produced in me. Indeed, these were people who cared about me, and wanted the best for me. But the gall, and the extreme strangeness, of keeping such monumental information from me—I just didn't know what to make of it. The possibilities: the Reverend Coombs was murdered, my father wasn't my father, and my mother had been even worse than I'd ever imagined. And all the while there was a killer on the loose, shooting at Girlinda Needle and her children. After a moment of this tempest in my brain, I simply decided to concentrate on something smaller, as she had asked me to do a moment earlier: the gun in question.

"I don't know that I've ever heard of a town meeting in Blue Mountain." I shifted uncomfortably in the itchy brown chair. The feel of it couldn't help reminding me of doctor's waiting rooms.

"Figure of speech." She seemed glad to lighten the mood.

"All right." I let her off the hook completely. "So tell me about the pistol."

"It was the same," she forged ahead, all business. "I'm convinced of that all right. I told Skid—"

"So Skidmore put you up to this."

"That's right." She nodded slowly. "When he was here last night, he was asking all sorts of questions. I said why didn't he just check on the police computers and he said because Maddox had taken him off the case and would be watching to make sure that he stayed off."

"So you checked hospital records instead," I finished for her. "Good thinking. What *exactly* did you find?"

"Coombs and Thresher were both killed with an antique German Luger. Not the kind of gun folks have around here."

"That's quite a bit of information. There are a lot of years between those two murders." I didn't know what to do with my hands in that damned chair. I folded my arms, unfolded them, crossed my legs, and put my hands in my jacket pockets. "Sheriff Maddox will get hold of it, though, and it will help his investigation."

"Not likely," she shook her head. "He doesn't know that Coombs was murdered, I don't guess. So I don't believe he would have any reason to even look at these records. He might make some kind of little surprise out of seeing that the murder weapon was a Luger, but otherwise—"

"I know it was slightly before his time." I didn't know if I wanted to wade into those waters or not. "But there aren't police records?"

"Coombs was listed here at the hospital as a suicide, that's what most people who knew about it thought—or *said* they thought." She lowered her voice. "People don't like word getting around that a minister would kill himself."

"All right, then." I drew my hands out of my pockets, slapped my knees, and stood, moving around her desk. "Let's have a look at the form you were staring at when I came in."

She was happy to oblige. She followed me around the desk, sat in her chair, and we both watched the screen.

The space after "Cause of Wound" was filled in as I'd seen it but as I stared at it, I realized that the space had probably said, originally, "Cause of Death." It had been typed over. Nowhere on the form was the phrase "Cause of Death" found. Only "Time of Death," and it was listed as 7:37 P.M.

"Coombs's body was taken over to Blue Ridge and given a real nice burial," Lucinda said absently, "is what Junie told me. Then the story went around that he'd been called away by God, left town, and Hek took over the church, and everything went on just like normal."

" 'Normal' is a word I think we should stop using when referring to anything about this."

"Okay." She shrugged.

"So what's the rest of the story? Was Coombs really a suicide or was he killed?"

"I don't know the answer to that," she said calmly, "but I get the impression that the suicide was just another made-up story." She looked up at me. The light from the computer screen was like a blue sunset, and her face was lovely. "I think he was killed."

"What makes you think that?" I tried to tear my eyes away from hers, but they wouldn't budge.

"Everybody goes out of their way," she answered, "the older people, I mean—whenever the subject comes up—to talk about how he was called away by God and what a good man he was."

"Couldn't that have been explained by the fact that they just didn't want it getting around that a spiritual leader had taken his own life?"

"Yes," she said, "but it always seemed like there was more to it—more than they were letting on. You know how these things get all wrapped up around here."

"A fabrication within a fabrication."

"You've said yourself," she told me, "in these articles that I've read: The stories and songs up here, they're from the old-timey days. They have meanings within meanings, some of them coded, some of them hidden, some of them barely recognizable today." She smiled. "It's a gift we have, you said."

"You've read my articles?" Momentarily, that was more important to me than anything, that and the light on the contour of her cheek.

"Sure," she touched my arm. "Those ones that you wrote last year about the snake bowl over at Hek's church? They were real entertaining."

She's read my articles, I thought, my heart picking up a beat. Why was that such a thrill?

"What were they called?" she went on. She covered her mouth a minute, thinking. "Troubadours! In that big old article in the *Journal of American Folklore*. You know what I'm talking about?"

"Yes. Well." I was suddenly very happy, for some reason, to be asked. "These were traveling singers who, in a preliterate culture, were the only source of news, entertainment, information, and even mail, of a sort, in the world. The songs they composed would often have ten or twelve meanings, some coded, some obvious to the listener of the day but invisible to us now . . ."

"Like what?"

"Oh." I tried to think of an easy, quick example. "For instance, there were stories about Nelly Long Arms, a water demon from the Yorkshire area, that would have been common knowledge to everyone up until the eighteen hundreds, say. So much so that a song about a woman named Nelly would have immediately made the listener suspicious about a girl with that name, and it would be assumed that she was ultimately demonic, so that a perfectly nice song about Nelly the Milkmaid would have, to people of that day, a much more ominous undertone than we'd be aware of today."

"And these troubadours," she asked, "they still do that?"

"No, they were much earlier, in medieval Europe, but I'm saying that the tradition of wrapping stories in songs inside of riddles that suggested news . . . it can make these seemingly simple little folk songs as thick and rich as any novel."

"Fascinating."

I heard the tone in her voice. I saw the spark in her eye. I knew then what she'd been doing.

"Splendid," I said, acknowledging her work. "I *do* feel better."

She'd gotten me to talk about my work, and it had distracted me from the overwhelming nature of the news she'd given me. But it had also made clear to me, in a way that I would understand it, the true nature of stories in these hills: There was always more to them than met the eye—exactly the point I had been trying to drive home to Andrews.

"Now," she said, patting her desktop, "are you ready to take me to lunch or not?"

The sun slanted in through the blinds and colored her face in gold. She smelled of hyacinths and her skin seemed to radiate the life that was in her spirit. Her hair seemed impossibly soft, and her eyes seemed improperly amused.

"What ever provoked me," I struggled to ask her, "to go away from a person like you?"

"You," she said, standing and taking my arm, "have got no good sense."

"That's right," I agreed, and we headed out the door. "I knew it was something like that."

But we both knew that something more significant had compelled me to leave her, to leave my home. I didn't know what it was. Something happened to me in my past, in those hills, something that was buried, something of which I was not consciously aware. That event or circumstance, deep in the grave of my memory, was the cause of the black cloud—murders and shootings—that I had brought with me to Lucinda's world.

That—finding that buried truth—was more important to me than looking for a murderer.

"You know," she told me as I opened the passenger-side door of my truck for her, "you have to put aside your personal problems right now. You have to help Skidmore find this maniac that's responsible for shooting Girlinda. He's not got his whole heart into it, on account of his wife's suffering. You can see that, can't you?"

"The problem with that idea," I told her, "is that my personal problems happen to be, to me, the most significant clues in finding the person we're looking for."

Instead of protesting, as I thought she might, she just pulled the door to.

I walked around the truck and got in, turned the key in the ignition, and began to back out of the parking place before she spoke again.

"Shouldn't we try to find out who owns that Luger, anyway?" she asked me.

"We?" I pulled onto the road.

"This situation affects us all, Fever." Her voice was as dark as the clouds that rush up over the hills and change a pleasant morning into blackest night.

I thought about the times in the past several days that I'd tried to convince Andrews or Skidmore that there was more to the strange events surrounding my homecoming than met the eye. But hearing Lucinda's sentence, in that ominous and ultimately unfathomable voice, did more to chill my bones than to convince me I had been right.

Sixteen

That evening, Lucinda met me at June's house. Our lunch had been entirely innocuous: fast food, facile talk, forty-five minutes. It proved to be exactly what we needed, laughing about nothing, remembering school days, sharing light opinions about half-read books and recently loved movies. I spent the rest of the afternoon at last cleaning up the cabin. Andrews appeared at around two in the afternoon, registered that he was impressed with my domestic progress, said he'd learned nothing from Carson but that June Cotage was the greatest cook on the planet, and went immediately to take a nap. He was still sleeping when I left at just after five.

I had been looking forward to June's singing for weeks, and even something like murder seemed to pale beside the prospect of hearing that voice. In the first place, the sound of it would ease my mind. In the second place, it was another good excuse to see Lucinda. And in the third place, I thought I might be lucky enough to distract June the same way I had tricked Shoo earlier in the day. She might reveal something that she had been keeping secret.

A fine gray shadow was gathering around the tops of the moun-tains, a lazy fog that wandered from meadow to rock and swirled casually around until it arrived at the Cotage home. It was as if the breath of the earth were blowing on the house, warming it against the chill of night, sheltering it with unusual care. The sun was already beginning to sink behind the taller mountains, and it was impossible to tell where a Parrish blue sky ended and the Devil's black night began.

When I pulled up to the house, I could see Lucinda's Chevy already parked in the yard. I fished in the hiding place behind my seat and pulled out the reel-to-reel tape recorder.

I went around to the kitchen door, and entered without knocking. Inside, as usual, the place was spotless. Lucinda and June were seated at the kitchen table.

June was dressed in another of her endless navy blue dresses. She wore a gray and white apron over it, which meant that she had been cooking. The heavenly scent of the kitchen confirmed that observation. Lucinda had changed from her dark office suit into a pair of rust colored jeans and a lightweight black sweater. Her hair was down in a tumble around her shoulders.

I unzipped my black jacket and began some idle small talk, but June raised up from the table, spatula in hand, and I understood that we were not allowed to talk. June pointed to a seat, I took it, and she went immediately for coffee and wild blackberry pie.

The coffee was weaker than bad tea, but the pie was a portrait of the mountain: clear and fresh and sweet and tart. The crust was golden and lighter than spring sun. Each forkful was a different childhood memory: picking berries with Lucinda, hearing the church-singing off down the hillside, watching the clouds race overhead.

"This isn't pie," I told her in the silence of the kitchen. "This is God."

She only smiled, and when we were all finished, she got up again and cleaned up the plates while we sat in silence again. The silence was deliberate, a resting place for the singing that was to come, a vacuum for the music to fill.

I had recorded June's music many times before that night, and she was used to it. She'd even mass-produced several cassette tapes of her own to sell at fairs. So she did not seem nervous when I unpacked the tape recorder and started setting it up.

"Does Hek want to come in and listen?" I asked her absently as I plugged in the microphone.

With all the modern recording equipment available to me, I still preferred the romance of my old Wollenzak reel-to-reel recorder and the Shure Vocalmaster microphone. Most of the great Alan Lomax Library of Congress folk recordings had been made on similar machines, and I was in love with the notion of magnetic tape. I was also enamored of recording in the kitchen—the appliances provided small echo surfaces, and most of the female singers were more relaxed in that room than in any other in the house. June was no exception to that rule.

"Hek's already gone over to the church," she answered, drying her hands. "We've got the house to ourselves."

"Do you need help fetching your psaltry?" Lucinda wanted to know.

"I could use a hand with it, sugar. It's in the parlor."

The wooden part of the instrument was black-lacquered and polished like a mirror. The ornate top piece, which doubled as a carrying case when June played at fairs and competitions, was intricately inlaid with lighter wood in a pattern that looked, at a distance, so simple it seemed almost a part of the natural burl of the wood.

June and Lucinda carried the instrument into the kitchen. June took the top off and laid it against the wall by the sink. The psaltry sat firmly on tapered wooden legs, the trapezoidal shape belying its general spinetlike appearance. Lucy sat back at the table. June sat behind the psaltry on an antique three-legged piano stool with her back to the stove.

She touched the strings here and there, checking the tuning. They arched over double bridges and gave the appearance of a loom as much as a musical instrument.

We sat for a moment in silence as she gathered her thoughts. The wind, the birds, the entire world seemed to hush.

Then, in her still, small voice, June whispered, "What shall I play first?"

"How about 'The Black-Haired Lass'?" I started the tape recorder. She nodded and began.

She leaned over the strings and her fingers barely touched them. The golden light from the last moments of the sun coming through the window beside her seemed to attach itself to the notes. The room was filled with angel-sound. Like a harp playing by cold water, the instrument gave up the introduction to the song, coaxed from its soul by June's loving fingers.

Then she began to sing—like the first light of morning over the edge of the purple hills. Clear, simple, untrained; more honest than a saint, that voice lifted in the air.

The song was about a woman in the lowlands who waited for her mountain lover to visit one moon-pale summer's evening. She was unaware that her brutish brothers did not like her swain because of his highland heritage, and were lying in wait for him. When they saw him come through the pass into their part of the forest, the brothers fell upon him with their knives and took his life. The poor girl waited that night, and the next, and every night of summer—but her lover never came.

Then, in the twilight of the year, when the wind grew cold and the night was black, this lover's ghost finally paid a call on the girl. He told her what had happened, and that her brothers were to blame: "Maiden, maiden hear me well, false-hearted kindred here doth dwell."

To this very day, the end of the song suggests, that ghost will warn all hapless suitors to beware the brothers of the Black-Haired Lass. "Take heed my plight to all who go to tip a cup of kindness with her brothers, oh, in the lowlands low."

The song never failed to prompt a delightful shiver.

As she continued the musical interlude, coaxing ecstatic waves from the psaltry, I was struck once again, as I had earlier watching Shoo, that here was something that would soon be gone forever. In this case it was a kind of music, a way of making music, that would be gone from the earth when June died.

My tape of her voice would never be ample enough to communicate what it had been like to sit there in her kitchen and listen to her sing, watch her face, see her fingers. The live experience of true music, untainted by the outside world, was passing from the earth—and with it, the innocence of the human race.

All I could do, I thought sitting there, was to help in some way to preserve it, so that we as a race could at least point to the recordings and say, "That's what it was like. That's the way things used to be, for thousands and thousand of years."

That's what my mentor Dr. Bishop had taught me, had instilled in me: a holy mission, a salvation of our racial innocence. As June finished the song, I could almost see Bishop's face smiling, listening too.

Truly, I thought, *we only work by standing on the shoulders of giants.* I stood on his.

"That was always one of Dr. Bishop's favorites too," June said in the silence that followed her last notes.

"What made you mention him?" I turned off the tape recorder. "I was just thinking about him myself."

"Where is he these days?" June folded her arms. "I know he retired from the university."

"He spends a good deal of time in Scotland." I sat back. "He still owns a bed-and-breakfast there."

"Hear from him often?"

"Oh, a call now and then," I admitted, suddenly regretting the infrequency with which I had called. "But I e-mail fairly regularly."

"E-mail." She laughed at the sound of it. "How about you, Lucy sweetheart, what would you like to hear?"

"I always liked the 'House Carpenter,' " she said, "and you don't do that one so much anymore."

"I never get tired of it though," June smiled. "It's just one that's so old-fashioned, don't a lot of people like it much."

"That's what I want to record," I encouraged June. " 'The House Carpenter' has variants from all over the world, over hundreds of years."

"I learned it from my mother," June said, somewhat disingenuously, I thought.

"How long's it been in America, then?" Lucy asked—and I was aware that she was asking me even though I had probably told her the answer on a dozen other occasions.

"It's been popular here since the late sixteen hundreds." I took mercy on the women and cut my lecture short.

The song was about an extramarital affair. A woman falls in love with a builder. She abandons her husband and children, two daughters, to run off to sea with her paramour. After only a few weeks, alas, she begins to yearn for her babies, and grows sick with a mysterious fever. In some variants she simply dies then. Lesson learned. In others, the ship and all its occupants are lost. In June's version, visions of the children appear on deck, coaxing their mother to jump overboard and try to swim back to shore—which she does. Her lover jumps overboard to save her, but not before building them both coffins (a swift builder, we have to assume), because he fears they will not survive the swim. He tosses the coffins into the water, finds the woman's lifeless body, places it in the ornate bier, and then casts himself into the other, expecting to drown.

But the coffins wash up to shore, where the woman's *actual* daughters stumble on their mother's coffin and are so horrified by the sight that they instantly turn into old women. The husband finds the carpenter's coffin, with the carpenter still alive inside. After a stern chastising and a fairly gruesome bit of torture involving the carpenter's own tools, the husband uses the carpenter's bones to build a new house for himself and his now aged children.

It was a remarkable American Gothic take on the story—harsh retribution for infidelity and abandoning children. There was not, as far as I knew, another version of the song like that in the entire world—and I'd looked for over ten years.

June obliged us by playing a shortened version, only about twenty verses—nearly a half an hour's time. When she finished I did not turn off the recorder again, because I happened to glance over at the case cover.

"I've always loved that cover," I said idly. "Where did you get it?" I thought I might take a few pictures of the cover, the instrument, even June playing it, to go along with the tape.

"Oh, Shoo made that for me a long time ago," she said. "Isn't it pretty?"

"What is it?" Lucinda stared at the white image.

"Just some design, is all," June mumbled, not looking at it. "What should I sing next, Fever?"

"You don't remember when he made this?" I pressed. "How long ago?" I thought I'd get some accurate information on the tape.

"Let me think," she said, putting her hand to her mouth. "I guess it would be . . . oh, a good thirty-five, maybe even forty years ago— or more."

I leaned toward it, and shifted it a little so that the light from the overhead lamp fell on it. It looked familiar, and I tried to place where I might have seen similar patterns.

"Is it a quilting pattern?" I said. "It's not a typical woodworker's pattern, I don't think." I only took a second kicking myself mentally for not being more interested in material culture motifs. Then I scooted my chair over, moved in for a closer examination.

"Don't scrape up the floor like that." June watched nervously. "Looks kind of like a lion, don't it?" She turned to Lucinda. "What you want to hear, hon?"

I picked up the top, it was heavy and solid. I got the inlay in the light just right and put my face even closer to the design.

Suddenly my heart was beating so loudly I thought maybe the others could hear it. As the light glinted off the surface just right, I could see exactly what the pattern was. I nearly dropped the cover onto the floor. Both women were beginning to realize how excited, or alarmed, I had become, and Lucinda leaned toward me, touched my arm.

"Fever?"

All I could do was stare at the pattern. It had almost been worn away with time and use, but it was still clear enough to shoot electricity through my hands and directly into my brain.

"This is not a lion," I said to June, my voice actually shaking. "You can see the tip of a wing there in the corner. It's from a mythological creature—called a griffin. You have to try and remember when Shoo made this for you, all right?" I tried my best to stay calm.

The inlay was highly stylized: Squares and triangles in odd patterns, and the whole thing was so scuffed that I could hardly make it out at all. Still, two snakes seemed to wind their way up a crooked cross, and on either side of them two winged lions sat motionless, white, ready to pounce on anything that came close.

"Are you okay?" Lucinda was watching me carefully.

"This image," I turned to face her, "is a detail from a pattern on the Serpent Bowl in Hek's church—or very similar to it, anyway. Now, Shoo Walters has never been inside Hek's church, correct me if I'm wrong. Let alone studied the bowl."

"He wouldn't be caught dead in the place," Lucinda confirmed. "Shoo's a Methodist."

"And he would not to your knowledge have ever inspected the bowl in Hek's church."

"What is it, honey?" June was genuinely concerned. "Your face is so flushed. You having one of your spells?"

"I'm asking," I insisted, "when did Shoo make this cover?"

"Like I said," she snapped back, "it was a good long time ago. It was even before Reverend Coombs came to town I believe, but I can't be sure."

"But if he did this before the bowl was even here," Lucinda began, trying her best to understand the significance of the image, "then where did he get the idea for the design, if it's the same?"

"It could just be a coincidence," I said slowly. "But this pattern is very much like the one on the bowl. And it's certainly not American. Dr. Andrews, in fact, seemed to think that it wasn't British either. He told me that he thought it was ancient Sumerian."

"How would Shoo ever know anything about that?" Lucinda's voice was thick with confusion.

"What does this mean, Fever?" June sat straight as a board on her piano stool. For some reason, her voice reminded me of my second grade teacher's—her question was like a math problem in school.

"I suppose it could mean a lot of things." I could not force my eyes away from the image. "But I've just heard that Coombs was very interested in Shoo's tools and methods. And I was also recently reminded that once Shoo gets a certain thing in his mind—an activity, an idea, a plan—he does tend to do it over and over again quite a lot."

"And what does *that* mean?" Lucinda was still considering the problem of the inlay—or was she staring at me strangely?

"I'd just like to know how Shoo got this particular image for your case." I finally turned to June. "And why."

Once I saw the look on her face, it only took me a few more seconds to realize that June and Lucy were not as much in the dark about this subject as I had thought. A growing paranoia—one that had been building since the first moment I'd come home, one that had been engendered by lifelong suspicions as much as by recent bodies and bullets—began to grip my core. "Of course," I said to June in measured words, "you've wondered about this very question before tonight."

My head was hot, the way it used to get when I was a child, dry and burning. But my hands were cold, and I jammed them into the pockets of my jacket to keep from shivering.

"I might have considered it a curious design when I first got it—way back in the old days." June looked down at the strings of her psaltry. "But I really didn't think too much about it since then."

For some reason, her stubborn denial grabbed my throat. I felt a welling up of hundreds of moments just like that one, in her kitchen or on a bench at Gil's or even in my own living room, when in the mountains older people so obviously had something on their minds but stopped short of saying anything about it. I felt a frustration that had built for years, an awareness of the weight of all the things they kept inside.

"I've just about had it," I seethed, my anger threatening to boil over much more suddenly than I would have expected, "with all of this hiding and dodging and innuendo."

June turned to Lucinda. "Fetch him a cool rag from the sink, sweetheart."

"Stop," I demanded.

Lucy didn't move, and the hounds of paranoia were, apparently, unleashed in my brain.

"Go on then," June said, still in her sweetest voice.

"Carson tells me his little secrets like some backwoods Buddha," I resumed, my voice growing in a slow, steady crescendo, "and you tell me yours with all that sugar in your voice. But you're all whispering behind my back, wondering if I'll figure out the depth of your strangeness."

"Fever . . ." June tried to interrupt, her face creased with concern.

The kitchen seemed to darken a little. Maybe the sun was setting, or a cloud overhead obscured the sky, but it made the kitchen seem less inviting, and more ominous.

"Even Shoo Walters," I crashed on, my face hotter, "a man who's one step above *village idiot* status here in town—he lords his esoteric knowledge over me, trying to get me to guess the right answer."

"What do you mean 'right answer'?" Lucinda seemed genuinely troubled, afraid for my state of mind. "The right answer to *what*?"

"You all want to see if I'm still one of your *tribe*." I stood emphatically. "Damn."

I thought June said to Lucinda, "Didn't he used to have some pills for this?" But the blood was pounding in my ears.

"If you all have something you want to tell me—or if you know something you think I ought to know," I demanded, steadying myself against the kitchen table, "why don't you just come out and say it?"

Both women were clearly uncomfortable with the volume of my voice and the growing force of my ire. But it still seemed to me that they were watching me closely. It almost seemed as if they were testing me, and it seemed to me to be the same test I had undergone at Skidmore's house, listening to my song.

All of these people are conspiring, I thought, *to engage me in some sort of bizarre contest.*

"Say it!" I slapped my palm on the tabletop. The kitchen seemed liquid.

"Say what?" June seemed almost afraid.

"Whatever it is that you all are hiding from me."

"Hiding from you?" Lucinda reached out for my hand.

"Lucinda." My eyes implored her. "I feel as if I . . . I might have some sort of note pinned to my back, the way children used to do in school—something that everybody else is reading. And no one is willing to just come out and tell me about it." I swung my head in June's direction. "You all just keep hemming and hawing and trying to get me to look at it, but I don't know what it is you want me to see. Just tell me what it is. God damn it."

They were both frozen. As it was most likely the first time that last phrase had ever been uttered in June's kitchen, I thought she took my cursing well. Her face went white, her eyes rolled back, and it seemed, for an instant, she might just pass away.

"Is that what you think of us?" Her voice was wounded to the quick, and barely audible. "That we're playing with you, like a cruel game at school? Don't you realize what's going on up here?"

"You're an idiot." Lucinda's eyes were brimming.

"Well, I guess it's true that we know some secrets about you that we've held back," June finally allowed, smoothing her apron over her knees in a distracted manner, "but that was only on account of how sensitive you used to be. You're a grown man now, Fever, and we're trying to tell you about all that as best we can. The rest of this—you think we know some big riddle that we're trying to make you see?" She locked eyes with me. "We don't." Simple. Straightforward. True.

"You're supposed to be the clever one," Lucinda's voice was almost bitter. "You're the one who went away to get all that education and learn all there was to know."

"All we're trying to tell you," June folded her arms again and pulled her sweater a little closer around her, as if a sudden wind had chilled her, "is that we've all got questions we've all had in our heads since before you were born. About all this mess. We don't have any of the answers. That's what *you're* here for. We look to you for that. That's why you've come back to us. To find the answers."

"You're the smart one," Lucinda reiterated, only a little more gently.

I felt like a statue. I stood immobile in that room, as if someone had made me out of concrete, moved me in, and left me there.

How could I have been, I thought, *so absolutely ignorant.* My face cooled, the rumble in my ears stilled, the river of fear moved past me, leaving me on the banks: wet, cold, dull.

"I don't know what to say," I finally managed. "It's just that you act strange when you feel like a stranger, maybe." I was still searching for the root cause of my odd reactions.

"You're not a stranger here," June said softly. "Not in this house, not in these hills."

Lucinda cleared her throat. "I reckon," she began with more of the mountain accent than she usually used, "that when you get shot at and then somebody tells you that your father's not your father and then your best friend's wife nearly gets killed—well, it's apt to make a person a trifle on the odd side." She offered up a wry little grin.

There was another aspect of the peculiar culture of my home that was as worthy of recording as June's voice: friends will pick at friends, needle them, tease them, fuss, and taunt—until that person snaps. And then when the person snaps, his friends will forgive him, almost instantly and with a kind heart. My friends and neighbors had always used the phrase "hard to know, easy to forgive" to describe themselves. I'd seen a hundred demonstrations of it in my life.

"Not to mention that I'm an idiot," I agreed, "and a paranoid freak and I'm really sorry."

"Yes." Lucinda folded her arms. "You certainly are."

And then the cycle of needling and picking would start all over again.

"I was only looking at the situation from my own weird point of view, my own subjective observations of this set of phenomena." I looked out the window. There was no light outside at all. "It never occurred to me that you all have been confused about all this for—quite some time."

It was just beginning to sink into my sad little brain that this community had been torn apart by some mighty forces. Most mountain communities had not survived the tripartite invasion of two world wars, electricity, and rabid tourism. But this little town, if my growing suspicions were in any way accurate, had been savaged by much more than time and tide—and the savagery had been deliberate, somehow.

Part of the problem had been my mother, clawing a swath of amorality in the deeply conservative fabric of this world. But if I was right about my newly developing theories, there might have been a darker force at work—darker and more purposeful.

I sat back down, but I seemed to be sitting down in an entirely different room from the one in which I'd stood only moments before.

"All this time," I continued, "since I've been back, I've wasted my energy on thinking that all of these events were my fault. It shoved me close to a precipice. I've wasted a lot of time thinking I was to blame, or that you all blamed me in some way, for all of these events. And I mean all of them: Mother and Daddy, the trouble in the town because of them, and this murder and the shooting over at Skid's— I thought you all were my parents, trying to teach me some sort of lesson. I realize now . . . I've just realized that you've had in mind, from the beginning, something like the *opposite* idea, in fact."

"And what would that be?" Lucy asked, sitting back, the sun of a smile dawning across her eyes.

"You thought I was the teacher," I told her simply.

"You are a teacher," June said right back. "What have you been doing for the past eleven years?"

"Teaching."

"And you forgot all that in one night when you came back up here?" June glanced at Lucinda.

"Okay." I leaned forward. "All I can say to that is: I hope you never come home and find a dead body on your front porch. It can alter your mood considerably."

"I found a dead body in my office once," Lucy offered wryly, without batting an eye. "Some new orderly said he thought it was the morgue on account of the way my office looks—but I always thought it was just a joke."

And with that, the last dust of uncomfortable atmosphere between us vanished from the kitchen: Gone like smoke.

"Your office does look like a morgue." But I hoped that my eyes conveyed something more than a resumption of the teasing.

"All right." June rocked back and forth a little. "If you're all done horsing around, junior, are you ready to get you some *answers?*"

"Yes." I folded my hands and waited.

"Good." She seemed genuinely relieved. "We've been waiting an awful long time for this, one way or another."

"What's first?" Lucy leaned forward.

"I think I'd better go talk with Shoo again, don't you?" I suggested. "I need to find out when and—more important—*why* he made that particular design." I inclined my head in the direction of the psaltry case.

"You have an idea about it, though." Lucy could tell.

"I do have an idea," I confessed, "but I wouldn't like to talk about that sort of thing until I have facts to back up a hypothesis—especially given the mistakes I've made so far."

"So you have to talk to Shoo," she concurred.

"Right." I stood again. "I'm going now."

"Now?" June looked out the window. "It's after seven. He'll be asleep."

"You know you stole an angel's voice when you were born," I said to her. "I'm not done recording it. Come back tomorrow?"

"Shoot." She looked down, trying not to grin.

And she made no further objection to my leaving.

"I'm going with you," Lucy told me firmly.

"I don't think that would be so good." I shook my head. "Shoo won't be as free to talk with you around."

"Are you serious?" she bristled. "I've known Shoo Walters way longer than you have, with all the time you've been away."

"But I'm not a beautiful woman," I said simply. "And women make Shoo nervous."

She didn't want to agree, but she knew I was right. It only took her a moment to agree. "All right, but the minute you find something out you call me."

I nodded.

I looked for a second at the psaltry case and then around the kitchen, sighing.

In another week or two, there would be a fire in the living room hearth every night, and the stained-glass leaves on the trees all around would make a cathedral of the entire sky at sunset. I truly couldn't wait to come back into that room and listen to the music.

"June," I said, sliding my chair under the table, "I'm really glad to be home."

"You're a mess." She looked up at me, not standing. "But I think about you like you're family, you know that."

"Yes, ma'am." I touched her shoulder, then I offered my hand to Lucinda. "Walk me to my truck?"

"Now we're getting somewhere," June said immediately.

Lucinda stood, adjusted her sweater, and took my hand. "We surely are."

"Good night, June." Lucy's hand still fit perfectly into mine. I was relieved, more than happy, to see that time had not altered that.

"I'll try to save you some pie," June suggested as we were closing the door behind us. "But you know how Hek eats."

The night air was like a cold apple, and Lucy pressed against me, taking my arm with her free hand.

I zipped my jacket to my chin, and walked as slowly as I possibly could toward the truck.

The moon was not yet up, and the stars gave white, fierce fire to the sky but could not illuminate our path. And I was grateful. In that darkness, Lucy held me tighter.

"Do you know about Xeno's arrow?" I said, my voice somehow

an intrusion on the other night sounds—black cricket song, wind sweeping the tops of the trees.

"What is it?" she asked lazily.

"He said that in order for an arrow to get to a target, that arrow first has to travel halfway to the target. Then when it got halfway, it would still have to go halfway between its *new* position and the target. He said you could go on and on like that—dividing that distance, and then halving it—for infinity."

"What would be the point of that?" she said, almost at a whisper.

"It's proof that the arrow can never reach its target."

She considered for a moment, then squeezed my hand more tightly. "You'd like to use that now," she said, leaning her head on my shoulder, "to keep us from ever getting to your truck."

"Yes I would."

I leaned my head on hers, and for a moment there was no sound on earth but the sound of our breathing.

And then we came to the truck.

"And *that*," I announced, tapping the hood, "is the trouble with philosophy in general. It's good in theory, rotten in practice."

"You be careful driving up to Shoo's at night." She patted my arm. "You forget how dark it can be up there."

It was harder to let go of her hand than it had been to leave home when I was seventeen. It was all I could do not to kiss her then, in the dark. I don't know why I didn't.

We stood for a moment, still and silent, and then I climbed into my truck without another word. The rush picked up in the top of the trees, and in my head, nagging and taunting me, were the words of my song: *It blew away the kiss from a pair of osculators; it's a great high wind that blew the low post down.*

"Maybe that man ought to have used a kiss instead of an arrow," she said, closing the driver's door behind me. "Sometimes *they* don't ever meet."

I was surprised to learn that I had retained almost every curse word I had ever heard from any of my students. I used them all on myself as I pulled the truck out of June's yard and into the blackest part of the night.

Seventeen

The night was pitch and the mist was thicker up on the mountain. Even my bright lights didn't seem to dent the cool air and the growing fog. I drove excruciatingly slowly, and I missed a turn to Shoo's house. I had to double back, so it took me nearly three quarters of an hour to finally creep up the dirt path to his little vine-covered home.

All the lights were on, which alarmed me. Shoo would ordinarily have been in bed after the sun set. As I drew closer, I could see several cars parked in front of his house. Shoo rarely had visitors.

When the high beams finally hit them, I could see that all the cars were from the sheriff's office.

I pulled up beside one, and got out quickly. I could hear the rattle of men's voices from inside, but they all stopped when I shut my door. I slammed it deliberately hard. I had no intention of sneaking up on a police interrogation of Shoo Walters. I wanted to announce my presence.

After an infinite second of complete silence, one of the uniformed deputies appeared in the doorway with a blinding flashlight.

"It's Devilin," he called back into the house after another second, surprised.

Instantly Maddox shoved the deputy out of the way and came barreling in my direction. I could tell who it was from the way he was walking, even though the deputy's beacon was still shining directly in my eyes.

"Dr. Devilin." His voice was colder than the bottom stone in the well. "This is very interesting to me that you're here."

"Sheriff." I shielded my eyes from the light with my left hand and held out my right to shake.

"Why are you here?" He only glared at my hand, and he didn't stop walking until he was inches from where I stood.

"I was here earlier—videotaping Shoo while he made one of his chairs—for the Georgia Folklore Archives. I just had a few more—"

"Where's the tape?"

"What?"

"If you were taping, where is the tape?"

"Right here in the truck."

"Let me see it now." His voice was hard.

I took my time opening the truck, digging in the space behind the seat, deliberately trying to annoy him. I finally picked the camera out of its case, and turned it on.

"You look through here," I told him, pointing to the viewfinder.

"I know where to look," he shot back.

I ran the tape for him as he stared into the camera, one-eyed.

"What's he saying?" Maddox continued to watch. "I can't hear it."

"He's just talking. Telling me how he makes a chair." I lowered the camera. "What's going on, Sheriff?"

"I'll tell you what's going on." He grabbed the camera. "Shut up. That's what's going on."

"I see."

The moon was low on the horizon, almost purple, and jagged behind several mountain peaks. It did little to shed any light on the world. Tree frogs and wild night birds called all around us, unafraid of the deputy's harsh light or Maddox's grating voice. High above, the stars twinkled so angrily in the box of night that they seemed to spin out of control, their light shooting like sparks.

"Sheriff?" one of deputies called from inside. "Can I call the Peaker Brothers now?"

The Peaker Brothers Mortuary had been a thriving business in Blue Mountain since 1937.

"Get lost, Devilin," he told me quickly, handing me back my camera.

"Is Shoo all right?" I started to follow Maddox, then called out, "Shoo?"

"Didn't I say 'shut up'?" Maddox stopped in his tracks and turned around very deliberately. "And you're going to have to yell a whole lot louder than that if you want an answer out of Walters." He took a menacing step in my direction. "He's dead. And if you want me to run you in for interfering with *another* murder investigation, just say one more word."

Not waiting to see if I would respond, he spun around again and disappeared into the house.

I stood for a moment, not believing what he had told me.

The deputy in the doorway let Maddox past, watched as the sheriff turned in the direction of Shoo's kitchen, and then lowered his flashlight and started my way.

"You'd best get on out of here," he said, but his voice was gentle. "Sheriff ain't one to mess with."

"I know." I was still staring into the house—my voice as vacant as the cold hollow at the top of the mountain. "Shoo's dead?"

"Maddox found the body hisself," the deputy nodded. "Up at the Heart."

Instead of thinking about Shoo's body inside his house, all I could think about was the way that locals sometimes pronounced the word "hearth" that way, omitting the *th* sound that was difficult to create for a tongue that spent most of its time farther back in the mouth. Sometimes the mind works overtime with insignificant details to protect the heart from a sudden wound.

"The Devil's Hearth?" I finally asked. "What was he doing up there?"

"Sheriff or Shoo?"

"Either one." I leaned against my truck, still reeling from the news.

"Sheriff was up there on unrelated official business that I don't know a thing about," the deputy intoned. "And he found Shoo. Brought his body back down to home and called the ambulance— but he was real dead." He looked toward the house. "Pretty strange your showing up before the medics even got here."

My eyes were adjusting to the darkness. The boy was no more than twenty. I thought his name badge read CUNNINGHAM.

"Are you kin to Howard?" I asked him.

The boy smiled. "He's my uncle."

Fiddlin' Howard Cunningham was a legend in the South—his

home was in Hiawassee, Georgia, but he had traveled the world with his music. The Georgia Mountain Fair, an institution for decades, boasted Howard as its king.

"Well, tell him Fever's back home when you see him, would you?" I said. "Tell him I said 'hey.' "

"Okay." He tapped the flashlight against his leg. "Don't see him all that much lately."

"When did the sheriff find Shoo?"

"Just after dark." He lowered his voice. "Said it looked like he was up there to meet somebody."

"Who said that, the sheriff?"

The boy nodded.

"And then the sheriff," I said more slowly, "lugged Shoo's dead body all the way back down the mountain, to this house."

"Um," the deputy began, "he had to bring it where everybody could get it. You know how hard it is to get up there."

"Cunningham!" Suddenly Maddox's voice pierced the quiet. "If it's Dr. Devilin still out there that you're talking to, you moron, and he's not getting into his truck this second, arrest him."

The deputy grinned at me. "You want to ride in a police car?"

"I believe I will rely on the better part of valor," I answered him, opening the truck door. It wasn't easy.

I took one last look at the house, wanting desperately to go into the kitchen, shake the body, wake him up.

The deputy must have read my expression.

"I'd like to say about a hundred things right now," he began tentatively. "The kind of thing you say when somebody's friend dies."

But that was the extent of his ability at consolation. He put his hand on my door, shoved it shut, and turned back toward the dead man's house.

Eighteen

As I headed back down the mountain, slowly in all that darkness, the only thing I could see was the angelic, contented look that Shoo had worn when he was turning rough tree limbs, making them into chair legs by the golden light from the windows in his shed.

For the first minute or so rolling downward, I didn't even know where I was going. I was gripping the steering wheel, trying to keep my eyes clear and my head cool.

By the time I hit the main road, I had a destination in mind. I headed the truck toward Skidmore's house. It couldn't have been later than eight-thirty. The drive was difficult, even though I would have known the way in my sleep. The low, autumnal fog had turned into a shroud that covered the night.

I found my brain flying wildly between the thousand questions in my mind and the treacherous road in front of me—a sudden turn or an unexpected shot of light from someone else's high beams.

I finally wound my way up the other side of the same hill, pulled close to the house. A few lights were on. I was relieved to see only Skid's police car and Girlinda's four-wheeler parked in the yard.

I went around to the kitchen, tapped and entered at the same time, and found Skid drinking coffee and staring at the table.

He looked up slowly when I came in. His eyes were bloodshot, his hair wildly disheveled, his hand shaking a little, holding his cup.

"Hey, Dev," he managed.

"Skidmore." I sat at the table with him. "You look beat."

"I am." He started to get up.

"Sit," I told him

The percolator was on the table.

"I'll get one." I went to the cupboard and got a mug.

"Andrews says to call him at your place right away." He took another sip, still staring vacantly.

"Sorry?" I sat back down and poured coffee, my mind too distracted to clearly understand what he was saying.

"Andrews called here looking for you," he said again. "Call him back at your place." He gazed down into his cup as if the rest of the message were written there. "Said he thought it was important."

"I will." I was trying to think of a way to soften the worst news I had to give him.

"What's wrong?" He finally looked up at me. "I can tell by your face you've got something to say, Dev. What is it?"

"I don't know how to tell you." I set my mug down on the table.

The light in the kitchen seemed too harsh for the news, and the hum of the refrigerator too loud. The ordinary incidental things about the room seemed too trivial for the announcement of a death—the clock in the stove should have stopped, the ice-maker in the freezer should have frozen. The room had no respect for the terrible thing I had to say.

"Oh." His face was empty of any emotion. "You mean about Shoo. I heard."

"You heard?"

"On the police band." He tilted his head in the direction of a black receiver on the windowsill. "Heard Maddox call it in."

With the sound of Skid's voice, the click of the second hand in the clock seemed mournful, and the tight fluorescent light seemed like tears.

"So . . ." I trailed off.

What was there to say, exactly? The death of Shoo Walters was difficult enough to fathom on a personal level, but I could not ignore what I believed to be the greater loss as well—the loss to the world, and it did not seem hyperbole. It was possible that the last man alive on earth who knew how to make a certain chair a certain way—was gone. An entire heritage, one that had survived for a thousand years or more, was dead.

"How did it happen?" I asked after a moment. "Do you have any idea?"

All I could think was that Skidmore may have been privy to some special police information and would know more than I did about Shoo's death.

"Naw." He didn't look at me. "Maddox—he just said he found the body while he was looking for something else. Said it looked like 'foul play.'" Skid looked up at me, then, and managed something close to a wry expression. "I never heard anybody use that phrase except on the television."

"He thought Shoo had been murdered?"

"He did." Skid returned to studying his coffee. "But it was probably the two bullets in Shoo's head that made him think that."

"The deputy . . . I was just there. I mean, at Shoo's house, not the Hearth. Anyway, Maddox had several deputies there, and one of them—what's the Cunningham boy's name?"

"Bernard." Skid smiled. "There's some that call him Barnyard."

"He was at Shoo's," I went on. "He told me that Maddox thought Shoo was at the Hearth to meet someone."

"I was wondering," Skid nodded, "what in the world Shoo would be doing up there this time of night."

"How's Girlinda?" I suddenly asked, ashamed that I hadn't sooner.

"Fine, fine. Better than me, probably." He shook his head. "You know this is not the first time she's been shot up. She was just reminding me of the time her brother shot her."

"What?"

"Yeah. Her brother—you remember Able . . ."

"Yes, the shy one."

"Right," Skid set down the empty coffee cup. "He accidentally shot her when they were young'uns out hunting birds one Thanksgiving weekend. Shot her in the foot. She laughs about it to this day. Able carried her everywhere she went for the next six months." He looked up at me. "She says it made them closer than they ever would have been otherwise."

"Girlinda's a remarkable woman."

"I know," he agreed, "but anyway she says that time was lots worse than this. This didn't break bones."

"On the other hand," I felt compelled to point out, "this time it wasn't a family accident."

"Right." He looked back down at the table.

"We have to find the person who did this." I tried to keep my voice steady. "I think if we do, we'll find the person who killed my so-called half-brother, and who shot at us—all the same person. All because of something my mother knew about, and wrote in her diary."

"That's a mouthful," he told me, "and I don't want to agree—but I do. I guess if you think about it, your mother knew a lot of secrets about the people here abouts—when you're kind of a free wheel like she was? You get in on the slippery side of things easier. No offense."

"The slippery side," I smiled. "Delicate."

"You know what I mean—"

"Oh, yes," I stopped him, "I know what you mean. She was much more apt to know about what people did wrong than what they did right." I stood. "Let me call Andrews and see what he wants, and then I think you should get some rest. Then why don't you call someone . . ."

"I already did, if you mean call somebody to watch Linda while I go out and work."

I stared. "First, you're not going out to work, you're going to bed. And second, whom did you call?"

"Able," he shrugged, as if it should have been obvious.

"I see."

"And I am going out to work." He sat up straighter, squeezed his eyes shut for a moment. "If you think I can sleep while all this is going on—and Maddox is out there somewhere gumming up the works—you have done forgot a whole bunch about me." He was determined as a bull.

"When Able gets here—"

"He's already in back." Skid sat back in his chair, exhausted by good posture. "He walked over the hill when I called him."

I'd forgotten that the Carter place, where Girlinda's family still lived, was actually within closer walking distance from Skid's house, over the top of one little hill, than driving all the way around on the main roads.

"All right, I'm calling Andrews, then," I told him, and walked over to the phone on the wall beside the stove. "What's my number, again?"

"Two-five-two . . ."

"Right, right, right," I suddenly remembered the rest and dialed, only a little embarrassed at having to be prompted to remember my own phone number—it had, after all, been a good many years since I'd called it.

Andrews picked up on the first ring. "Hello?"

"Andrews? I'm at Skidmore's, he told me you called."

"Yes, God." He sounded relieved. "I have news."

"About?"

"Two things. First, I finally did get Carson alone this afternoon and he told me more about this so-called business arrangement between Bishop and Coombs. It had to do with the Serpent Bowl and *starting* the church—although the details are a little murky. So I spent some time on the old laptop computer—"

"You brought your laptop?" I broke in.

"Ask me what I found."

"Andrews . . ."

"I found out that I was right." He began to ramble. "The image on the Serpent Bowl is Sumerian in origin, and would not have been indigenous to the Celts in any way. It would be highly unlikely that that image would have been found on anything authentically Scots. So I read all of Bishop's early articles on the thing. You know he started off talking about how amazing it was that an image so old would have survived all the way to America in the twentieth century—then, when his *find* gained momentum and there were more and more articles, he began to insist that the only worthwhile scholarship on the subject would be found in firsthand accounts of the *effects* of the bowl—on the people in the church. Still, plenty of other scholars wrote about the bowl itself, and everyone was amazed at what became the obvious anomaly of it all, and the thing seemed to gain a minor status as one of the great folk mysteries, owing to the fact—"

"Andrews," I had to stop him. "I've based a lot of my career on the things you're telling me. I already know all of this."

"But you don't see what it all means." His voice was like a boy's.

I smiled. "What do you think it means?"

"It means," Andrews told me plainly, "that the bowl is a fake."

It wasn't as if the bowl's origins hadn't been questioned for years, but no one had ever suggested it was an out-and-out fabrication of any sort—not in print, at least.

"That sort of talk's gone around about the thing for years," I told him. "But with all that Bishop has written about it . . ."

"No one's ever dated it," he reminded me. "You told me that when we were at Hek's church just . . . yesterday?"

"Seems longer ago," I agreed. "And I know the thing's never been officially dated—"

"Not to mention Piltdown man," he interrupted.

It took me a second to recall the famous hoax, partially perpetuated by none other than an eventually very embarrassed H. G. Wells, who had written about it in his *The Outline of History*. Supposed for many years to be a sort of "missing link," Piltdown man was eventually discovered to be a hoax deliberately perpetuated on the scientific community—a prank invention, a monkey jaw and a human tooth, an old skull, and a little varnish. Wells was forced to print a retraction and refutation of the find.

"But the likelihood that someone in Scotland deliberately perpetuated a hoax," I insisted, "that went undiscovered until Coombs found it, and then said nothing at all about it when Coombs took it, has always seemed, to the academic community, quite remote. Hoaxers like for you to *know* you've been duped."

"Aren't we talking about the land of crop circles?" Andrews's voice was growing louder. "What if the thing had been faked years before, and the person who created it had died?"

"You might as well give up this line of thinking," I told him. "Bishop covered it in the journals long ago. Your thinking is headed in the wrong direction."

"Well, I'd still like to date it, wouldn't you?"

"I don't know that I would," I said honestly. "I'm not certain it's the folklorist's business to completely muck up folk icons."

"Doesn't matter if the Shroud of Turin's a fake?" he began.

"Not that it doesn't matter; it's just not what I'm interested in studying. Let some scientist determine the carbon dating of things. I'm more interested in the folk behavior around those things. The effect that the bowl has on the people in that church is more interesting to me now."

"Psychological anthropology is your field now?"

"If you like," I shifted the phone, finally out of patience. "Look, I've got some more important news—and we've got work to do. Shoo Walters is dead." It seemed to me that the moment called for being so blunt. "I think he's been killed by the same person responsible for these other shootings, and I think that some information in my mother's diary is at the heart of it."

There was a static of silence on the other end of the phone.

Then: "Shoo Walters is dead?"

"Yes, and it's changed everything." My voice sounded cold, even to myself. "It's time to stop all this idle speculation and the stupid, pointless research, and the self-indulgent self-analysis. It's time to find the person responsible."

"Well . . . obviously." He adjusted quickly. "All right. What do we do?"

"We find the diary. We get the facts. We need facts more than these idle speculations of yours . . . and the vague, lazy internal analysis in which I personally have been indulging."

"Facts." He could see that. "Where do we start?"

"Where Shoo was killed." I looked at Skidmore, still talking into the phone, he nodded back, and I told Andrews: "The Devil's Hearth."

"You think there might be something Maddox missed." Skid stood up.

"Christ." I smiled grimly. "I think Sheriff Maddox could miss breakfast if it were brought to him in bed." I spoke again to Andrews. "We're on our way to pick you up, are you ready to go?"

"To the Hearth?"

"Exactly."

"I'll be waiting on the porch." Andrews hung up without even saying good-bye.

Skidmore went in to tell Linda's brother, Able, that he'd be gone for a while. I heard them talking softly, their voices warm in the other room. When he came back into the kitchen, he had his departmental jacket on.

"You ought to pick up a sweater to wear underneath that cloth jacket, Dev," he told me. "It's chilly up on that mountain."

"All right." We began to move toward the door. "Don't you agree that Shoo wouldn't be up there after dark unless it was someone else's idea?"

"Knowing his feelings about the place, and his sleeping habits? I'd say that's definite." He locked the door behind us, which was unheard of in our little town. "It must have been something big to get him up there at night."

He headed toward Girlinda's Jeep four-wheeler, the only vehicle likely to make it anywhere close to the Hearth. And I knew that we'd still have to climb the last part of the journey on foot.

"You follow me back to your place, so you'll have your car at home," Skid said as he stepped up into the Jeep's cab. "The three of us can go up to the Hearth in the Jeep." Skid gunned the engine and peeled out of the yard before I had a chance to answer.

I jumped in my car and followed, but it was all I could do to keep up. I drove the truck down the hill much faster than I should have, taking curves at a frightening rate, leaving the road for seconds at a time, flying over the little bumps.

We arrived at my place in ten minutes—a record. Andrews didn't even wait until we'd come to a complete standstill.

"Everything happens at once," he said breathlessly, running over to the side of my truck and leaning in my window. "June Cotage just called here and said you had to come to her place now. Right now. She sounded terrible."

"She called me now?" was all I could think to say.

"She said it was about your mother's secret—something you had to know tonight."

"Damn." I looked over to Skidmore. He had his widow down. "Did you hear? What do we do? Should I call her?"

"I mean it, Dev," Andrews insisted. "This sounded like a serious emergency. I don't know the woman very well, but I think she was nearly hysterical."

"Why don't you run over there first," Skid called over to me. "It could really be something important. Me and Andrews'll get on up the mountain. You meet us there quick as you can. Tell Junie you've got business that can't wait. Okay?"

Even though I didn't like it, his suggestion seemed a sensible plan. If June really had information—especially if it had anything to do with the diary—it might be essential to our needs. Meanwhile Skidmore and Andrews could well explore the Devil's Hearth for clues that Maddox had missed.

"Damn," I said again, but I gunned my engine and Andrews went to hop in the passenger seat of the Jeep.

Before the door was even closed, Skid had thrown the vehicle into gear and started off up the mountain. I only watched a moment as they roared off before heading in the opposite direction, down the mountain and away from the Hearth.

Nineteen

There was a strange car parked close to the Cotage house.

What a night, I thought to myself.

"Fever?" June threw open the front door, as if she'd been watching for me. "Is that you?"

Her face was white as a ghost, her hair was more unkempt than I had ever seen it.

I leapt out of the truck and up the steps, taking her hand. It was ice cold.

"June," I asked her, "what's the matter? You came running out of your house like it was on fire."

"I wanted to get you ready . . . before you went inside." She glanced for a second over her shoulder. "I didn't want you to just walk in on it."

"Walk in on what?" I peered anxiously past her into the darkened house.

"Lord, God," she said, staring out into the night.

"June." I was worried more about her than whatever it was inside the house; she seemed on the verge of a heart attack.

"Fever—you got to prepare yourself."

"What is it?"

She sipped a little breath. "Now that you're standing here," she said, on the verge of tears, "I don't know how to tell you."

In the maddening moments she used to collect her thoughts, shiny black crickets and crawling tree frogs raised a clatter that echoed only slightly louder than the pounding in my ears. Suddenly there was a shadowy form silhouetted in the front door frame.

"Why don't you just come out and tell him plain?" The voice was calm, sweet, simple—and icily familiar.

She stepped onto the porch, and the light from inside the house was no longer at her back. It spilled onto her face as she turned sideways to close the door. She was older, heavier—her hair was different—but the eyes had not changed one molecule. Still, it didn't seem possible, and for an instant, I forgot how to breathe.

Some ghosts come unbidden in the bright daylight—but some step out of the light into the darkness.

"Mother?" I didn't even recognize the sound of my own voice.

"Hey, kiddo." But I did know hers. "Your hair sure did go white."

June Cotage was holding both my arms and staring into my face. "It's your mother, Fever."

"Come back from the dead." The familiar stranger smiled.

June finally let me go and collapsed into one of the rocking chairs on the porch.

I stood on the top step, staring at the old woman by the doorway. Her hair was only barely controlled wire, and she was shorter than I remembered—very short, five feet and little more. I couldn't tell much about her figure, she clutched her thick brown sweater around her and kept her arms folded tightly to her chest. Her skin was not as wrinkled as I might have imagined it would be. She wore expensive shoes, black, the kind I had seen some of my students wearing when they had to dress up for church or job interviews. I imagined that the shoes I saw had been mail ordered. Only her eyes seemed not to have aged, and they were alive with a devil's coal.

"You surely are, as they say in the funny papers," she croaked out, "a sight for sore eyes."

"They do say that." I was motionless. Even my blood stood still.

She glanced over in June's direction. "Why don't we go on inside for a while. I can't stay long." She shot me a wry enough grin. "Not that I'd be welcome here anyway."

June looked away, studying the black horizon for the proper response.

"Let's do go inside," I urged June. "I think I need to sit down where it's a little warmer."

We all moved, like a troupe of zombies, through the door, down the hall, and into the bright kitchen. It was the same kitchen where I'd been sitting only hours earlier, but it seemed to me that a decade had passed since I heard June singing.

I sat at the head of the rounded rectangular table, and the scuff of the chair on the floor seemed an insult to the cleanliness of the room. June stood by the stove, ready for a culinary emergency. And the third of our coven sat beside me, perched erectly on her chair like a gnome, delighted to be indoors.

"I'll get right to the point," Mrs. Devilin said. "I heard the news that Thresher was dead—somebody said it might have been you that was killed too, Fever. So I came running. I guess it was a little foolish, after all these years of playing dead. Now I hear Shoo Walters is gone and even Girlinda Needle's been in the hospital." She made a loose fist with her right hand and she began to grind her fingers absently. "Well, it's all got to stop. So I had to come to do what I had to come and do. Because it's got to stop tonight."

She looked between me and June.

I stared at this woman as if she were a movie of a memory. I felt more removed from the reality of her sitting in that kitchen than from the reality that mastodons had once roamed the earth. I heard the sound of her voice, but I didn't quite understand the words—as if I needed an interpreter.

In my mind a thousand questions thrashed and battered, like birds trapped in a house, all clambering for an exit. Not a single one of them had a complete sentence attached to it. Like messages on carrier pigeons' legs, the phrases were coded, incomplete, and desperate.

I watched as her face, a face I had demonized and seared with scorn, wrinkled into quite a pleasant smile. There was an ordinary face, not a devil's mask—a normal expression, nothing ominous or cruel. There sat, at that table, a very nice country woman in her late fifties, no more remarkable than any of hundreds of others I knew. There was, in short, a person who was not remotely my mother—not the mother I'd created—or had needed to create—in her absence.

"It would be about this time, in my own kitchen at home," the nice country woman said to June, "that I'd offer a person a cup of coffee."

"Lord." June responded instantly without thinking. "Yes. I'm sorry. Let me get us a fresh pot started." And she went to work, a little relieved, I thought, for the routine activity.

"Fever, will you talk with me?" The ghost smiled.

I had imagined, when I was younger, a circumstance of this sort a thousand times, where I would blast Satan's Stranger with a litany of questions and demands and accusations. But in the light of that kitchen, I was just too stupefied, paralyzed on a plateau of shock waves—words meant absolutely nothing.

"So, right to the point, then," Mrs. Devilin began. "You never got my diary."

"No." I didn't know where to look. I wasn't certain who had spoken.

"And you don't know where it is." Her voice grew more urgent.

"I don't." I stared at the tabletop.

"My great plan," she sighed and sat back, "was that Thresher would come to you with my diary, and say that it had been my dying wish that you get it, because it told you things you ought to know." She shook out a slight coughing laugh. "Talk about bad timing."

"Bad timing?" I stared at her.

"How was I supposed to know all this would happen?"

"All this?" I had grown to love the repeating response.

"How was I to know that you were fed up with the college life and coming back here to live, for one thing?" She looked around the kitchen. "I always got the impression you hated it up here. Couldn't wait to get out. That's how I felt. That's why I took Thresher over yonder—thought he might have a better chance." A slight shrug lifted her left shoulder. "And how was I supposed to know . . ." She trailed off, suddenly losing her momentum.

The percolator started its familiar sound, June worked around us, setting cream and sugar and little almond cookies out. It was just a normal visit from a kindly old neighbor lady and a visiting professor from Atlanta—a homeboy who had gone to the city, and stayed, and only returned for strange and occasional visits.

I finally let one of the flood of questions find my voice. "Did you come to tell me who my real father was?"

"What?" Her head shot up, her eyes pierced mine, and then she pealed a clear, bell-like laughter. "My God, what difference does that make?"

"What difference—"

"Fuck these people in this goddamned town and their stuck-up ways," she shook her head at June. Then, back to me: "Is that what they've got you to thinking? What the hell difference does that make?"

"You don't think it matters to me—"

"I'm saying," she interrupted again, "that it doesn't *matter*. Period. Maybe you want to know now, but you never would have had the question in your head in the first place if it hadn't been put there by wagging tongues and little minds."

True. But: "So little," I exhaled slowly, "exists in any human mind that hasn't been put there by someone else. That's how we learn. That's why we have teachers."

"You never would have given it a thought," she waved her hand dissmissively, "if these little Christian soldiers hadn't started putting ideas in your head and messing you all up."

Partly true. Still: "But now that it's in my head, it's *there*." I leaned forward. "I have to know the answer."

"Well." She gave a carefree toss of her head, like a girl thirty years younger. "It's just not that easy to answer."

"Why is that?"

"I don't have time," she shifted in her seat, "to spend here on this foolishness. Out of all the millions of questions you could have asked me, this is the thing that you're obsessed with? Look, I aim to be home in bed before midnight. So let me just say this: Around the time you were born, I was seeing three men. Fletcher Devilin I was married to, the Reverend Coombs who taught Fletcher a lot of his magic tricks, and Taylor Bishop, Coombs's friend—but you know him too, now, they say. It could be any one of those three that's your father, and there's the closest I know to tell you." Her voice softened a little. "Naturally, after I heard about everything that you did in college, I always figured it was Bishop that was your dad. He thought you were his, you know. He was very proud of you." She squinted. "I think Thresher was probably one of Coombs's pups, but I never named the father there either—not in public nor on the birth certificate."

"You gave Thresher his own birth certificate," I realized, "so that I'd believe what he was saying."

"That boy was always on some kind of mission from God," she nodded, "and it made him kind of hard to take. He surely did love to sing, though—especially the religious songs. Coombs loved playing the preacher, too, you know—always on some grand adventure, like the one that . . . that Thresh was just on. The one that got him killed." And even though I would never in a million years have predicted it, I thought her eyes moistened for an instant. Then, pointedly: "Though I understand there's some who think he wanted money from you. That's Christians for you: They're always mistaking the fervor of God for the love of money."

"Coffee?" June asked, as if the previous speech had not taken place.

"Thanks," Mrs. Devilin said, with one single sniff.

June poured for me too.

"I guess you could say it's on account of Taylor Bishop that I'm here," the woman went on. "It said in all the papers that you were coming back up here to continue your *research*, especially on the snake bowl in Coombs's church."

"What?" I blinked at her, squeezing my eyes shut for a moment. They were burning and hot.

"That's right—that's all this was about." She sipped coffee genteelly. "At first. It all started just because . . . I sent Thresher here to see you mostly, I reckon, because I didn't want you to be embarrassed."

"Embarrassed?" My voice seemed gravelly, and the coffee burned my esophagus.

"It was just that simple," she confirmed. "I didn't want you spending a lot of time on that thing only to find out what it really was. You're a smart boy. Always were. You would have figured it out eventually, but you would have wasted a lot of time on it, and I thought I could help you out." She stared down into her coffee cup. "Too little too late from a mother that still don't know the first thing about being a mother. My pride; my fault. You always said you were more interested in stories and songs than all that *stuff* anyway, and I just thought . . . I thought I could help." She set her cup down. "That's what I get for thinking I could help anybody."

"I don't understand." I looked to June for help, but June's face was sour ice. "What did you have to tell me about the *bowl*? What's that got to do with anything?"

"The damn thing's a put-up job, Fever." Her voice was filled with a righteous fierceness. "It was for the rubes. Bishop made it up."

Christ, I thought, *there ought to be thunder or an earthquake or some sort of blinding flash.* The implications of the thing she had just told me shook the foundation of my life, a cornerstone of south-eastern folklore research, and my own personal wading pool at the edge of the universal unconscious.

But instead of a heavy downward string section spiraling chord, all I heard in my head was a little voice—a voice that had been growing steadily louder for the previous few days. It was saying, *I thought so.*

"Poor old Bishop," Mrs. Devilin went on, oblivious—as she always had been—to my internal storms and strife. "He didn't find anything remotely interesting to study up here. He was kind of lazy, and usually drunk, so after a while he just made something up." She shook her head. "We all thought it was kind of funny at the time. Bishop knew some people took up serpents here abouts, that much was true. So he came up with the idea when he and his pal Coombs were drunk one night. That's what they did best in those days: drink. Still, Coombs was one of the most remarkable sideshow magicians I ever saw, especially up close. Fletcher and me, we knew him from the show circuit over several years. He taught Fletcher so much about misdirection and making things disappear. Anyways, Bishop and Coombs figured to start something. For Coombs, it was a way to get off the road—or maybe it was just a good joke. He liked it here." She gave another harshly evaluating look around the kitchen. "God knows why, but he decided to stay. For Bishop it was more important: something big to set him up in the college world, so he could keep his job and his reputation."

"And they got Shoo Walters," I said, "to help them make it."

"That's right. I knew you'd figure that much out. Bishop said that anybody looking at it would reckon on modern tools right off. But you know how Shoo is about that old crap."

205

"So." I could barely focus my mind on the next question. "The only reason you sent Thresher to find me was to give me your diary—still fostering the misconception that you were dead—so that I would know that the Serpent Bowl was a fake."

"Doesn't matter now." She leaned across the table. "What matters now, Fever, is that you find out who killed Thresher. I don't care what you think of him—or me. He was your bother, and you have to get the one that killed him." She sat back. "I reckon it to be the some person that killed Shoo."

"Yes." My eyes were steel.

"Oh." She seemed to read something in my expression, and the color of her eyes seemed to change. "You know who it was, don't you?" She stayed very still, holding her breath, waiting for an answer.

"I have an idea."

"You know who did this?" June froze too. "Who is it?"

"Well, who's the one," Mrs. Devilin sneered, turning to June, "that's most involved with this thing now? Who stands to be hurt the most if the truth comes out now? Why the hell do you think I chose this house to make myself known, June? It's your husband that did it. It's Hek."

June nearly fell to the floor. She put her hand on my shoulder and I stood to help her into a chair.

"It's not!" She stared helplessly between the other two people in the room, then her eyes fell on mine. "It's not Hek. Tell her it's not, Fever."

"What a thing to say." I remained standing, and looked at no one. "I'm not saying any more about this to anyone. Too much gossip and innuendo—it's gotten in the way so badly I nearly couldn't see at all—it was like a blind fog."

"Tell her, Fever," June's voice was a whisper.

I looked at Mrs. Devilin. "I don't know who you are. I have nothing to tell you, and you have nothing to tell me. I know you're not my mother, no more than the woman I've created in my mind—partly out of my own memories and partly out of other people's gossip—is my real mother. I am an orphan—and believe it or not, that's a very enviable thing to be, because it is absolutely unfettered. That's all. And I thank you for it."

Both women stared at me. I would have stared at myself if I'd been another person in the room. After all the years of wondering and wanting, cursing and praying, hoping and hating—that was all I had to say to the woman.

"Perhaps there is one question you could answer," I told her, taking a menacing step in her direction, "as an antidote for all the others that will never be spoken—if you even remember or know the answer."

"What is it?" She stared back at me, expressionlessly.

"I recently found dried Cherokee roses in the hiding place in your room."

Her face warmed like the sun, and would have melted a heart of granite. "Those roses." Her fingers darted to her eyes for an instant, as if she'd been struck there by a sudden point of light. "You don't remember? I sent you to gather those for me the day you went off to college." She shook her head. "That's the last thing I ever put in my special place. Not too long after that day, I left the house for good. I can't believe they're still there." She tried, but failed, to look me in the eye. "That means something, I guess."

This was the only hint I would ever have, I thought, of a mother's love. All the years of standing in the darkness of the hallway, watching her, praying she would see me—wanting a mother—paraded, mocking, past the window of my eyes.

And my only response to her implied and glancing affection was to feel the urge to get on with the work at hand. Some things that have grown cold during a long night will never warm again; certainly not in so mere a suggestion of sunlight. Some things will stay dead, even when hope and the promise of a certain kind of life urge them from beyond the grave. Some things that have taken a lifetime to destroy cannot be built back in a single, strange moment in a kitchen on a mountain in the first days of autumn.

Sometimes all that remains is weary work, and a determination to see that work through.

"Skidmore and Andrews are up at the Hearth now, June," I said coldly, "and I need to go. Are you going to be all right?"

"All right?" She glowered up at me. "No I'm not going to be all right. This *woman* has no right to come into my house and accuse my husband . . ." she shot a fiery gaze in the direction of the other person at the table, but continued to talk only to me. "You get that woman out of my house!"

Mrs. Devilin stood. "I think I'll be going now."

"You should never have come back from the dead!" June hissed.

"Sometimes the dead," she said to me as she drew her brown sweater around her, "just can't stay dead."

"Get her out of here, Fever!" The pitch of June's voice had grown high, and howling, and barely human.

But Mrs. Devilin needed no urging from me. She headed for the back door.

"You go, too," June said to me. "You go up there to that awful place and you find out what there is to find out. Then you tell her it wasn't Hek, you hear?"

"Fever." Mrs. Devilin looked at me. "Don't see me out," she told me, even though I hadn't moved to do so. "You just keep on thinking of me as a ghost. That's what I want to be, and that's what you want me to be."

"Why would I want you to be dead?" My voice was as black and cold as the grave.

"You don't need to trouble yourself with me," she said, soft as an angel's wing. "You're a grown man. You don't need a mother. Alive, I'm a stone in your belly. You were better off thinking I was dead— that was my idea. If I'm dead, you can go on with living. You're the kind to chain hisself to the past. Let it go. It's the ending of the year, and I'm just one more falling leaf. You don't want to get to know me, or to find out who I really am. Fact is, there's nothing much to know." Then, utterly incongruously, I thought, she smiled again. "My gift to you is nothing but a wild tale. Sorry as I am at being your mother, I surely did spin you a good story for your life. And look how you turned out: You're a mess, but it's a fine mess, and I'm proud, because you are *all kinds* of interesting. That's not much for a mother to give you, but it's got to be good for something."

And she instantly stepped out through the doorway, vanishing— something from a scene out of her old magic act. The door closed; she started the car up and drove away before I took another breath. In my mind I heard my father's voice—or the voice of the man who raised me: "She's vanished, brother. Or was she ever really here at all?" Which was all I could ever think about my mother.

June collapsed on the table, her head on her arms.

I put my hand on her shoulder.

Without looking up, she spoke to me. "You go on now. You get to work. You fix this. Finish it tonight!"

"I don't want to leave you in this condition," I began.

Her head lifted. "I survived the dying of my own baby—and even my own death, they say." Her voice was soft. "I reckon I can get through this."

I stood a second longer, and felt the strength in her voice pour over me.

I was out the door and into my truck in seconds. My mind was a red cauldron. My heart was as cold and dead as the distant moon. The engine roared. I careened out onto the black road, squealing tires and spitting back dirt—into the Hellmouth of night: toward the Devil's Hearth.

Twenty

Even though I tried to hold them back, memories flooded my mind like the icy torrents that plunged down from the high rocks. I sped through the sullen air, somehow thinking that the truck might outrace my mind. But image after image of my parents played in the theater of my head, looped and twisted, Mobiuslike and dreaming. There were disappearing boxes, loud raucous songs, eerie shadows made by the footlights—a vile serpent twining up the forbidden tree of my mother's leg.

Then, as if I'd hit a deer on the highway, a memory so clear and sharp slammed my entire body, and it caused me to stab my brakes and squeal off the road. I skidded onto the shoulder and nearly down a steep embankment.

I stared at that memory, the internal vision, as if it were a picture taped to my dashboard. It was of a night so long ago, when I was a child and I had been playing hide-and-seek at someone else's house—the night I had just told Andrews about. It materialized before me like a magic-lantern show. I was hidden in the woods, not near the house, and I heard angry voices. I drew closer, and found myself nearly at the edge of the church property, Hek's church—only before Hek was a preacher. I could clearly see the Reverend Coombs arguing, then wrestling, with a man who had his back to me. There was a vicious struggle, and a sudden pop. The man with his back to me stood, and Coombs was covered in blood. The other man lumbered a step or two, then stared down at the body. I was frightened out of my wits—I was certain the man standing was my father, though I didn't know why, I still couldn't see his face.

I ran like an animal back toward the house. The group inside had just begun to sing "The Great High Wind" and I raced inside to tell everyone what I'd seen, but when I got to the doorway of the parlor, there was my father, sitting in the midst of the group, smiling and singing, and it so disoriented me that I couldn't speak for a time. I thought perhaps, somehow, I'd imagined the entire scene. That's when he called me over and told me it seemed to him that I'd been called into the house, away from play, by the music.

Just as suddenly as it gripped me, the vision left. Somewhere in the other world, where dreams and visions are controlled and scheduled, a strange administrator had waved a hand, and I was ripped from the scene of my childhood, and thrown backward into my future life. I was staring down the embankment and my truck had stalled.

All I could think was that the shock of seeing my mother had served as the catalyst for such a revelation, so long buried in the cemetery of my thoughts. I took a moment to consider how right all my friends had been to suggest that therapy might, in fact, be a good thing for me. Then I started the truck.

Even though I knew I would have to deal with these memories in more depth later, at that moment they only seemed to confirm a growing theory: The recent murders on Blue Mountain were connected to my personal past, and to another more secret murder long ago.

After a few moments of spinning my tires and rocking the truck, I managed to get it back on the highway and I headed up toward Blue Mountain. The fog was confounding, and the high beams barely cut into it at all. Still, I slowed when I thought I might be getting close to the turn up the backside of the mountain toward the Devil's Hearth, and I didn't miss it.

The way was rocky and very steep. The truck shuddered in second, and I shifted down to first just to make it to the plateau where I thought I could park. It was a small flat surface, the last such level place before the cliffs and the Hearth, a place where we used to park as teenagers, watching stars, making out, scaring each other with stories about the haunted place not far above. The place was empty.

Skidmore, in the Jeep, might have made it to a graded plot five hundred feet further up. It had a clearer view of the whole area and some of the boys from the forestry service used to sit there and fire-watch.

I was certain that my truck could not go further, that it had made a valiant effort to make it as far as it had come. I nudged it the final few feet, and then turned onto a grassy step. The headlights showed the old, dilapidated picnic table, the barely readable sign: SCENIC OVERLOOK. It was left over from the prewar WPA projects in the area. The trees and rhododendrons had grown so much since then that whatever view that the sign had referred to had long since been obscured.

I reached into the glove compartment and grabbed my emergency flashlight. I also found, as if it had been waiting there for me, a small spiral notepad with a stubby pencil shoved into the loops.

Not so much trying to remember as spilling words out onto the page I made a quick list:

antique Luger
Deveroe brothers
and their connection to Hek
Hek's arrests
Trio: Coombs/Thresher/Shoo
phenomenological fields

It wasn't complete and seemed, as I glanced at it, more like bad modern poetry than a list of thoughts. I knew I wouldn't even refer to it again, it's just that the process of writing things down always made them solidify in my mind. I had an odd intuition that I might need that solid foundation before the night was over.

I stepped warily out of the car. For some reason, I locked the doors, utterly uncharacteristically. No one I knew in these mountains ever locked their cars—I never did when I was home. Maybe I'd done it, somehow, because of the fog or the strangeness of the night in general. I didn't even think about it.

I just began to hike up the mountain path. The moon had risen nicely, and despite the swirling fog, everything was flowing eerily—not clearly, the light was diffused, almost dreamlike. To my left I knew that the cliffs fell away, nearly half a mile down, with nothing so much as a shrub or a stone to stop a misstep. The mountainside was nevertheless rich with pines and blackberry brambles and looming boulders larger than a car. To my right there was a sheer granite cliff, decorated with weeping rivulets of mossy water and unearthly lichens, ashen-gray, bone-white, gangrenous. The path before me was well worn but rocky. It was easy to stumble—even the beam of my flashlight only suggested objects; it did not entirely reveal them.

I remembered, then, that Skid had told me to bring along a warmer jacket, and I wished I had taken his advice. The damp air was already chilling me to the marrow. I tried walking faster, partly to keep warm, partly because I was anxious to meet up with Skidmore and Andrews. No matter how sophisticated an adult grows up to be, there was still a child somewhere in the brain who had been raised on violent and terrifying stories about cold foggy nights just like this one.

Unfortunately, it had been five years since I had climbed a mountain of any sort, and my thighs gave out after only a few hundred yards of quick hiking nearly straight up. By the time I saw Skidmore's Jeep, I felt like sitting down more than celebrating. But the urgency of the moment drew me on.

High above, I was beginning to see the eerie glow of the Hearth. It did not give off light, exactly—it was more as if the air itself were mixed with colored illuminations.

I reached the top of the path, and the effect of the phosphorescent lichens was quite disturbing, and disorienting. The color seemed to come from the fog all around me, and the moon's beams only added to the diffusion of the luminescence. I couldn't see anything at all more than fifteen feet in any direction, so I walked very slowly with my flashlight focused mostly on the ground at my feet. It was as if I were suddenly in no place, no time, a white smoke tablet upon which anything might be written. To make the trek even more difficult, the rocks and mosses were slick and slippery. I lost my footing with every third step. I stole my way up the steep path more slowly, stabbing my flashlight into the fog, as if it could lay hold to something firm, something substantial. Even the typical sounds of night seemed stilled by the cotton of that fog, and the only thing I could hear was the struggling of my feet and the gasping of my breath.

At last I came to the end of the incline, and the beginning of the rock outcropping. I looked backward for a second, surveying the way I had come. The path was narrow, and the fall downward was absolutely deadly. Even in daylight and dry conditions, people had been known to plummet from the place.

I stood on a precarious shelf. On a clear day in autumn, I would have been looking on the river valley so far below. I was glad I could not see it, glad of the illusion that everything around me was close.

I gathered my strength, took a breath, and turned forward. There it was, looming, unreal: the Devil's Hearth.

Dramatic upward thrusts of granite and bizarre formations of petrified wood created the genuine illusion of a mammoth fireplace. All around it the rest of the landscape looked like the tumble-down remains of an enormous stone cabin. The rocks were round and covered with mosses; the petrified wood was likewise layered. It seemed as if some giant from the days before humans walked the earth had built a cabin, lived long and lonely, and died in it—that it had never been used since. The illusion was so complete, that around every boulder it seemed possible to find huge bones.

My flashlight pierced as far as the middle of the Hearth, but not beyond to the other side. I knew that there used to be a small trail on the other side. It once headed over the mountain, around to a gentler slope, to a riotous meadow which had been part of the Department of Agriculture's wildflower reclamation project—a place where Lucinda and I had rolled and kissed and watched the summer clouds. But it was impossible to get to the beauty of that meadow without first having to brave the Devil's Hearth.

I hesitated on the rock shelf. I thought that I ought not to venture any further unless I caught sight of Skidmore, who knew the place far better than I did. I knew I should not venture onto the worst part of the rocks. They were treacherous in bad weather, a certain fall.

So I drew the light upward along the thick mantellike formation that had given the place its name, afraid to call out—afraid that the sound of my voice might betray the fear in my chest. I was hoping Skidmore and Andrews would see my light—or that I might even find them, crawling along the crags.

When my light hit the largest boulder I caught sight of movement, but the hulking figure slipped out of the beam and behind the stone. I stood very still. The place was not unknown to bears, drunken teenagers the likes of the Deveroe boys, and other potentially dangerous creatures.

I saw the movement again, just outside my light, and I called out before I could stop myself. "Andrews? Skidmore?"

Thick, wet silence followed, and the movement ceased altogether. I waved my flashlight, trying vainly to make the beam some sort of a threat. All I succeeded in doing was further disorienting myself. I lost my balance and nearly tumbled.

I thought, then, that a bluff might do the trick.

"Oh, there you are," I called out, waveringly. "What are *you* doing up here?"

It was a complete act of hopeless bravado. Not only did I not see anyone, but I had more than five hundred guesses about who might actually have been hiding behind the rock.

But the unsteadiness of my voice had given away the uncertainty in my brain. There was no response.

Gingerly, I took a few steps further on the rocky shelf. I dared not look all the way down to my left. Because of the fog I was certain that I would not see the roiling waters hundreds of feet below, but I didn't want to risk a bout with vertigo in addition to all the other fears coiling in my stomach.

I trained my light directly at my feet, and chose my steps with more care than a man on ice.

Suddenly, just above me to my right, in the rounder rocks above the actual fireplace formation, I heard a knocking. I swung my flashlight wildly in the direction of the sound and lost my footing. I fell hard on my left elbow and hip, slid downward, and scraped my hand raw on the rock before I stopped, sending my flashlight skidding across the Hearth, then straight downward, finally blinking out, soundlessly.

Without any warning, a very large man had thrown his bulk upon me before I could even catch my breath.

I had no time to maneuver or defend myself. He had my jacket in his hands, ripping the shoulder seams, shaking me violently. His face was close to mine for only a second before he threw me sideways and I went sprawling onto the base of the Hearth.

His breathing was labored to an alarming extent, and even

though I was splayed facedown and helpless, he couldn't seem to muster his forces to do me any further harm.

I'd had the wind knocked out of me by the fall, and I was having difficulty getting a breath myself, but I tried to draw my knees under me and turn to face my attacker. Before I was completely turned, he spoke, and his voice froze me in half-motion.

"That was close, Mr. Devilin. You nearly went tumbling." His voice was punctuated by heavy breathing. "I was afraid you might go over the side. They've always told me it's quite a way down, although you'd have no way of knowing that tonight." He stopped for more breathing. "I've never been up here before, myself. Quite a spot."

I finally found the muscles I needed to turn and sit up. He was right beside me, in his old, familiar greatcoat. He could not seem to catch his breath. By the weird, ambient glow of the lichens on the rocks, I could see that he was smiling—it was the smile of a demon.

"Hello, Fever."

"Dr. Bishop." I exhaled wearily, and struggled to sit up. I did not smile back. "I was hoping not to find you here."

Twenty-One

As far as I could tell, he looked much the same as the last time I'd seen him. He had thick, wiry-gray hair. His eyes were deep-set. His jaw was solid and his shoulders were broader than most. He'd added some weight to his already substantial frame, but otherwise he was the image of the legendary man I'd first met years ago at Burrison University. It even seemed that the long black greatcoat he was wearing was the same one he'd always worn.

"Ah. 'Hoping against hope,' don't they say?" His voice was still lively. "I love that." He was beginning to recover from his exertions, though he did not move. "I thought you'd be happy to see me. It's been a while."

"It has." How had I managed to make my voice colder than the stones? "And it's *Doctor* Devilin, actually."

"Now, correct me if I'm wrong," he continued pleasantly, "but didn't I just save your life? Isn't that the sort of thing for which people often find themselves grateful?"

"Of all people, I thought you might realize that any set of phenomena is devoid of any valuation," I intoned, "save the interpretations we bring to them ourselves. That's what you taught me, at any rate."

"So I did." He continued to beam at me very warmly, but the green glow only made his expression more menacing. "Still my prize pupil."

"I hope not," I muttered.

"What?" His voice lost a little of its twinkle. "Why would you say a thing like that?"

"Because I had hoped, tonight," I began, exhaustedly, "that I was a poor scholar in some regard. I was hoping that I'd assembled the facts incorrectly—and that I'd come to a faulty conclusion." I was suddenly more tired than I could ever remember being. "I still hope I'm wrong."

"Well." His buoyancy returned, and he settled into a more comfortable sitting position, tapped my knee with the back of his hand, and assumed his familiar, parental professor's voice. "Let's see if you are. Let's discuss."

I felt a churning in my stomach, an aching in my marrow. I hated the sound of that voice. There sat a man who, for all practical—if not, in fact, biological—purposes, was my father. All my thinking processes owed more to him than to any other person alive. My odd assessment of phenomenological fields, a bizarre obsession that took the place of most of my emotions, was almost exclusively inherited from him. The Freudian interpretation of all folk culture, though certainly not his invention, was something he had driven into me when I was at the perfectly impressionable age of seventeen. And in some way, however limited, he had loved my mother. Those three things combined to give him an almost certain claim of parentage. Still, I refused to think of him as my father, and I would not play the part of his student.

"What are you doing here?" I opened.

"Hm." He approved, palm to his cheek. "Good first question. I suppose 'vacation' would be a useless ruse. Let me think for a moment." He closed his eyes. "I'm sterilizing the field." Eyes open wide. "How's that?"

"Yes." I kept my eyes locked on his face, and I was unable to breathe. "That's exactly what I feared most."

" 'Feared' " He seemed genuinely puzzled. "Why?"

My mind was racing. What to tell him? What to hold back? Where were Skidmore and Andrews? I feared for their safety. How insane was this man? Was there anything left of the teacher I had known? Or was the person I had always known only a mask? Was I seeing who and what he truly was for the very first time in our long history?

"Do you even realize," I began, caution to the wind, "what you mean when you use a phrase like 'sterilizing the field'? What you're really saying when you use it in this context is that you've murdered two people." I let the coldness of my voice mingle with the fog, then added, "Or three, including Coombs." Whether that was another gambit, another bluff, or an actual accusation—I didn't even know.

"Christ." He growled and shoved himself laboriously forward. "What are you talking about?"

"I'm talking about you," I spit. "I wish I weren't. I came up here thinking I might find Hezekiah Cotage, though I didn't want to find him either. Perhaps I was most hoping to find the benighted Deveroe brothers."

"Who?" His voice was losing its shine.

"At the very least I thought I might stumble across evidence of some sort. But all the time, in the back of my mind, in a hiding place, I was afraid I'd find you here. It wasn't conscious. I didn't even know it until I saw your face. It was a hypothesis that was supported by all the facts, but one I was unwilling to admit." I shook my head bitterly. "And why would you shoot into Skidmore's house with all his children . . . you know you nearly killed Girlinda."

"You're babbling," he began. "What are you talking about? Who are all these people? You've lost your thread of reasoning, Fever."

"No." I stopped him. "I'm stalling."

"Stalling?"

Good, I thought. *The repeat-response works for him too. He doesn't know what to say, or what to think about that.*

"While I gather all my thoughts," I lied.

"Then tell me exactly what you're trying to say, why don't you?" His voice had grown irritated, but it was the scholar's ire at faulty study. "We'll examine it together." As we had done when I was his student.

But I could tell—was it an intuition or was it a result of all the years I had known the man?—that he was really saying: "Let's see how much you really know about all this—and then I'll deal with you properly."

Not many people would have heard the menace in his voice, but I was a dutiful son, and knew that voice too well. I'd heard it many times before: years of scholastic challenges, dozens of encounters defending dissertations and papers. And always behind the ruse of pedagogy I'd heard the voice of self-doubt in his words. I knew he harbored fears that I actually might know more than he, and later that I might engage his students better than he ever did. And I had just come to realize that he had always dreaded that I might discover that he was, in fact, an utter charlatan.

So I chose my words carefully, harboring hopes that if I spoke slowly and carefully enough, two things might happen: He might be disarmed by his own self-doubt; and Skidmore and Andrews might eventually come back to where we were sitting.

I knew I could never subdue him by myself. Especially since I suspected that somewhere in the pockets of that huge black coat he might have a pistol—a vintage Luger—loaded and ready.

"Where to begin?" I mustered a wry expression, I thought, leaning back on one elbow.

"You tell a story better than that." He sat up, matching my tone exactly. "You know where to begin."

" 'Chapter one: I am born.' " I nodded.

"Oh for God's sake."

"You don't think that's appropriate?" I looked out into the vague white air. "I know all about you and my mother."

"All about what?" But his voice was losing a little of its swagger.

"I know that you and Coombs and Fletcher—all three—knew her quite well. Around the time I was born."

"If you're suggesting—"

"I don't see the point of denying it now," I went on. "It's all in the diary." That was my biggest bluff so far. I wanted to see what he'd have to say about that.

"It's . . ." he began, then took a deep breath and collapsed onto his back, staring upward. "So you do have the diary after all. I was convinced he had hidden it up here somewhere. That would be about Thresher's speed, from what I've heard of the boy. He would have thought it would have been so . . . poetical."

"Actually," I enunciated searingly, "I have no idea where the diary is. I don't have it; I've never seen it. But you've just answered the first of a series of questions I have on the subject."

He only took a second to recover. "Very good, Fever. Bravo."

"Still, I know all the secrets it contains." I knew he wouldn't be tricked that way again, so I plowed on in earnest.

"No you don't." He was firm on that point.

"Let's start at the beginning, then, shall we?" I darted my eyes back to the path that led to where Skid's car was, hoping I might catch a glimpse of aid, but the fog was too thick, and I could barely see past the edge of the Hearth.

"Go on," Bishop said impatiently.

"Some thirty-five years ago you were just beginning to build a folklore department at the university. You were doing field research, but you weren't very good at it. You were much better at drinking the local illegal beverage and stealing other men's wives."

"This is a harsh supposition." His voice coiled sarcastically, hissing to strike.

"You wasted the university's time and money," I went on, "maybe even a series of grants, and had nothing to show for it. You weren't merely embarrassed, you were on the verge of losing your job. You had to find something big to redeem yourself. Something big. So you came up with a cheap parlor trick. You invented it one drunken night, in the company of a sideshow huckster."

"Coombs was more than that," he cautioned me. Then, still dripping with irony: "God rest his soul."

"The problem was," I barreled on, piling guess upon intuition, "that your invention was too big. It was too unbelievable. No one would have bought the idea that an object of such ancient origins would have just appeared here in these hills, so you had to come up with the odd story of the 'Reverend' Coombs having found the thing in Scotland." I shook my head. "You should have rethought the design then."

"I agree I should have," he shot out impatiently, the way he always did when I got something wrong. "That wasn't the real problem. You're forgetting the historical context. Remember that we're talking about a time, really, before computer research, when folklore was essentially, for all practical purposes, still a nineteenth-century discipline. The *Golden Bough*, Child's ballad categorizations, Thompson's motif index—these were still the dominant sources of the day. We were an arcane bunch." He sipped a little breath. "And people were more trusting then. It was a better time."

I was a little surprised that he hadn't even bothered to protest the idea that the thing was a fake. I suppose he might have thought he'd taught me too well to be fooled.

"Still, something happened." My voice had gathered momentum. "After a few years, Coombs wanted to get out of the deal, and you had a violent argument about it." I took a deep breath. "And you killed him."

I didn't know what effect that accusation would have on him. The professor I thought I had known would simply have nodded and considered it an interesting hypothesis, one among many to consider. But the man beside me on those cold stones—I wasn't certain I knew that man at all, or what he might do.

"You're baiting me again." He seemed delighted. "That won't work twice, you should have guessed."

I didn't bother mentioning that I had, in fact, already guessed that.

"I'm not baiting you," I told him simply. "I saw you do it."

The silence was more palpable coming after words of that ilk. Fog swirled, milky moonlight shifted, the green glow seemed to pour something foul over everything—nothing was real.

"I remember the evening quite well, actually." I started to tell him about my shocking and near-fatal recollection of that very event on the highway only a short time before, then thought better of it. "I was playing hide-and-seek, and I heard you arguing. I came to the edge of the wood, and saw you wrestle, heard the gun go off, saw you walk away." I tried to ready my muscles, in case he got it into his mind to attack me in some manner because of my prodding.

"So, you expect me to believe that you saw a thing like that and never told anyone?" His voice was utterly foreign.

"I thought you were my . . . I thought you were Fletcher." My throat weakened. "I ran back to the house to tell everyone, but Fletcher was already there, singing in the parlor. It confused me. I thought I'd imagined it all—"

"My God." His short, chopping laughter echoed out across the stones. "You had trauma amnesia." He shook his whole body heartily. Even under the circumstances, I still had to admire his piercing intellect, his immediate grasp of the facts. "Classic." He reached out and gently, even warmly put his hand on my shoulder. "You really ought to find a therapist."

"Well," I responded wryly, "at least we can all agree about *something.*"

"What made you remember it? When did you remember it? How did you come to the conclusion that I was the man you saw? Tell me everything." He dropped his hand back to his lap.

"Perhaps some other time," I told him. "I'm anxious to move on to the rest of the story."

"Sorry. Do go on." Odd manners dripped from his words.

"You thought that killing Coombs would end it—" I took up.

"End what, again?" he interrupted, feigning confusion.

"Your fears of being exposed as a total fraud." I tried to soften the import of the words, but the sentence still seemed too hard.

"You don't know how far off-track you are," he hissed suddenly. "Especially about Coombs—but please continue. This is amusing."

"Here's your psychology," I continued, trying to ignore his increasing menace. "It's the psychology of anyone who is basically a good person but does some inexcusable deed: You wanted to get caught."

"Textbook clichés." He waved his hand. "They do you *such* a disservice . . ."

"You wanted to get caught," I pressed on, "so you steered me—your image, your younger self, your alter ego, your own son—into the very field of endeavor that would lead me to discover your sham. You trained me in folklore research, you fostered in me an intense curiosity about the folk community, you even goaded me into being interested in doing the research here in my own home, the snake-handling churches, for God's sake. I only wanted to study the music—"

"Any idiot can tape-record folk songs in a kitchen, Fever." He was genuinely disgusted. "You needed to distinguish yourself in the academic world. Hackneyed reiterations of second-rate commentary on the nature of the 'folk song,' Christ—that was no way to *excel.*"

"Why did you even bother with me in the first place?" I tried to overwhelm him with the suddenness of the question. "I would never have known that Fletcher was not my father."

"But I would have," he said, his voice momentarily hoarse.

Yes. The ego. The subjective perspective. And that admission only reinforced, somehow, my thought that he actually longed to be found out.

"So, to return to the point," I muddled on, trying not to think too much, "you shouldn't dismiss my theory that you wanted to get caught."

"But I do dismiss it." He sighed heavily. "There was nothing to *catch*."

"Nothing? Then why all the panic when I began my series of articles last year about the Serpent Bowl in the *Journal of American Folklore*?"

"Panic?" What was in the repetition of *that* word?

"Isn't that when you began your move," I stated plainly, "to shut down the folklore department?" Might as well try out a few of Andrews's theories as well, I thought. Especially since I was beginning to agree with them.

"What?" he thundered. "You can't possibly think that I would want to shut down my own department?"

"That's just the thing," I shook my head. I knew his denial was a lie. I could tell from the hesitation in his voice. "It wasn't your department anymore. It was mine."

"Same thing. Jesus." I couldn't tell if the sound of his voice held affection or arrogance.

"Forging ahead," I rambled, "you thought that if I spent any real time researching the bowl, I'd discover that it was a fake, and your life's work, your reputation, your place in the textbooks—all wiped out. Then came my articles a year ago, questioning them. So you panicked."

"And only a moment ago you told me I *wanted* to get caught," he shook his head. "Now you tell me I was—what?—working overtime *not* to get caught?"

"Classic double bind." I shifted a little in his direction, still tensed, in case he might attack. "The irony is, Andrews was the first to postulate the problems with the damned bowl, not me. And I was so loyal to you that I dismissed the possibility without even thinking about it at first."

"Loyalty is a fine trait," he said plainly.

"The problem ultimately was that I could not ignore the mass of evidence for long. I realized that Andrews had not even considered that you and Coombs might have created the fabrication. He only suspected fakery, and thought it was the product of pranksters in Scotland."

"It might have been." He was testing me.

"But it wasn't." I dismissed that thought outright. "And by the time I . . . received the information in the diary, it only confirmed what I had already suspected."

"How could you *receive* information in the diary without talking to Thresher or reading the thing, which you haven't done?" He shook his head, lying there, staring upward, blankly.

"I'll get to that in a moment. First I was hoping you might tell me," I pressed, "about the actual symbols on the bowl? What made you choose something so outrageously ancient, and then gloss over that fact in the articles?"

"Let's say a young, imaginative academic," he drawled laconically, "wanted to invent something upon which to forge a reputation. His first impulse might be to create something astronomical—because he *is* young and because he has no subtlety—something that would turn the academic world on its ear. But let's say he has a friend who understands the value of understatement, the power of obscurity. Then our young—and I may add: entirely hypothetical—academic might begin to appreciate the grandeur of mysterious notoriety. As opposed to glaring stardom."

"Especially if you'd created something," I pushed, "so astonishing that it would bring a great deal of attention and scrutiny."

"Precisely. So I changed my tack from the bowl itself to the bowl's effect." He locked me in a grotesque gaze. "And that's how I educated you."

"So your articles became more and more experiential than observational." I was deliberately drawing out my case, still stalling for time. "That's very interesting. You were obscuring your blunder."

"You seem to have more to say." Suspicion edged his voice.

I wanted to lower the boom, hammer him with accusations, beat his head with a bludgeon of questions. How much of that impulse was left over from my encounter with Mrs. Devilin I couldn't be bothered to consider in those moments on the Hearth.

"No, I think I've just about concluded this business in my own mind," I answered softly.

"I doubt that," he finally said, sounding very good-natured. "I scarcely know which of your significant errors to correct first."

"What if we approach it this way, then?" I answered him quickly. "Look me in the eye and tell me why you were trying to kill me."

Shock, I thought, might provoke him.

"Trying to kill you?" For the first time, he seemed genuinely perplexed. "What are you talking about?"

"You thought you were shooting at me when you killed Thresher."

"What?" More sincere incredulity flooded his words. "I knew that was Thresher."

The old Bishop, my mentor, my friend, would never have been tripped up in so simple a net of words—would never have admitted to what his sentence had suggested.

It seemed to me that he realized what he'd said a second or two after he'd spoken. I could see the play of emotions on his face, even in that grim light, and then another one of his effete grins plastered itself there.

"You know," he began calmly, "if I weren't so tired, you'd *never* have gotten me to this point."

"No." I glared at him. "I don't know that."

"I'm tired, Fever," he said again, and for the first time—perhaps my eyes were finally adjusting to the weird light—I saw the circles under his eyes, and the deep wrinkles on his brow. "I haven't slept well in a great many months."

"When did you come back to the States?" My voice softened, almost imploringly. "How long have you been up here?"

"Up here? In these mountains? Not long. Back in the States—what?—half a year? I think." He heaved a sigh so heartbreaking I nearly forgot the rest of the world. "Now, then. Since it seems you believe I killed Thresher, let me just say that I never, at any time in my life, confused the two of you. Thresher was Coombs's boy."

I could see that he'd brought up the subject deliberately to throw me off balance. But that knowledge did nothing to save me from being utterly disintegrated by what he had said.

"Coombs?" *If only the repeat-response had some sort of rescue effect attached to it*, I thought.

"So." I knew that look on his face. I'd given something away to him. I could tell. He leaned back, and seemed to relax for the first time in our meeting. "You really don't have the diary."

"I *told* you that I didn't . . ." I began, but he waved his hand to stop me.

"It isn't that I know exactly what's in the goddamned diary, you know," he continued.

I was completely off balance. He had the upper hand. So I played for an aggressive strike of my own. "So then why would you bring up Coombs now? Unless his death was no accident."

His face betrayed nothing.

"I could buy that Coombs's death was accidental," I pressed, packing my voice with venomous irony. "You struggled, the gun went off—just like in the movies."

"The thing of it is," Bishop told me slowly, his right hand moving to his coat pocket, "Coombs really was an accident. You have no idea."

"I think I do. I saw it. It looked like an accident."

"No," he said, gazing into the fog, "you have no idea what the argument was about." He looked me in the eye, and his face was filled with questions. "Even after all we'd been through, he and I—everything we'd fabricated—not to mention his life as a . . . what did you call him? A sideshow huckster? Even after all that . . ." Bishop shook his head.

"You were arguing about the bowl?" I could not hide my incredulity. "After nine years?"

"No." His face recovered, once again, some of its composure. "Since you brought up the concept of phenomenological fields—even though you seem scarcely to understand the actual concepts involved—let me say this. You're shocked that I created the Serpent Bowl, that it's not 'real,' that it's not 'genuine folk art.' My God. What difference does that make? A thing is real if somebody believes that it's real. That's all it takes. Reality is what you make it."

"People in Coombs's church," I agreed, "they believed the bowl was real. They believed, and still do, that if you wish to take up a snake in the service, you ought first to touch your fingers to the water in the bowl, dab a bit on your lips, the rest into the hands. This prevents the poison from proving fatal to the true believer." I sat back a little, thinking.

"Right," he nodded, "there's the rub. The thing worked—really worked. That was true."

"What do you mean?" I grimaced. "I thought you knew that?"

"That's what *Coombs* thought—that was his problem." Bishop fiddled with something inside his coat pocket with his right hand and came to a partial sitting position. "People dipped their fingers into the water in the bowl, were bitten by rattlesnakes, and didn't die." He shook his head wildly, as if trying to get something out of his mind. "Coombs, on the other hand, suffered from the poison of faith. He couldn't explain it, so he cast his intellect to the wind and reduced himself to the position of an acolyte. I mean, it didn't happen overnight, but Coombs got religion. There came a day—a day you seem to remember quite well—when he wanted to stop lying to his 'flock' and come clean, as it were, about the bowl. Of course, I didn't want him to do that. I tried to convince him that he had come to a time of Nehushtan, the broken bronze serpent figure of Moses. I told him, in short, he ought to just eliminate the snakes altogether." He seemed to rouse himself then from the memory. "In short, we argued, and the gun went off—just like in the movies. The gun went off." His hand darted out of his pocket like lightning, and I was face-to-face with a black pistol. "This gun, in fact."

I hadn't thought about what the gun would look like, the instrument of at least three murders. It was black as thunder and seemed to take light away from everything around it. The hand that held it looked darker than the rest of Bishop's body. And it looked familiar—I had the idea that it might be the gun I had found in my mother's hiding place so long ago.

"I can't say this hasn't been entertaining," he continued casually, "especially all the mistakes you've made—they were very amusing. But all good things must come to an end. Since you don't really have the diary, I need to continue my search for it. I followed Thresher up here when he first came to town. I was certain I'd seen him hide it up here. I intend to find it tonight. Now—you're just in the way." He sat fully up.

"You murdered Thresher," I stalled, trying to grasp the enormity of his actions, "just because you *thought* he would talk to me? Even if he didn't give me the diary?"

"All right." He was giving nothing more away.

"So you didn't mistake him for me." I tensed, ready to jump. "You were really trying to kill him."

"Haven't I already said that?" He leaned to his left, rolling to stand. "Get up."

"So why were you trying to kill me the other night?" I didn't move.

"I don't know what you're talking about." He twitched the gun. "Get up, now."

"So," I took a deep breath. "You're willing to kill me."

"A man like me, Fever," he said lightly, as if he were discussing superficial philosophy at a cocktail party, "has very little in his life save his reputation. You know how the academic community is: Everyone wants you to fail, even your friends. Achievement, excellence, accomplishment of any sort—these are viewed with extreme suspicion. They're even, ultimately, frowned upon in the general scheme of things—no one really wants anything superior in the university world. And yet excellence is the only coin of the realm, the only real power. It is a hellish dung pit of poisonous, flesh-eating vipers, the university is. Now if you don't get up I'll just shoot you in the hand or the arm to encourage you to move."

I rocked forward, my mind racing for anything that would forestall what seemed to be the inevitable. "Shoo was a different from that," I said. "That was your biggest sin. Shoo helped you to make the bowl, but he would never have told anyone about it. You never realized how close-mouthed he was, you never understood him—"

"Be that as it may. Damn." He tapped the gun on his thigh impatiently. "Shoo knew everything." He blew out his breath wearily. "Everything."

"What do you mean 'everything'?" I got slowly to my feet, every muscle screaming for me to jump. Still—I had to have answers. "How could he have known everything?"

"I saw him talking with Thresher one night. Between the two of them . . ." He let the sentence finish itself.

I paused for a second to think about this shadow of a human

being hiding in the woods while Shoo and Thresher sat quietly in front of my house.

"Only for a moment or two on the porch," I said. "Shoo told me all about it."

"Well." He tossed the gun cavalierly, waving it in the air. "Not *all* about it. They spent more than a moment. They spent the entire evening together drinking, smoking cigarettes, laughing—"

"Camels!"

"What?" he was momentarily startled.

"Damn damn damn." I shook my head. "Just something I should have thought to add to a list I was making a moment ago."

"Lists," he smiled. "Still making lists the way you did when you were an undergraduate? I remember that about you. I don't see why you ever did it. You never looked at them. What's this about camels?"

"Camel unfiltered cigarettes," I told him. "Shoo left crushed-out butts in my house, but I didn't make the connection until just now. He *did* spend time in the house." I stared at him. "You do realize that you've single-handedly wiped out an entire tradition?"

"Shoo Walters's death, you mean? And that's more important to you," he goaded, sneering, "than the death of an old friend?"

"You know that's not what I'm saying." *Jump—rush him.* But the rats in my brain still had to have more information to eat, still had to know more.

"Isn't it?" He checked the pistol, making certain the safety was off. "Shoo told me he had convinced Thresher to hide the diary up here at the Hearth—that no one would find it up here."

"Shoo told you this?" I didn't believe it.

"Yes, but when I saw you videotaping him—"

"You what?" I knew that my fear showed through that small net of words.

"Oh," he said casually, "I've been monitoring your activities for some time. Ever since I've been back in the States, actually. I followed you around Atlanta, and I came up here with you. When I saw you videotaping Shoo, I began to suspect you might be trying to get information as well as 'folklore' out of him. That would be just like you."

"But if Thresher had hidden the diary up here," I asked, pouring out genuine confusion, "why did you ask Shoo—"

"Because Thresher was dead," he interrupted impatiently, the way he always had in class. "Shoo was the only one who might have been able to help me find the thing—it being his idea to hide it in the first place."

"But why would he?" I shifted my weight. "Why would he help you?"

"Well," he began, "you know how simple the man was. I told him we needed to find the diary so that we could give it to you—so you could know all the secrets it contained. He did it for you."

"But . . . why did you kill him, then," I whispered, and found that the words were attached to a small sting of tears, "before you found what you were looking for?"

"He was foolish enough to attack me." Bishop slid his finger into the trigger ring. "I don't know why. I wouldn't have thought it possible that he could figure out what was really going on, but once we were up here, he came at me. I pulled this gun. He was very close." He let out a little breath through his nostrils. "I have to confess, though, I really didn't expect to see you up here tonight. I hadn't planned . . ."

But he didn't finish his thought.

There were voices coming from the direction of the far side of the Hearth—where the wildflower meadow was.

He instantly lowered his voice to a whisper. "If you call out or make any sort of noise, I'll shoot you this moment and take my chances with whomever that is."

"I thought you were going to shoot me anyway," I answered, more boldly than I felt.

"Maybe, on second thought, I'd better just throw you over the side," he whispered. "That way there's no dead body to worry about because the word is that the water of that river down there, it just takes you away. No messy cleanup afterward." He glanced in the direction of the voices, then toward the edge of the cliff. "Go on."

"You imagine I'll just toss myself over the side?" My voice was steady and at a normal volume. "Not tonight."

I was certain that Skidmore and Andrews would appear any

instant, and then Bishop would not be able to do a thing. He must have seen in my face something that indicated my confidence.

"You're awfully calm for a man in your position." He glanced again in the direction of the nearing voices. "Oh. Is it because of that noise—those voices? You think you know who's coming?" His smile was really quite reptilian. "You're wrong, you know. I've been up here for a while, tonight, you see—and I happen to know that your friends—yes, I recognized Andrews, and the deputy with him is doubtless your childhood chum, what's-his-name—I saw them coming, hid behind that boulder over there, and watched them search." His eyes were black coals. "They're gone now."

"Why couldn't they be coming back?" Then I had a terror that Bishop had killed them, too, and was about to tell me as much.

But in the next instant, as if it were part of a shoddy magic act from another era, the mist parted around the approaching figures, and in the diffused moonlight I saw at once that the voices were coming from the Deveroes—all three brothers.

They saw us immediately as well, and the one in the lead hit another on his arm and they all began running our way, whooping like berserkers.

Bishop—startled by their sudden burst of speed or the bizarre noises they were making—reeled and fired his gun several times wildly into their midst. One of the boys instantly clutched his knee and tumbled onto the rocks with alarming heaviness, dizzyingly close to the edge of the precipice.

The others seemed utterly unaware that one of their number had fallen, and raced on. It seemed obvious to me that they intended to sweep us across the cliff top and over the side. They seemed completely unafraid of the gun, and Bishop began making involuntary fright noises, clutching his chest.

How could I have been so completely wrong? I thought. *The murders were all part of the Deveroe madness, and we're next.*

The thought was something that had always played at the back of my mind. Perhaps we had invaded their territory, somehow, or perhaps we had even stumbled, unaware, on a moonshine still hidden close by. Whatever the cause, the effect seemed certain: They were going to kill us both. Neither Bishop nor I had any hope of outrunning these younger men, and where I had slipped and fallen on the untenable wet surface, they seemed absolutely sure-footed. And utterly insane.

Bishop whirled in my direction, and pointed the gun directly at my face, but it clicked wheezingly, jammed. His expression was nearly as mad as our attackers'; he was white with fear. There was simply no telling what he had in mind.

Instinctively, I flailed my arms in front of me in a ridiculous effort at self-preservation, and I accidentally sent the gun flying. In the second that it took for Bishop to register amazement, I kicked his left leg as hard as I could—an unwise move on my part, as it turned out. Bishop fell forward, effectively tackling me, sending us both plummeting down the slippery rocks and moss—toward the edge, the sheer drop-off.

I tried to speak, to reason, even to beg—but everything was moving too fast. My heart was pounding, and I was gulping air in loud gasps. So was Bishop.

The two Deveroes were suddenly all over us. One of them kicked my arm where I had ahold of Bishop. I let out a yelp and rolled into a ball, letting go of Bishop entirely.

My eyes were closed, waiting for other kicks, other blows, and I was skidding with increasing speed toward the edge of the cliff. I thought I could hear the water below, and the air all around me was filled with the grunting animal noises of the killer boys.

In what I imagined to be my last attempt at life, my eyes flew open and I thrust out my hand, hoping to grab one of my attackers.

A thick arm shot toward me, and I could see I was inches from dropping over the edge. That stumpy arm would provide the final thrust, it seemed, to propel me over the edge and downward into the icy black water so far below.

I cried out just as the arm reached my neck and the wild boy gripped me with both hands, like a vise. I saw, in slow motion, his heavy boots dig into the moss and mud and rock fragments.

Just as my legs tipped over the side, I came to a frozen halt, my feet dangling.

"Hoo," the boy holding me said, grinning. "That's better'n a ride at the fair." He let out a louder whoop. "Don't you move too much, though, Dr. Devilin, hear? I ain't got that good a grip on you, and I don't believe you'd care to go any further down this here hill."

"Pull him up, Dover." The other remaining Deveroe was standing five or six feet to our left, looking over the side into the darkness below, talking to my savior.

"I'm trying," Dover said. "He's heavy."

"I believe," the other continued, "I might have lost mine."

"Cuss!" said Dover, tightening his grip on me. "And double cuss! You mean that one went over? Do you got any idea how mad that's going to make Officer Skidmore?"

"Real mad?" the other ventured.

"Well, come over here and help me reel this one in."

The other lumbered over to us, leaned down, got a handful of my belt and trousers, and lifted me, like a mechanical crane, up, over, and down onto a softer part of the incline.

Dover Deveroe fell back, breathing hard. "You okay, there, Dr. Devilin?"

"You had quite a tumble-down," the other one grinned.

"You like to got shot, too," Dover offered, "it looked like to me."

"Was that some kind of kung fu," the other one said, looking down at me, "that you was using on that man to knock that gun out of his hand? It was real fancy."

"It wasn't kung fu," I said, unable to sit up. "It was panic."

"Pa-Nic," the other repeated, and I couldn't tell if he was making a joke or was really that stupid.

"Are you saying," I addressed him haplessly, "that Dr. Bishop . . . fell over the side?"

"That was his name?" the big boy wondered.

"Yes. Did he?" I managed to make it to one elbow. "Did he go over the side, is that what you said?"

"I'm afraid so."

"Shouldn't we try to get down there, or see if he . . ." but I didn't even bother to finish my thought. I knew he was dead.

Still, Dover apparently felt compelled to put it into words. "He's fish bait now, Doc. What's left of him? That'll come out by the dam down at Split Creek in a day or so."

Suddenly splitting the fog again, someone called my name.

"Dev!"

It was Andrews. I still couldn't see him, but I guessed he must be coming onto the Hearth.

"Andrews?"

"Thank God," he said, mostly to himself. Then he called out in a different direction. "He's here."

The two Deveroes helped me up, and we made it, with some difficulty, back up the slope and onto the rocky shelf of the Hearth. Skidmore and Andrews were there.

"Are you all right?" Andrews took my elbow and helped me to a small flat rock upon which I could sit.

"All right?" I could barely speak. "Not by a long shot."

"I guess not," Andrews nodded, gazing over the side. "This place ought to be roped off or something. Skidmore told me people fall to their deaths from here often."

"Always have." I was getting my breath back slowly.

"Then you ought to be more careful," Andrews scolded, "wandering around up here without a flashlight."

"Well," I glared at him. "I had a flashlight, but I lost it when I took a tumble." I looked around. "Just before Bishop attacked me."

"Bishop?" Andrews froze. "Dr. Bishop is here?"

"Was." I stared toward the precipice. "And he was completely insane."

Skidmore and the Deveroes were gathering.

Dover volunteered the needed information. "Donny let him slip a little, and he went over—that other man that was up here with Dr. Devilin." He turned to me. "His name was Bishop, you said."

The wounded Deveroe came limping up then. "I got shot," was all he said, and very matter-of-factly, I thought.

"Bishop was here?" Andrews was still shaking his head in disbelief.

"Yes," was all I could say at that moment. I looked to Skidmore. "Did you send these boys to my rescue?" I could hardly make my mind accept the thought.

"We're deputies," Dover grinned.

"Unofficial," Skidmore said clearly. "We just ran into them up here about half an hour ago. But I knew we'd need some help scouring this area, and the boys, here, are more familiar—"

"We come up here all the time," Donny interrupted.

"I thought so." I nodded. "You have a moonshine still somewhere up here."

"No, sir," Dover shook his head, a little insulted. "This is where we come to get the snakes."

"Snakes?" *Repeating.*

"Let's get off this damned mountain," Skidmore croaked, "and I'll tell you all about that. Then you can tell me what the hell happened up here."

"What happened," I blew out a heavy breath, "is that I heard the implied confessions of a multiple murderer, and I have absolutely no proof whatsoever to back me up."

"Except maybe this here." The wounded Deveroe fished in his pants pocket. He produced—holding it by the barrel in a very professional manner—the black, antique Luger.

Twenty-Two

The Luger turned out to have belonged to Coombs. It had been remarkably easy to trace—a legacy from his father who had fought in the German army during World War II, when the family name had been Kumpz. I proposed that it had been Coombs, not Bishop, who had produced the weapon on the day I'd seen Coombs murdered, and that the death had actually been accidental.

Ballistics experiments proved conclusively that bullets from the gun had killed Thresher Devilin and Shoo Walters, and had been fired into the Needle household. The gun was also found to have been insured by Bishop over the course of nearly thirty years as a collectible weapon.

Among Bishop's effects that Skid allowed me to see—found at the nearby Dillard House, where he had rented a room under the name of Renard—was a curious set of letters. They were all from doctors—fertility experts—spanning years, telling him that he was, indeed, sterile and incapable of ever fathering a child. What he intended to do with the letters, or why he had them with him at all, would remain a mystery, something to talk about later—with the therapist I would surely soon engage.

I had an odd vision thinking about those letters, though. I saw Fletcher Devilin performing his perennial final trick in the magic show.

It was an easy illusion: turning water to wine. He muttered some religious quotations, things that went with my mother's *Dance of Eve*. Then he'd hold up a clear, empty wineglass, and a plain glass pitcher of water. As he poured the water into the glass, it transformed into wine. All that was required to make this happen in reality were a few drops of red food coloring placed in the bottom indentation of the wineglass.

He would then drink the "wine," break the glass into an upturned top hat on his table, and out would fly a burgundy-colored dove. The dove would circle him three times, land on his arm, and turn snow-white before our eyes.

"All things lose their guilty stains," he would always say, "under the watchful eye of the Father. Good night, children."

I had no idea what the trick meant, only that I found some sort of peace in remembering it.

Since there was only my hearsay evidence—and since, in fact, Bishop had never actually confessed to anything—Skidmore was forced to suggest that the case be marked as unsolved. He had filed all the necessary paperwork that night, after we'd come down from the Hearth, while Sheriff Maddox had slept.

Bishop's body had not been found. Recovery teams waited at the Split Creek dam, but no body had yet presented itself.

Sheriff Maddox had tried, unsuccessfully, to fire Skidmore and to arrest me. But since we were unofficially credited with solving three murders—however coincidentally—his objections were deemed moot. Skidmore began to suggest to Maddox just how questionable it seemed for him to have moved Shoo's body before calling anyone. I went so far as to insinuate that he had been in league with Bishop. When Andrews pointed out, in front of the sheriff, that Maddox didn't have the brains to be in league with spinach, the entire matter was dropped.

No one, of course, asked any questions about the Serpent Bowl in Hezekiah's church, and I naturally volunteered absolutely no information on that subject either—nor on anything else of a more personal nature.

So on the day of the inquest, a particularly brilliant autumn day, when the sun was hot and the breeze was cold and the sky seemed polished like a mirror high above all the world, Deputy Needle, Dr. Andrews, and I were standing outside the courthouse watching the leaves blow like ruby birds all around in the air.

The town square was more or less as it had been when I was a boy. The courthouse, the government buildings, and the mayor's office all surrounded a small park and garden. The obligatory statue commemorating our Confederate dead stood proud and gray— more a memorial to a time before the close of the twentieth century than a testament to long-gone soldiers. Huge trees, hundreds of years old, filled the yard, and underneath were fire-red mums planted in knotty patterns all along the brick walkways. Here and there a bench dotted the grass, some in sunlight, others in shadow.

"No one ever told me, you know," I began to Skidmore as he fished a cigarette out of his coat, "what the Deveroe boys were doing up there on the mountain that night."

"I guess it'd be all right to tell you about it now." He lit his smoke. "Seeing that it's all cleared up."

"They said something about snakes?" I ventured. We began to walk down the steps.

"Yup." Skidmore blew out a breath, making white clouds all about his head. "It was snakes. For Hek."

That stopped me.

"Maybe you heard that I had to run Hek in," Skidmore went on, "a couple of times recently."

"Yes," I nodded, "I'd been wondering about that."

"Some kids—young kids," he went on seriously, "they got bit up at Hek's church in a service one Sunday, fooling around with those damned snakes that he keeps up there. I told him if he didn't get rid of them, I'd arrest him on a reckless endangerment. He didn't believe me, so I had to haul him in once or twice to prove a point."

"I understand," I said.

"You probably don't know this," he drawled to Andrews, "but since that Alabama boy used a rattlesnake to murder his wife back in the thirties it's kind of been accepted, at least around these parts, that snakes can be considered deadly weapons—under certain circumstances." He shook his shoulders. "I personally hate the things."

"Alabama boy?" Andrews didn't know what else to ask.

"His name was Major Raymond Lisenba," Skid went on. "Not a major like in the army, his mother *named* him that: *Major*."

"Some mothers will name their children anything," I offered.

"He changed it to Robert James when he grew to be a man," Skid said, nodding. "I guess on account of how odd his given name was. Some people surely do have funny names."

"I guess," I agreed wryly.

"So anyway, about the snakes." Skid tossed his smoke on the bottom step and crushed it out. "Hek hit on a plan that he thought would make us both happy. He hired the crazy Deveroe brothers to go get rattlers, milk the poison out, pull out the fangs, and sell them to the church."

"But don't the snakes replenish the poison . . ." Andrews began.

"That's right," Skidmore confirmed. "Not to mention that a snake has a hard life in them services, getting batted all over the place. A lot of them don't make it more than a month. So just to be sure, Hek got the Deveroes to supply him on a monthly basis. It was an entirely new business venture for the boys. Providing safe snakes. This all happened while I was gone with Alan Jackson. In fact, that's why they were shooting at us when we were on your front porch the other night."

"What?" I stumbled. "The Deveroes were the ones shooting at us? Not Bishop?"

"Naw, not Bishop." Skid gazed out across the courtyard. "Remember we heard a hunting rifle, not a pistol. Apparently there was a big bag of rattlers under your porch." He reeled his head in Andrews's direction. "They didn't want me to see them on account of the boys have one or two felony convictions, and they knew my thoughts on the subject of snake as weapon. They thought I was there on account of their stash."

"They were shooting at you, not me?" I asked incredulously.

"Yeah. How about that, Fever?" he offered. "Not everything in this entire world is about you."

"And there was a bag of snakes under the porch that night?" I stared, ignoring his jibe.

"Snakes for Hezekiah," Skid answered.

"What made them stop, then?"

"When they moved around to get a better angle on the house," he said, "after we went behind your car? They saw Thresher dead on the steps. They thought they'd killed him."

"Does that have anything to do with when we saw them racing by Gil's the other day?"

"Yeah." Skid was quieter. "They'd come up my way to apologize for shooting at us and to confess to killing Thresher." He shook his head. "But they heard the shooting—Bishop, as it turned out, though I still haven't figured out why—and they took off scared. Weird timing, that's all."

There's more to it than that, I thought.

"Could we get back," Andrews's voice sounded skeptical, "to Hek and this arrangement with these sterile snakes?"

"Hek just told me," Skid said to both of us as we reached the sidewalk, "that he reckoned it didn't matter what the truth of the thing was, as long as the people in his church had the faith—the blessed assurance. Faith is what matters, not miracles. And I agreed."

I thought that to be a fitting inheritance from the man who had invented the church and from the object the church housed. The truth was only more shards of painful knowledge best left unrevealed.

The bowl was a sham, the snakes were harmless, the whole thing was just one more carnival show. But what did that matter? These beautiful magic tricks brought redeeming grace, faith into the hearts of people who needed it, and one more dab of color onto the autumnal horizon.

God's sideshow, I thought. *And thank God for it.*

Of course, I would eventually have to write about the bowl, address its true origins. I would just have to do it in such a way— and in such a publication—that the true believers in Hek's church wouldn't have to be confronted with it. And it probably wouldn't matter anyway: There is no fact that can't be fractured by faith. And as an object of faith, the Serpent Bowl was certainly more powerful than any fact I might muster. Best to leave a few unanswered questions.

"There are so many questions left unanswered, it seems to me," Andrews began, tugging at his earlobe, reading my mind. "What was Maddox doing up there on the Hearth? And Shoo? Why did Bishop kill him?" He lowered his voice. "And your not-so-dead-as-we-thought mother, where's her diary?"

"I think Maddox knew something," I said slowly, "or suspected something about Shoo, and followed him up there. I think it's possible Maddox saw Shoo's murder. And obviously Bishop killed Shoo because of what he knew about the bowl. He was a loose end that could corroborate my suspicions." I thought about my mother's last words to me, about how it was better for everyone if she remained a ghost. "As to the rest: If a question is the beginning of a quest, then the *answer* is the end. And if it's true that the journey is more important than the destination, maybe it's better to leave some things unanswered."

With that admission, I finally felt I had come home—reassumed my place among a race of people who all felt it was better to leave so many things unspoken—buried away. It was clear to me that Shoo had made the Serpent Bowl, that he had been summoned to the Hearth by a ghost from his past, and that ghost had shot him with an equally ancient pistol to keep him quiet. But what honest good would come of that revelation? And I did have, after all, a fine tape to show at Shoo Walters's funeral—that was more important than the truth.

"Christ!" Andrews looked around. "Who said that? Certainly not our Dr. Devilin."

"I'm just saying," I told him, "that sometimes faith is more important than proof."

Andrews offered me his opinion on the subject in the form of several four-letter words.

"Not sure I can completely agree with you about Maddox," Skid said softly. "He's been meeting someone up at the Hearth for several years now, on and off." He sniffed. "We don't ask too much about it around town—they say she's married, whoever he's meeting up there. I think he just stumbled onto more than he could handle, and wrestled Shoo's body away on down the hill so no one would know about his little secret—which we all do anyway."

"But no one says anything." Andrews looked my way. "Because the main part of the mountain is under the ground."

"Everybody's got secrets," Skid offered.

As we started down the brick walkway toward Skidmore's police car, an older woman dressed in a thick gray sweater, sitting on one of the benches by the garden in front of the courthouse, waved at us.

"Hey, Fever Devilin," she called out. "I heard you was moving back home. You up here for good, now, son?"

"Well," I smiled at her, "I'm here for a while, anyway."

"That's right, that's right," she beamed. "We've missed your likes up here since your parents passed away. You're a mess." She coughed a laugh. "But you surely are an interesting one to know about. We need more like you up here at home—crazy young people."

I waved, then, and we moved on toward the car.

"Who was that?" I whispered to Skidmore as soon as I felt we were out of her earshot.

"Her?" he looked back over his shoulder. "You remember her, Fever. That's Ida Shump."

"The one that gets baptized every week?" I grinned at Andrews. "Did I ever tell you about her?"

He shook his head.

"Of course she thinks there ought to be more like you up here." Skid shoved me a little. "That way she's not the only odd duck around."

"I see," I told him as we stepped up to his car. "Well, I'm going to pay her a visit very soon. Odd ducks need to flock together."

"You know they say she and your mama used to have an act." Skid jangled his car keys

"What?" I thought I hadn't heard him right. "An act? What are you talking about?"

"Junie told me. Before your daddy married your mama, she and Ida Shump used to waitress together over at the Dillard House." He lowered his voice. "But they were also fan dancers over at the movie house every first Saturday night of the month—men-only show. Gossip is that they were completely necked and they would wave a fan away and the men would go crazy. Some says that's where Fletcher first saw her. And you know that somebody carved both their names—Ida's and your mama's—in that big old oak tree Ida's sitting under. But that was about a hundred years ago." He laughed. "They also say that's why Ida gets washed by the reverend as often as she does now, on account of her past. All that baptizing is just heavenly insurance against the sins of the flesh."

"A hundred years ago in another world." Andrews turned to me as we all got into the car. "I know I told you that I couldn't understand why you were moving back up here." He slid into the back seat. "Now I'm thinking of moving to the mountains myself. It's very entertaining."

"I have a guest room with your name on it any time you like." I got into the front seat of the squad car.

"I'll definitely take you up on it," he answered, piling into the back.

As we pulled away from the courthouse, Ida Shump, in a slanting shaft of golden September sunlight, waved to us again.

In that moment I saw her clearly as a wild young girl in a small mountain town. I saw her walking arm in arm with my mother down those same streets late at night—after a show at the movie house—staring at their names newly carved into a tree, giggling and sharing secrets that no one else would ever know.

And I saw, in my mind's eye then, my mother's diary, like hidden treasure, under some loose stone or wedge of moss, high up on the Devil's Hearth where someone had most likely buried it.

A sudden wind caught orange chestnut leaves and showered them all about Ida. She held out her hands, delighted with the sweet rain of them on her face and hands. All around the leaves swirled, some like kites in the air, some like lanterns hung in the crisp breeze, filtering sharp sunlight. Some went east, toward the ocean, and some swirled aimlessly, with no direction.

I watched the ones that showered downward, homeward, to the solid ground below. They made an impossible, glowing carpet underneath that tree, in and around the ruby mums—around the tree of knowledge at the center of the garden.

Maybe it wasn't Eden, but it was home.